SEAR

WHITLEY GREEN

PROLOGUE

Drew

My best friend's photo pops up on caller ID and I debate not answering—I still haven't started class, thanks to the pseudo-celebrity I'm waiting on. But I haven't heard from Bailey in weeks.

The students can wait a couple more minutes. I duck around the corner from my classroom and open the call.

"Hey, Bailey girl."

"Drew! I'm glad you answered," she says. "Do you know anything about dyeing clothes? Like, to fix a color?"

Uh-oh. If Bailey's making repairs, something's wrong.

"What did Peter do now?" I ask, referring to her fiancé. Bailey's got a bit of a bad track record with men. When things start to go south, she tends to get a little destructive.

"What? No, not Peter," she says. "I was trying to bleach out these jeans and I must have read the directions wrong. So once again: Do you know anything about dyeing clothes?"

"Not a thing," I say. "My best advice would be to donate them and buy a new pair."

Bailey sighs. After more than a decade of friendship, I know that sound. Something is definitely up with Peter.

"Peter's been staying late at the office again," she says quietly.

Shit.

Bailey continues before I can think of something supportive to say besides "dump that bastard, you deserve so much better."

"It's not what you think," she says. I'm glad she's not here to see me roll my eyes. "He's on this big case, and—"

"He's always on a big case," I say, trying to keep the anger out of my voice. She really can pick them.

"Yeah, but—"

"But nothing," I say. "Have you talked to him about this? About him being gone so much?"

"...Not in so many words."

"Bailey."

"He says I'm overreacting," she says, sounding forlorn.

"You do have a history of overreacting," I concede. "But that's not what this is. He's your fiancé. I don't think asking for an explanation or a compromise is unreasonable."

"He says I'm too available. Like I'm supposed to work the same crazy hours he is? I work full time just like most normal people."

I murmur agreement and let her rant while I check my watch again. If the guy I'm waiting on doesn't show in the next three minutes, I'm starting class without him.

"Anyway, enough about me," says Bailey, winding down. "How've you been? Wait—don't you have class tonight? Shit, Drew, you should have said something! I didn't mean to keep you."

"It's okay," I say, laughing. "I'm waiting on one of the guys from the network to come down. Archer Burke's making the big announcement to my class tonight about the cooking competition."

"Did they find somebody to host it?"

"Yep." The guy they picked to host is a royal pain in the ass. But fortunately somebody else at Sizzle TV will be in charge of managing him. I'm only a lowly production assistant. Though considering my boss put me in charge of coordinating the new cooking competition, I don't think I'll be a lowly PA much longer. Teaching these cooking classes after hours in the Sizzle TV test kitchen is just a side gig.

"I should sign up for your class," says Bailey wistfully. "I haven't done anything fun like that in ages."

"You cook all the time," I say, checking the hallway. Still no Burke.

"Yeah, but just for Peter and me," she says. "Is your class fun?"

"Of course it is," I say, making sure to sound offended. Predictably, she laughs.

Bailey's got a great laugh.

"Maybe I'll sign up for the next one," she teases.

Please don't. I have enough trouble concentrating these days.

And it's really, really inappropriate to be thinking about another man's fiancée in those terms, so I bow out of the conversation as gracefully as I can, promising to text Bailey after class.

Burke shows up as I'm shoving the phone back in my bag.

"About time," I say. He shrugs, offering no explanation. "Right. Okay. I'll go in first and introduce you."

The class isn't large, fifteen students total. All adults, all paying to be here to learn what I think of as cooking 101. My friend and colleague James is sitting toward the back next to his handsome dark-haired friend Ben. I've caught some vibes between them, but James and I aren't that close, so I've never asked if they're together.

I lay my bag on the counter at the front of the room and clap to call everyone's attention, shooing some of the stragglers back to their seats.

"Sit down, everybody. As you may have noticed, we've got a guest for the next few minutes. Put a sock in it and let him speak." They laugh and I smile at Burke, gesturing for him to take the floor.

He announces the brand-new cooking competition being held here in town, hosted by Sizzle TV. The students ooh and aah accordingly over the prize money and the promise of their very own pilot episode on the network should they win the competition. I spend most of Burke's speech pointedly ignoring the one man whom Burke came down here to talk about.

He's sitting in his regular seat, halfway to the back of the room at a table by himself. His dark hair is artfully mussed, falling over one eye. I've seen tattoos peeking out from underneath the seams of his shirt while he works, colorful designs I can never quite make out. His face...

Is staring right at me.

Cooper Lawson, kitchen klutz and pain-in-the-ass extraordinaire. Why aren't assholes like him ever ugly?

"And now for the reason I'm really here," says Burke. "Sizzle TV has finally found a host for this brand-new competition series." He pauses, then extends a hand out. "Cooper Lawson! Get on up here."

Cooper's smirk tells me all I need to know about how he feels about Burke's announcement. He doesn't care at all that the rest of the class has seen him set his own eyebrows on fire, or that he's made a spectacle of himself every week since class started. And not a good spectacle.

I grit my teeth, shoving my hands in my pockets, determined not to say a word one way or the other. It wouldn't be professional to roll my eyes, or particularly mature. That guy brings out the worst in me.

Lawson's got a significant online following, thanks to his videos reviewing unusual foods and restaurants. Don't ask me how, but he's got a reputation as a foodie—the network thinks he's perfect for the hosting gig.

Ignoring Lawson as he resumes his seat, I lead the class in a round of applause for Burke and resume the lesson as normal once he's gone.

All I have to do is get through a few more weeks of class, then a few weeks of filming, and I'll never have to see Lawson again. I can take it; no problem. Question is, can he?

1

BAILEY

A FEW MONTHS LATER...

Peter's a dick.

Yeah, I can laugh about him and his stupid name now, but seriously. As exes go, the guy is a straight-up rat bastard. Don't ask me how I missed that for the fourteen months we were dating. Or the two months we were engaged after that.

He was supposed to be here over an hour ago to pick up the last of his boxes. You'd think that because we've been broken up long enough that he'd have picked up all his crap by now, but no. In true pest fashion, I keep finding his shit in every corner of my apartment.

Not after today, though. I've combed every surface, nook, and cranny in this place, pitching the last of it into two final boxes. After this, I can draw a veil and pretend I haven't just wasted yet another big chunk of my life on a man who didn't respect me.

Not that I have a history of that. Much.

Alan, Stephen, Peter... and those are just the fiancés. Who's counting?

Sighing, I check my phone again. No word from him. Big fucking surprise.

I'm supposed to meet my best friend Drew for coffee in twenty minutes. If Peter's not here by then... Guess we'll see.

Thank God for Drew. If it weren't for him, I don't think I'd have made it through these last couple of months. Hell, maybe not even the last couple of years. He's been propping me back up ever since his brother, Alan, and I broke up back in college. Which, now that I think about it, makes Drew my longest-lasting relationship ever. Now that's funny.

He was a classmate (and we'll pretend I wasn't crushing on him all that semester) when he introduced me to Alan freshman year at a frat party. I thought it was love at first sight. Alan thought it was fun while it lasted.

Don't ask me how he got to "fun while it lasted" from his previous stance of "we should get married." But I'm pretty sure there was a lot of booze involved at the time.

I don't hate Alan, not anymore. Which is good, because Drew's practically family—without question the best friend I've ever had. I don't know what I'd do without him being my rock the last ten years.

I'll have to leave in five minutes if Peter's not here. Bad enough I'm waiting on that jackass; I'm not going to make Drew wait on him too.

Drew never liked Peter. Maybe I should let Drew screen my boyfriends from now on. God knows he's got better taste in men than I do.

The phone vibrates in my hand and I answer the call without looking at the screen.

"Where the fuck are you, Peter?"

"Language, Bailey," says my mother. I can practically hear her clutching her pearls from here. "Is that really how you answer your phone?"

"Sorry, Mom," I say, wandering over to peek out the window again. "Peter was supposed to be here an hour ago to pick up some boxes. I thought it was him calling."

"Humph," says Mom. "You know I'm no fan of Peter's, but that doesn't mean you have to answer the phone like some kind of trailer trash."

Right. Because to my mother's mind, people thinking we're from the "wrong side of the tracks" is the worst thing in the world that could happen.

Probably because that's exactly where we're from. And she thinks

I'm the one with issues.

"Is there something you needed?" I prompt, hoping to avoid the lecture this time. "I'm supposed to meet Drew in a few minutes."

Mom huffs again. "That boy," she says. "Honestly, Bailey. You know, if you spent a little less time with Andrew Hicks and a little more time on your own life you'd actually be married by now."

"That boy" is twenty-nine, same as me. And the amount of time I spend with Drew is another sore subject for my mother. It's unthinkable to her that men and women can be friends and friends only. You'd think that since Drew and I have been friends for a damn decade, she'd have changed her mind, but nope.

She also still invites him to church every time she sees him, just in case he's given up "the whole atheist thing"—her words. Drew tells me to take it with a grain of salt.

"Maybe I don't want to get married anymore," I say instead. Mom gasps.

Damn it. Why did I say that? I don't have time for this.

"What exactly do you think you'll be doing with yourself, Bailey?" starts Mom. "When I was your age, I'd already birthed two children and lost a husband."

I yank open the junk drawer in the kitchen, looking for... I don't know what, but my hand closes over the handle of some old scissors. They'll do.

I don't see how it made you any happier. Out loud, I just say, "Yes, Mom."

Stepping into the tiny bathroom on my way to the front door, I set the phone on Speaker mode and lean over the sink. Mom continues with a lecture I've heard so many times I could probably recite it for her and save us both the trouble. But if we didn't go through this at least once every couple of weeks, she and I wouldn't have much else to talk about, so I let her get through it while I put the ancient scissors to use.

"Are you listening to me, Bailey?"

"I'm here, Mom," I say, observing my handiwork in the mirror. "Just getting cleaned up. I have to get going, though. Can I call you back later?"

"If you insist. But I still think—"

"Love you too, Mom. Bye," I say, hitting the screen with my elbow to end the call. "This was probably a bad idea," I say to my reflection, now sporting brand-new, uneven-as-all-hell bangs.

Fuck it.

I chuck the scissors back in the kitchen drawer, grab the stray book of matches I'd originally been looking for, then shoot a text to Drew telling him I'm going to be a couple of minutes late.

Peter's boxes aren't heavy as I haul them out to the curb. They're actually pretty small.

Like his dick. The thought makes me snicker. I don't even care if I'm being petty right now. That rat bastard made it perfectly clear he had no respect for me while we were together. I'm just returning the favor.

I look down at the matchbook in my hand and do a quick check up and down the street, just in case my neighbors are hanging around.

I scan the boxes one more time, just in case there's anything I want out of them, or maybe something of any value. It's all bullshit knickknacks and old paperwork, and I'm sick to damn death of looking at it. If Peter cared, he'd have packed it all up when he left three months ago. Or maybe he would have shown up today. Or asked me to mail them. Something.

So I don't feel bad when the first lit match finds its mark. Pretty sure burning trash inside the city limits is against the law, but today I'll take my chances.

I stay long enough to make sure the fire dies. It's so damp from all the rain lately the flames barely take the cardboard. Par for the course lately.

By the time I get to the cafe, I'm feeling better than I have all week. Drew said he'd meet me outside, so I take advantage of the last bit of warmth we're likely to get this year and sit at one of the tables near the door. Suits my mood just fine.

Working at the bank the last couple of years means I don't get to spend a lot of time outdoors. Guess that's my own fault for not trying a little harder in college, or at least picking a line of work that would let me get out more. Turns out business management isn't a terribly useful field of study if you don't actually intend to run a business. But the bank's local and I like my boss. More or less. I mean, it's fine. I've definitely had worse jobs.

I always figured this was the reason Drew and I hit it off so easily. He's a regular jack-of-all-trades, after he figured out public education wasn't his dream job. He just takes work as it comes and keeps the ones he likes.

I'm not an idiot or anything. My grades were pretty good. I have skills. I'm a damn good cook, for one thing. I guess that's another reason Drew and I are friends.

And don't ask me why I'm thinking about our friendship like it needs to be examined. Drew's the most solid thing I've got in my life. He's sure as hell stood by me more than anybody else I know, including my girlfriends. And God knows, more than my exes.

Hopefully, this means he won't be scared by the bangs.

I'm perfectly aware that there's a good chance Drew and I would have lost touch by now if he hadn't introduced me to Alan at that party all those years ago. Alan, the big, blond, built senior, swept a mildly intoxicated nineteen-year-old Bailey off her feet in the span of about five minutes, in large part because Drew had already friend-zoned her lame ass.

It had been humiliating at the time; thank God we can laugh about it now. Drew still swears I'm the only person—guy or girl—who's ever tried to get with him by asking about his other hookups.

I still think it's really freaking hot that Drew is bi. Don't know why it gets to me, but it does.

And that thought can go right back into the box of "shit Bailey doesn't think about." Along with just how much I loved hearing those hookup stories, on the rare occasions when Drew got drunk enough to tell them.

We're grown-ups now and friends only—always and forever, he likes to say—so any thoughts containing the words "Drew" and "hot" are not welcome here.

I shake my head to derail that weird train of thought and catch a glimpse of somebody through the store's solid glass picture window. I can't see his face—there's a sign in the way—but God. Damn. I'm pretty sure there's no possible way Chris Evans, aka Captain America, aka finest motherfucker on the planet, is really standing in Bill & Jillie's Market Street Market on this particular day. Not that I stalk him on Twitter or anything. Much.

But I'm pretty sure he's filming on location right now, so the body I'm looking at is probably not Chris Evans. But sweet Christ, what a body. Shoulders for days. Fitted T-shirt showing off a seriously well-developed chest. If I were sitting any closer, I bet I could see his abs through the fabric.

Get a grip, girl. It's not like it's been forever since you got laid.

Maybe not, but it's been a damn age and a half since anybody got me off without battery-powered assistance. And there is no way God would put a body like that on this earth and make it anything less than amazing in bed.

Whoever he is, the people he's talking to seem to like him well enough. I watch as the two guys sitting with the girl laugh at something Not-Chris says, then wave him off as he walks up to the counter. I wonder briefly if Drew would be pissed if I ditched him to introduce myself to Not-Chris.

Except I'm off men, damn it. Focus, Bailey. Three fiancés in four years means I've got a serious problem and until I figure out what that is, no real-life penises for me. Not even the super kind.

Saying a heartfelt mental goodbye to that perfect male body, I pull out my phone, determined to ignore Not-Chris if he walks out the cafe door. I start tapping out a text to Drew—he'd get a kick out of that guy, which is another reason we're friends; Drew has excellent taste in men—when the bell over the Market door jingles. I don't look up, just in case it's Not-Chris and my clothes somehow evaporate without permission.

Sitting outside the Market, waiting, loser. Where are you? There's a guy here you should see—

As I'm typing, footsteps approach my table and stop. I ignore whoever it is as hard as I can, rewording the message. Before I can finish, a voice stops me.

"You don't have to text me, genius, I'm standing right here."

I freeze, my finger hovering over the Send button. A cup appears on the table in front of me.

Sneakers.

Fitted jeans. And yep, that's America's ass all right, though I'm only seeing its profile right now.

That damned see-through T-shirt. Wholesome, all-American good looks, topped off by warm brown eyes.

Brown eyes currently full of humor. Drew's clearly trying not to laugh.

"Everything okay?" he asks. I erase the text as fast as I can, setting my phone down as I pick up the coffee cup.

"Great," I mutter, choking on my drink. Drew laughs as I splutter and try to basically drown myself.

In my defense, I didn't know it was Drew, but Jesus. Did he swap bodies or something? Maybe my bangs were somehow attached to my good sense.

It's not like I didn't know my friend is good-looking. He can be downright beautiful sometimes. I don't know what's wrong with me.

I take another sip of coffee and strive to bring my brain back online.

"Caught me off guard," I say. "Thanks for the coffee."

"You're welcome," he says, taking the seat across from mine. He stares at me a minute, long enough I can feel my cheeks warm.

"What?"

Drew taps his fingers on the table. "You want to talk about it?"

"No!" I set the cup down so hard, coffee sloshes out over my shoes. "I mean, what are you talking about? Talk about what?"

Drew just points to his hair.

Oh. Right.

"Oh, that," I say, mopping up my mess. "That would be the last vestige of my relationship with Peter going down the drain. Or in the trash can, in this case."

Drew's expression hardens.

"What happened?"

2

DREW

"Mr. Hicks, my name is Anthony Olstein with the Calaveras County School District. I'm calling regarding your application for the middle school science teacher position." The brisk tone of voice is par for the course in my experience with the public education system. Experience that is pretty far in the past. Experience that definitely does not include applying for any jobs with the local school district.

"We'd like to bring you in for an interview," continues Mr. Olstein without waiting for my response. "We've got to get this position filled pronto, considering the academic year is already underway."

"Mr. Olstein," I say. "I'm sorry to disappoint you, but I have not applied for the position you're talking about. I haven't applied for a teaching position anywhere." Not in the last six years, but he doesn't need to know that.

My father, on the other hand, has submitted no fewer than ten applications for open teacher positions this summer. In my name.

"Sorry for your trouble. Thanks for calling," I say and hang up before he loses any more time on me.

I used to take more time explaining. The first few times it happened, I even went on the interviews. I've learned not to waste anybody's time like that anymore, least of all my own.

Dad's getting pushier about jobs, that's for sure. It's second only to my lack of a committed relationship on his list of things wrong with my life. I wonder—not for the first time—if my family has an actual list they consult when I'm not around.

Doesn't matter to him that I tried—I really did. I spent two soul-sucking years teaching basic biology to middle-class suburban teenagers. Nobody goes into education planning to strike it rich, but I made enough to pay my bills. It wasn't like I was putting my life at stake every day, unless you count death by spitballs and eye rolling.

For those two years I could do no wrong in my parents' eyes; even coming out as bisexual barely caused a blip. But two years of teaching in a school was enough to give me ulcers, and my chosen profession was already starting to more closely resemble a terminal illness. The last day of the year, I walked down to the principal's office and let her know I wouldn't be back in the fall.

Leaving the building that day was the greatest physical relief I've ever experienced. I practically flew my car home.

Since then Dad's made it his mission to persuade me that I was just in the wrong place, that teaching really is for me. It gnaws at him that the career he's had for thirty-odd years is the absolute last place I want to be. No matter how many times I agree with him—teaching is for me, I fucking love it—it doesn't count in his mind since I prefer to teach outside the school system.

My phone pings and, sure enough, it's a follow-up email from the school district. It's bad enough I've let my dad down, bad enough he hasn't let me forget it at the start of every single semester these last few years. Now he's got me letting down all kinds of people I've never even met.

Not likely doing my reputation any good.

Of course, not that I'm going to need much reputation in those circles. Makes tutoring a little more challenging, though, when I can't just approach the local science teachers and tell them I'm taking on new students.

I'm pretty full up working for Sizzle TV—one of the bigger cable cooking networks—these days anyway, and my boss runs a damn tight ship. Ty's a great guy. Probably. Deep down. As bosses go, he's demanding and exacting. Which is great because you always know exactly where you stand with him. He also doesn't sugarcoat anything, which means he can be a little hard to take.

In short, it's one of the best jobs I've ever had. Keeps me so busy, I don't have time to think about the clutter in my head, or my father's unending disappointment in my lack of a "real" career. Or my family's opinion that I need to settle down and get married.

I shake off the automatic irritation his name brings to mind and push open the door to the Market Street Market. Bailey's not here yet, so I head to the counter to order our coffee. I chat with the owner a minute then catch a familiar face out of the corner of my eye.

James Flores works with me over at Sizzle, and he and his friend Ben took my Cooking Basics course this summer. They're sitting near the big picture window with a pretty, wholesome-looking brunette. I make my way over to say hello.

James asks me to join them right as I spot Bailey pulling up a chair outside.

"I'd love to," I say, pointing to the window, "but I'm meeting a friend."

Ben glances at Bailey and smirks at me. "Friend, huh?"

"My best friend," I say. "Since college."

It's all we've ever been and all we'll ever be, since she damn near married my brother Alan.

"Say no more," says Ben, holding up his hands.

"I won't keep you. I just wanted to say hi and ask if you've reconsidered entering the cooking competition. Starts next week, you know," I say. Most of this is directed to Ben; since James works for the network, he's not eligible to enter. He's also not what anybody would call an amateur.

"Thanks, but I think I'd rather watch," says Ben, shaking his head and grinning. "With Cooper Lawson hosting, it should be quite a show."

Right, I'd forgotten. Lawson was in the same class with Ben and James. They got to see the natural disaster up close.

"You're working with Lawson?" asks James.

"We have to be in the same place sometimes. It's not a big deal," I say, immediately feeling about twelve years old when I say it. "So far we've managed to avoid each other quite successfully."

Cooper Lawson, professional pain in the ass and my personal cross to bear. I've had troublesome students before—whether it was ninth-grade biology class, basic cooking class, or some of the kids I tutor in the evenings. Cooper Lawson could give them all lessons on trouble.

Why the network had to go and hire him to host the competition next week, I'll never understand. I don't give a damn how much of an online presence he's got. The guy is a walking disaster in the kitchen and a prick to boot.

Some people just can't get the hang of things, or think they can't when it comes to cooking. I know how to handle that type. It's all in the approach.

Fucking Lawson, though. That guy gets under my skin like nobody I've ever met. And because I'm in charge of logistics during the competition, it's apparently my job to make sure he doesn't blow the whole place up with his hosting demos, or set somebody on fire while he's doing interviews with the competitors.

Tutoring and teaching, I'm good at. Babysitting... not so much. Especially not him.

James makes a joke about paying off emergency medical services to hang close and I excuse myself, picking up my order from the front counter and heading out to meet Bailey.

She's staring hard at her phone, not looking up even when I step up next to the table. Leaning over, I see she's got our text thread open and is typing a message.

"You don't have to text me, genius, I'm standing right here," I say. Bailey takes her time meeting my gaze, clearly preoccupied. She looks up at me slowly, like she's never seen me before.

"Everything okay?" I ask. Bailey takes her coffee and gulps some down before I can warn her it's still too hot, sipping too fast and choking a little.

"Great," she gasps. "You caught me off guard. Thanks for the coffee."

"You're welcome." Something's not right, but it's obvious she's not keen to share, so I wait until she looks at me to start prodding.

"What?" Bailey says.

"You want to talk about it?" I ask.

"No," she says quickly, her eyes darting around like she's looking for an escape hatch. Bailey's wound a little tight these days, but this is next-level touchy. "Talk about what?"

I give her a break, because that's what friends do, and instead of asking what burr got stuck in her saddle, I point to my hair.

Bailey's hair is currently a gorgeous, creamy blond, a few shades lighter than mine. Every now and then she likes to do something crazy with it—a few weeks ago she went with pink tips, until her boss at the bank shut that down and made her change it back—but this is new. She's cut the hair across her forehead into bangs, I guess, but they don't look quite right.

She's been having a hard time lately. And when Bailey has a hard time, she kind of goes a little crazy. Not boiling-a-bunny-level crazy. Just randomly-cut-your-own-hair crazy, apparently. It's charming as hell, even though sometimes it worries me to damn death.

"Oh, that. That would be the last vestige of my relationship with Peter going down the drain. Or in the trash can, in this case," she says.

"What happened?" I growl.

Bailey rolls her eyes.

"Down, boy," she says, patting my hand like a dog. "Nothing happened, really. He was supposed to come pick up the last couple of boxes from my place today and he no-showed."

She wants to play it that way, fine. Gloves are off.

"How did you get from Dickless Dick to crazy ex-girlfriend?" I ask, pointing at her head this time.

"Funny."

"You know what I mean."

She leans back in her chair and crosses her arms.

"I don't know," she says, sighing. "Just the last straw, I guess."

"It's not exactly the first time he's bailed on you," I point out.

"I know that," says Bailey. "Don't you think I know that? Maybe that's the problem."

"What?"

She studies her nails a minute before answering me.

"I wish I knew."

We sit and sip our coffees a minute until a thought occurs to me, something I know for sure will help cheer her up.

"So remember I told you about that guy from my cooking class at the studio?"

Bailey perks up, nodding.

"He's hosting the cooking competition next week," I tell her.

"Ooh," she says, rubbing her hands together, an evil, gleeful smile on her face at the thought of my obvious torment. "I'd like to be a fly on those walls."

My turn to roll my eyes. "Of course you would."

"Hey, don't get me wrong. If he's picking on you for real, I'll kick his ass," she says. "But I always got the impression you liked bickering with him."

"I do not like bickering with him. If you even call it bickering." Who says that? Bickering. "He's a pest. A menace. And at this point, a necessary evil, at least until this competition is over."

"Is he cute?" she asks. For some stupid reason, that makes me choke on my drink.

"What the hell do you mean, is he cute?"

Bailey shrugs like she didn't just try to lobotomize me with that question. Honestly. I mean, if you want to be objective, he's marginally attractive. For an asshole. If you like the dark, lean, lightly muscled, tattooed, pierced hipster type.

Which I absolutely do not.

"He's not my type," I say, ignoring her raised eyebrows. "And anyway, you could meet him yourself, if you're dead set on it." I take a deep breath and brace myself to broach the question I called her here to ask. "I need a favor."

"Anything," she says, shrugging easily.

"Maybe not this," I warn. "I need a date. Specifically, I need a date to the competition kickoff gala this Friday."

Bailey rolls her eyes and sips her drink. "So get a date. Never known you to have trouble finding one."

"That's the thing," I say, rubbing the back of my neck. "I kind of need a girlfriend type of date for this."

Bailey lowers her coffee cup and looks me in the eye.

"What's going on?"

"There's this woman at work," I say. "She's been a little... overenthusiastic about trying to get me to go out with her again."

"You can't just tell her no?" Bailey asks, raising an eyebrow.

"I have," I say. "Repeatedly. But she keeps coming up with other ways to ask me out, or other events to ask me to."

"You said 'again,'" says Bailey. I nod.

"We went for a drink after work once." At her arched brow, I put my hands up. "Just a drink. *One* drink. And it was just that one time a couple of months ago." Mila's attractive enough and we've never had a problem working together, but I didn't feel any sparks. At the time, I assumed she felt the same. I was wrong.

"Have you reported her?" Bailey asks. "Because that sounds an awful lot like harassment to me."

"I don't think it's quite that bad," I say. "Mila's just really... persistent."

"So you, what? Told her you've already got a girlfriend?"

I nod again.

"And now she'll be at this big party for Sizzle and if you show up without a plus-one—"

"She'll know I lied," I finish. "Right. What do you say, Bailey? Be my fake girlfriend for a night?"

Bailey purses her lips, skeptical as all hell.

"You get to wear a fancy dress," I say, singsongingly because Bailey loves dressing up. But I saved the kicker for last. "And you know the food is going to be spectacular."

"Will I get to meet the kitchen disaster guy?" she asks, and I know I've got her.

"If you insist on meeting yet another jerk, yeah," I say. "I'll introduce you to him."

"Hell yeah, I insist," she says. "Anybody who gets under the skin of the unflappable Drew Hicks that bad deserves at least an introduction. All right. Count me in."

3

COOPER

"Cat got your tongue, cutie?"

The brunette standing at the bar is not getting the hint. If she got an invite to this self-important shindig, that means she works for the network, or she's with somebody who does. I'm going with current employee. Meaning, somebody I cannot afford to piss off.

Nothing personal, she's just not my type. Love it or hate it, I'm a sucker for blondes. Always have been, always will be.

"Sorry," I say, turning to face her. "What did you say your name was?"

She purrs, leaning into my arm. "I'm Mila."

"Nice to meet you, Mila," I say through my teeth. *Make a good impression. Make a good impression.* "You work for Sizzle?"

She laughs like I've cracked a joke or something and launches into a lengthy explanation of just how important her job is. It's a dick move, but I tune her out, she doesn't need me here for this monologue; I figured that out about ten minutes ago and survey the room for a possible escape.

Problem is, I don't know a damn soul here.

That's the whole point, jackass. Network. Make a good impression.

These people need to like you if you're going to stick around past just the one contract.

Trouble is, I'm not exactly good with people. Not on the ground anyway; face-to-face is not my jam. I'm great in front of a camera. And fortunately, being on camera is what Sizzle is paying me for.

I hate schmoozing and I'm no ass-kisser. Which makes this kickoff gala basically my worst nightmare, complete with—

Yep, there he is. Dickbag extraordinaire, Drew Hicks. And wouldn't you know it, he's got the hottest woman in the room on his arm—a petite blonde, exactly my type—to boot.

I hate that guy.

Bad enough he appears to have absolutely no clue that we went to college together; we even had a couple of the same classes. Then he got to witness my total lack of kitchen skills up close and personal.

Granted, I'm not exactly the scrawny nerd I was back then. Still. Guys like him, they're all the same: can't see past the fog of their own ego.

I turn back to the brunette at my elbow—looks like she's waiting for an answer again—and gesture to the bartender to bring us both another round.

You can't afford to be rude. Play nice, Coop.

"Ugh, I can't believe he brought her here," says the brunette, whose name I've already forgotten. Again.

God, I suck at this. I check my watch on the sly, trying to calculate just how much longer I have to stand here before excusing myself to find the bathroom.

"Who?" I ask, not caring at all. She jerks her chin toward a small crowd nearby.

"My colleague over there, with that trashy blonde." The brunette sneers into her second martini. She gets my attention when mentioning the blonde, but if she means Drew's date, there's nothing trashy about that particular woman. I prod her along anyway.

"You know Drew Hicks?"

She snorts. "Know him? We were together until she came along."

Ah, a jealous ex. This would normally be my cue to exit, stage left, except this gala is a work function. And maybe there's some merit in the old "the enemy of my enemy is my friend" expression.

"Who is she?"

My companion shrugs and sneers. "Hell if I know. I thought for sure he was making her up until they showed up together tonight."

"Ah," I say, laying on all the sympathy I can fake. "I take it things didn't end well?"

"You could say that," she says vaguely, her eyes narrowing at Hicks and his date. "I still don't buy it."

"About his girlfriend?" I ask. Hicks's arm around the blonde's waist looks awfully comfortable. Whatever she is to him, they're not strangers.

"Come on," says the woman—Mira? Miranda?—as she sinks her fake nails into my wrist, pulling me away from the bar. "I'll introduce you."

"You don't have to—" I shut my mouth, mainly to keep from yelping because those nails are fucking sharp and I'm pretty sure yanking my arm away would knock her over, given how fast she sucked down those martinis.

Drew Hicks and his petite companion are surrounded by a small group of people I only sort of recognize and whose names I probably ought to know by now. When the network hired me to host their new local cooking competition, they made it clear during the interview process that if I impressed them, it might lead to other work. Nobody actually used the words "regular show host," but it was heavily implied.

It's all I've ever wanted, that kind of recognition. This is my chance to earn it, the real deal too, and not just as an "influencer" because let's face it, social media influencer is barely even a trend. A full-time hosting gig on a reputable network, on the other hand, now that's the start of a real career.

So I let... Mila, thank God, that's her name, drag me along and don't mention that I'm already more acquainted with Andrew Hicks than I ever wanted to be.

More or less. A ten-minute college crush doesn't count. I'm old enough to know he's a twatwaffle. And twatwaffles are not attractive, not even the ones built like a goddamn action movie hero.

"Drew!" cries Mila far too loudly. Half the room turns our way. "Look who I found loitering by the bar all by himself. Have you met our charming host?"

Mila's drawing a blank, waiting for me to introduce myself and I let her hang. She wanted a scene. Looks like she's going to get it.

I steel myself for whatever wave of condescension is headed my way.

"We've met," Hicks says blandly.

"Oh, of course," says Mila, giggling. I get the impression little miss razor claws knows the exact nature of my relationship with Hicks and is prepared to let us costar in whatever drama she's looking to play out.

Sorry, sweetheart. You got the wrong guy.

"This is my girlfriend," Drew says, his voice thawing substantially. "Bailey, this is Mila Hague, a colleague at the network. And this is Cooper Lawson."

"Cooper?" Drew's date is eyeballing me hard and a sudden wave of recognition almost knocks me off my feet.

"Bailey Ross. Jesus, is that you?"

An instant later my arms are full up, squeezing the breath out of a girl I never thought I'd see again in my life.

"Holy shit," she says, squeezing me just as hard. "Coop. Seriously. I can't believe it's you! What are you even doing here?"

"I was invited," I say, breathing her in, flooded by decade-old memories. "Damn, it's good to see you."

"You too," she says, pushing me back a little to look me in the eye. I can't believe I didn't recognize her, but then it's been ten years at least since we last saw each other.

She made my heart pound back then, too.

"Look at you," I murmur. "You look amazing. How are you? How have you been? What are you doing here?"

Bailey beams up at me and the silence around us starts to register, louder than Mila's shrieking just a minute ago.

"We're making a scene," whispers Bailey.

24

"Yeah," I whisper back. "Fuck 'em." She giggles just like I hoped she would and Christ does that sound bring back memories... swapping whispered jokes in the back of the lab while an ancient professor droned on about lab etiquette.

Hicks clears his throat loudly, and Bailey pulls away, bringing me back to the here and now.

"I take it you two have met," says Hicks, looking like he just swallowed a whole truckload of lemons. For a minute I consider downplaying my satisfaction at having a surprise connection to his date.

Nah. Sorry, not sorry, dickbag.

"Bailey and I go way back," I say, beaming at him.

"Hang on," she says, wrapping a delicate hand around my bicep. "How do you two know each other? Do you work for Sizzle too, Coop?"

"Actually—"

"Lawson here is hosting the cooking competition next week," says Hicks. He didn't say anything strange, but Bailey must have heard something I didn't. Her eyes go wide as dinner plates and her mouth drops open.

"You're kidding me," she says. The disbelief chafes, especially coming from her.

Bailey Ross was my lab partner freshman year at State. It took me all goddamn year to work up the nerve to ask her out, and when she said yes, I knew I was using up all the luck of a lifetime in one fell swoop. That night was... definitely not something I need to be thinking about right now. Not with all these cameras around to witness a potentially embarrassing and highly personal reaction.

At any rate, I'd been right about using up all my luck since I never saw her again after that spring. Until today.

Bailey starts laughing her head off, drawing every eye in the room. Not that most of them weren't staring at her in the first place. Her dress is—

Something else I shouldn't be thinking about, considering she's here with another guy.

Dickbags don't count.

God, it's a tempting thought. For one brief moment, I wonder just how hard it would be to pry her away from Dick Hicks... But I can't do it. I can't stand the guy, but this is still a work function for me. I can't afford to give anybody else at Sizzle a reason to hate me, and Hicks certainly doesn't need the ammunition. Still. I'm having a hard time wrapping my head around the two of them together, though. Maybe Mira/Miranda/Mila has a point.

"Is that so hard to believe?" I ask Bailey. The question sounds defensive even to my own ears. She pats my arm.

"Don't get your back up," Bailey says quietly. "I didn't mean anything by it. I heard through the grapevine somebody was giving Drew a hard time lately."

"Hard time, huh?" I look over and watch, fascinated, as the color rises in Hicks's face.

"It's a good thing it's you, Coop," Bailey continues, still grinning. "I thought for sure I was going to have to beat some ass. But you'll do."

I can't help but grin back at her. "Yeah?"

"Yeah," she says, leaning up to kiss me on the cheek.

Mila elbows her way in between us. "I don't believe we've met before," she says to Bailey. "You're Drew's girlfriend?"

Bailey squeezes my arm and returns to her place next to Hicks. I resist the urge to cover the spot where her hand was resting to trap the warmth she left behind.

"I am," says Bailey, the humor in her eyes cooling. "I'm sorry, I've forgotten your name. You are...?"

"Skeptical," says Mila.

"Excuse me?"

"I don't believe you," says Mila, over-enunciating each word. We don't have the attention of everybody in the ballroom, but anybody close enough to hear doesn't even pretend not to watch the drama unfolding. "If you're really here with him, kiss him."

"I just did," says Bailey. She'd kissed Drew on the cheek just a minute ago; I know Mila saw it because she's been staring the whole time.

"Not really," sneers Mila. "I think you're bluffing."

"Mila, I don't know what you think you're doing, but this is absurd," says Drew. "Excuse us." He keeps his voice low and tries to walk away with Bailey in tow, but she pulls him to a stop.

"Really, Drew," she chides. "I know how much you hate PDA, but if the woman wants a show, it's the least we can do."

I find myself grinning and crossing my arms. Why Bailey putting on a show with Drew Hicks should amuse me so much, I don't know. If anything, you'd think I'd be jealous considering our history.

Then again, our history is of the ancient variety, so I've got no call to be jealous at all, not of either of them.

Not that I'd be jealous of her for kissing him. That'd be beyond ridiculous. And gross. Because he's an uptight jerk and I'm not into jerks, male or female.

And because I hate him, of course.

Oblivious to my mental ping-pong match, Bailey pulls on Hicks's hand until their bodies meet and wastes no time wrapping a hand around his neck to draw him down for a kiss.

Hicks looks stunned for a minute as Bailey leans up on her tiptoes to touch her mouth to his. An instant later he wraps his arms around her tight, kissing her like he means it. This draws some cheers from the people watching nearby. I guess Mila doesn't like that much because she pivots wildly on her stilettos and stalks away. Everybody else goes back to their conversations, except Bailey and Hicks.

And me.

Watching them makes my chest hurt and my heart pound, like something's coming for me and I should run, but I can't make myself look away. Bailey's the most beautiful woman I've ever met in real life, and while it galls me to admit it, Hicks might have some appeal. I mean, he's not my type—gross—but them together...

I tug at my tie, trying to buy a little more breathing room around my collar. It's stuffy as hell in here.

When Hicks sets Bailey back on her feet, he looks like somebody's hit him over the head with a frying pan. Bailey reaches up to wipe away a hint of lipstick off his mouth, and why the hell that move goes straight to my dick, I have no idea. Surely, it's because I remember what kissing Bailey was like and I'm jealous.

Surely that's it. It couldn't be anything else.

4

BAILEY

"Uh," says Drew, uncharacteristically speechless. I spot a smudge of lipstick on his bottom lip and flush, reaching up to wipe it away.

"Well, that was entertaining," drawls Cooper.

Somebody's got to get this shitshow offstage. Honestly. I thought Drew was supposed to be the sane one in this relationship.

Not that it's a relationship. Obviously. It's a fake relationship with my real best friend.

Best remember that.

Drew and I kissed exactly one time before today, and that had been an accident. Too many tequila shots plus a kiss on the cheek gone wrong. He'd been mortified and I couldn't stop laughing.

I'm not laughing now.

"Cooper," I say, grabbing Drew's hand and avoiding his gaze. "Come get a drink with us?"

When Cooper smiles, it's full of innuendo.

"You sure about that, Ross?" he asks me. Coop had called me by my last name every day of the school year, right up until the minute he'd finally asked me out. "I thought three's a crowd."

"Not tonight," I say. Cooper's eyes shoot wide and Drew's hand tightens around mine. "I mean... shit. You know what I mean."

"Maybe Lawson would rather go check on his new friend Mila," says Drew. He keeps the venom in his voice dialed back, but Cooper hears it anyway. I can almost see the chip on his shoulder get heavier every time Drew speaks. What the hell is it with these two?

I know they ran in majorly different social circles back in college, though they'd both been science majors of one flavor or another. Kind of odd they hadn't met until recently, now that I think about it. But the school was huge even back then.

Still not thinking about that kiss. See? We're going to be just fine.

"What's that?" Drew asks as we approach the bar.

"I didn't say anything."

"You were muttering," says Cooper, drawing up a stool on my right. "Something about science."

My face is going to catch fire if I blush any harder. I focus on charming the bartender out of the largest glass of wine he can pour.

There's a limit to just how crazy I let myself get. Like, there's a little wild, then there's maybe needing professional help. And, okay, maybe I've gotten a little too comfortable toeing the big, fat line between them lately.

Kissing Drew like that? That was certifiable. We have officially surpassed post-breakup-crazy and have entered padded cell territory.

Not that it wasn't good. On the contrary, that memory is going straight into the spank bank, though I'd never in a million years have guessed one PG-rated kiss in a ballroom surrounded by Drew's coworkers would ever have been hot enough to qualify.

Turns out I was wrong.

"I have to ask," says Cooper, pitching the question just loud enough that Drew can hear him, too. "How did you two lovebirds meet?"

My first inclination is to tell Coop the truth, that I'm just posing as Drew's girlfriend to get rid of that obnoxious woman Mila, and that Drew and I are really just friends.

Only friends. Tongue-kissing notwithstanding.

But Drew gets there first. "We've been friends a long time, right, Bailey?"

I nod. "Since college," I agree.

"So you've been together a while," says Cooper, prodding. His expression is all polite inquisitiveness, but I hear the hint of an edge in his voice. He knows something's up.

Drew hears it, too. "What can I say? When it's right, it's right." Drew puts his arm around me, shooting a hard look at Cooper and squeezing me tight to his side. Ignoring the tingling heat brought on by his hand on my hip, I focus on the wineglass in my hand, wishing it would magically refill itself. The mirror behind the bar is partly obscured by row after row of bottles I don't recognize, but I can see our faces clear enough: Drew on my left, Cooper on my right. Wide-eyed, red-cheeked Bailey right smack dab between them.

A split-second fantasy of being sandwiched between these two men under slightly different—slightly naked—circumstances flashes before my eyes, making me suck down a sip of wine.

"You okay?" Drew asks, pounding my back as I cough.

Cooper hands me a napkin, concern in his eyes. I wave them off and wonder if jumping out the first-floor bathroom window would be enough to kill me or if I'll just have to die of embarrassment where I sit.

At least Drew's not holding onto me anymore. Which is good. No need to go overboard with the touching. Definitely no need to be imagining anybody naked.

Drew is silent again, glaring at the room at large—the glass in his hand, the mirror. Cooper. Back down to the glass.

"Where did Mila go?" I ask tentatively.

Drew shrugs. Cooper shifts to prop his arm on the bar, stepping a little closer to me and turning to face us both.

"She's back behind the sound booth talking to somebody," Cooper says, jerking his chin in that direction. "You want me to flag her down for you?"

"No," Drew and I both say sharply. Cooper gives me that same crooked half-grin.

"You haven't changed a bit," says Cooper.

"I can't say the same for you," I say, unable to stop the smile. "For a lab rat, you've filled out pretty nicely." Back in school, he'd been talking about medical research as a career. But Coop shakes his head.

"Turns out med school and I weren't a good fit," he says blithely.

"Shocker," says Drew.

"Drew," I say, floored by his rudeness. I don't think I've ever heard him be deliberately rude to somebody before.

Cooper lays a hand on my arm and squeezes gently. "Don't sweat it, Ross," he says. "Typical needle-dick jock response. I'm used to it."

The bartender does a double take a few feet away. I hide behind my wineglass, eyes on the mirror, watching Drew's face get redder by the second.

Damage control, Bailey. Get on it.

I should probably intervene but, God help me, listening to them harass each other feels like foreplay. Yep. I've lost it.

"I have no desire to debate the size of my dick with the likes of you, Lawson," says Drew, his voice pitched low. The bartender's lips twitch anyway. I suspect he's enjoying this at least as much as I am.

"The likes of me," sneers Cooper, no longer masking his irritation. "What is that supposed to mean?"

"I think you know," says Drew.

"Spell it out for me, teach," says Cooper. He's not loud, but people nearby can hear. At least they've moved on from dick sizes. The bartender notices my empty glass and nods in question.

"Oh, yes," I say, handing back my glass. "Maybe I should come back there and hang out with you instead."

"I'd let you if I could," says the bartender. His name tag says Beck. Drew and Cooper are still exchanging insults, leaning around behind me to snipe at each other. "But I'm a little afraid of getting caught in the crossfire."

"You and me both, Beck," I say, raising my fresh drink in thanks as he walks back to the end of the bar. In the mirror I see a woman approaching—lithe, lovely, perfect hair. I already hate her.

She stops right in front of Drew, interrupting the guys' argument.

"I swear to God, I'm going to get you two matching muzzles if you don't knock it off," she says in a sweet, light voice. I snort at that, turning around to get a better look. The voice is a direct contradiction to the fierce expression on her face, a look that softens when she turns her eyes on me.

32

"Hi," she says. "I'm Kenna Burch."

I pause in the middle of shaking hands with her. "Kenna Burch, class of 2009?"

She nods, narrowing her eyes at me. "Do we know each other?"

"I'm Bailey Ross," I say. "We had World Civ 105 together."

"Well, hot damn," she says, smiling. "Nice to see you again, Bailey."

"Did everybody here go to the same damn college?" gripes Cooper.

"Not everybody," says Kenna, though I'm pretty sure the question was rhetorical. "But there's a few of us. How do you know these two?" she asks me, waving a hand between Cooper and Drew.

"Bad luck," I say. Cooper snorts. Drew goes still.

Kenna laughs. "I like you," she says, patting my arm. Kenna looks at Drew, pointing a thumb back over her shoulder. "Ty's looking for you. I think he was headed back to the buffet."

"Ah. Duty calls," he says mildly. Drew finishes his drink, sets the glass on the bar, then kisses my cheek. "I'll be back in a few minutes. Will you be all right by yourself?"

I'm about to mention that I've somehow managed the last twenty-nine years just fine, but Cooper speaks up.

"I'll keep an eye on her," he says, innuendo pouring out of every word. "She's in good hands." Kenna's eyes go wide. Drew looks like his head might explode, but he's told me more than once Ty Wilkes is not a man to be kept waiting. He stalks off.

Good thing Drew and I aren't really a couple. I'd have to take him down a peg or two for that "will you be all right" nonsense. But it's all pretend.

Even the kissing. Especially the kissing. *So don't get any ideas, girl.*

Kenna accepts her glass from the bartender and slides into Drew's abandoned seat.

"So Bailey," she says, surveying the room. "Are you competing next week?"

"What, the cooking competition?" I ask. Kenna nods. "No."

"Why not?" asks Cooper.

"Um, because." I stammer a little, completely caught off guard "Reasons?"

"You cook, right?" Cooper asks.

"Well, yeah, but—"

"You should enter," says Kenna. "It's going to be awesome." Cooper nods his agreement.

"Aren't there some rules against me competing?" I ask. Not that I'm actually considering this. It's a silly idea. Sure, it might be fun, but there's no way I can take the time off work for it. "Because I'm... with Drew, I mean. Dating Drew."

Bet your ass I'm going to blame the stammering on the wine and not the fact that I keep thinking about Drew's body pressing against mine. That, or the night Cooper and I—

"You mean because Drew works for Sizzle? Nah, you're clear. That rule only applies to employees and their spouses or immediate family members," says Kenna, waving a hand.

"I'm surprised you're not already competing," says Cooper.

"Why's that?"

"You always talked about running a catering business," he says. "Is that not what you're doing now?"

"I work at a bank," I say, feeling lamer than the lamest lame who ever lamed. I'd all but forgotten that. It was all I'd talked about after high school, having a catering company. I still cooked for people from time to time but it wasn't something I usually got paid for.

How could I have forgotten that? And what does it mean that Cooper remembered?

"Well, if you change your mind about it," says Kenna, standing up and straightening her already perfect cocktail dress, "the forms are all on the website. Registration is open until Sunday night."

Somebody calls Kenna's name and she excuses herself, leaving me and Cooper alone at the corner of the bar.

"So you and Hicks, huh?" says Cooper. There's no sly grin this time, no suggestion in his tone. Just a straightforward question.

"Yeah," I say. I hate lying to him, but I don't dare tell him the truth, not when we're surrounded by so many of Drew's coworkers who might spread the word if they heard us talking. Plus, I doubt

Drew would want me confiding in Cooper of all people, considering all they've done this evening is fight like schoolboys.

"You're happy?" Cooper asks, not making eye contact as he tosses back the rest of his drink.

This one is harder to answer.

"I'm happy with Drew," I say, as honestly as I can. Because I am happy with my friend. He's the best guy I know.

Cooper looks me in the eye, like he can see right into my head. He knows something's up.

Before he can call me on it, though, some suit from the network comes over to talk to him and for the next twenty minutes, I nod and play Drew's attentive girlfriend for his colleagues, ignoring the speculative looks I get from Coop here and there. Surely it doesn't really count as lying. I haven't seen the man in ten years—God only knows when I'll see him again after tonight.

The thought makes my stomach twist a little. Coop was a good friend. Maybe he could have been more.

Drew had introduced me to Alan just a week after my one date with Cooper. It hadn't seemed fair to ask Coop if we could be friends when I was head over heels for somebody else, so I never tried to find him after the school year ended. I could cuss myself for being so shortsighted, but there's nothing I can do about it now. Especially since Coop's under the impression I'm with somebody else now.

So I breathe through the regret—the wine helps—giving myself these few moments to think about what might have been. I think Cooper sees something of it in my face. When the production staff people wander off, Coop moves closer and ducks his head to look me in the eye.

"Bailey," he says.

"There you are," says Drew, coming up behind me. "I've been looking all over for you." He bends down to kiss my cheek, his arm around my waist again.

Cooper glares at him. "We're literally standing right where you left us."

"Hmm," says Drew, ignoring Cooper now. Cooper's shoulders

bunch, tension clouding the air around us. I still don't understand where it's coming from, but I'd have to be dead not to notice it.

"Actually," says Cooper, his voice sharpening, "I was just about to ask Ross here for a dance. What do you say, Bailey?"

This is probably a bad idea. There's no chance this is not a bad idea.

"Sure," I say, setting down my glass. I lean over to kiss Drew on the cheek, relishing his stubble against my lips. Drew's looking like murder, but it doesn't worry me. It provokes a tickle at the base of my spine. Bad idea. "Back in a minute."

Not that I want him to be jealous or anything. It's not like Drew's going to get jealous over me dancing with Cooper anyway; we're just friends. Fake kissing his fake girlfriend doesn't mean anything. And there's nothing unusual about a girlfriend dancing with a colleague at the office party.

No matter how many eyes that follow Cooper and me to the dance floor might suggest otherwise.

5

DREW

Lawson twirls Bailey around before settling his arms around her, and as much as I want to protect her from all that venom and spite, I have to admit they look good together. He's a much better dancer than cook, that's for damn sure.

I grit my teeth and force myself to smile, aware that a couple of my colleagues are watching me watch them dance.

Much as Lawson provokes me—and I know he does it on purpose—it's not usually this easy to get a reaction out of me. Tonight the stress isn't entirely his fault, and I'm not handling it as well as I ought to be.

I should never have kissed Bailey. Or let her kiss me, or whatever. However it happened, it was a bad idea. Asking her here, asking her to pose as my girlfriend, was stupid. This could seriously mess up our friendship and after a damned decade I'm not about to take that chance. Nothing else can happen between us.

Fortunately, the gala won't last forever. And Mila seems to have found other ways of entertaining herself. Ever since that first confrontation she's given us a wide berth, even her new pal Lawson. Of course, he's been Bailey's shadow for the last hour, which might have something to do with it.

"That's quite a woman you've got there," says the bartender over my shoulder. I glance back at him and raise a brow. He shrugs. "Just saying."

"Thanks," I say.

"You guys been together long?" he asks. When I turn to face him fully, the guy puts up his hands. "I'm not after your girl, dude. Just making conversation."

"It's new," I say, practically growling at the man. What the hell is wrong with me?

The bartender shrugs again. "You're a braver man than I am."

"What's that supposed to mean?"

He looks back out at Bailey and Lawson on the dance floor. "They seem pretty tight. Said they went to college together. If I had a woman like her, that kind of thing might make a man nervous, is all."

Bailey and Lawson went to school together? Which means Lawson and I went to school together, too. I wonder if he knows that.

"I've got nothing to worry about," I say. If Bailey's interested in Lawson, there's not much I can do. Except question her taste in men. Again. I just hope she can keep a lid on it until after the competition.

I watch Bailey laugh at something he says as he spins her around and dips her over his arm with all the possible drama, drawing applause from the onlookers nearby. An image of them together, tangled up and slick, all mouths and tongues and hips and heat, flashes in my mind's eye and I promptly inhale my whiskey.

"You okay, man?" asks the bartender. I wave him off, unable to speak and focus on getting my body under control. Choking to death on my drink is the least of my worries right now. Just what the hell could my dick find so appealing about the idea of my best friend in bed with a man I loathe?

The bartender's still watching me like he's afraid I'm going to keel over. I stuff some extra bills in the tip jar at the corner of the bar and wave as I head for the dance floor.

The floor is getting crowded. Like every wedding reception I've ever been to, the longer the night wears on, the braver people get. Some couples I recognize and plenty I don't, but that's no surprise. Sizzle's a good-sized company. I should know, I audited the invitation list myself.

Bailey and Lawson have their own audience. I'm not sure if it's because people know she came here with me or if it's because he's such a goddamned showoff. Or if it's because they move so well together. I have the sudden, strange sense they've done this before.

Which makes me wonder what else they've done before. It's that thought that gets me out on the floor and tapping Lawson's shoulder before I can think it through.

"What?" he says, barely glancing over his shoulder.

"I think I'm supposed to ask if I can cut in," I say, pitching my voice so nobody else can hear. "But instead, how about you just get lost so I can dance with my girlfriend?"

"Drew!" Bailey looks shocked. Shocked and freaking gorgeous. Dancing with Lawson brought color to her cheeks. Her eyes are bright, though if that's from dancing with him or the wine, I'm not sure. "Jesus, Drew. There's no need to be rude."

"I can think of a couple of reasons," I say. They stopped moving when I first spoke. If we didn't have the attention of the room before, we definitely do now.

"I'm not the one poaching another man's date," I say to Bailey, my eyes on Lawson.

"Poaching?" Bailey sputters. Lawson has the goddamn gall to laugh, turning to face me.

"Maybe if you hadn't abandoned your date at the bar, this wouldn't be happening," says Lawson, his lip curling.

"I did not abandon—"

"I'm standing right here," says Bailey.

"Insecurity is really not your best look, Hicks," says Lawson with a sneer. "Maybe next time you—"

"Enough."

Ty Wilkes comes barreling through the other dancers, all of whom are standing only a few feet away. I guess the music wasn't as loud as I thought.

"You're causing a scene," mutters Ty. "And there are reporters all over this room, not to mention three hundred guests with social media accounts being updated as we speak. While I am a firm believer in publicity by any means, I don't think this is the kind of

39

attention you two are after. Personally or professionally. Am I right?" He directs this last question to Lawson and me.

Lawson shakes his head at the same time I do.

"Good," says Ty. "Now get the fuck out of here. Get a drink, go for a walk, whatever. But you need to chill the hell out before somebody calls security on your asses."

"Don't have to tell me twice," mutters Bailey. She turns to Lawson. "Thank you for the dance, Cooper. It was nice seeing you again." She walks off the dance floor, head held high without saying a word to me.

Lawson watches me watch her go.

"What?" I ask, annoyed at myself for being defensive and asking the question in the first place.

"If you don't go after her, somebody else will," he says. "Namely, me."

"Is that a threat?" God, I hope so. Tomorrow I'll blame the whiskey, but tonight... nothing would satisfy me more right this minute than a good reason to punch him in the face.

Lawson's smirk returns. "Depends. You think me going after your girl is a threat?"

I step into his space and watch his eyes go wide, his pupils expanding until they're almost all I can see. My body goes tight and for one horrifying second I forget I'm about to hit him and I find myself staring at his mouth. His lips are lush, fuller than any man's have a right to be.

Cooper Lawson is the exact opposite of my type. He's mouthy, obnoxious, hateful, arrogant, and I don't care about his tattoos or how good-looking he is. I don't want him. I absolutely can't stand him.

My dick is obviously confused by the fighting, so I take a step back and take a deep breath.

"Right. Looks like my girlfriend and I are heading out," I say in a voice that doesn't quite sound normal. "See you next week, Lawson."

I don't flee, exactly, but I head for the main doors, hauling ass to catch up with Bailey.

. . .

"You don't have to escort me home, Drew," says Bailey for the third time as we climb into the cab. "It's not like it's a long ride."

"I'm not sending you out into the dark by yourself," I say, also for the third time. "I concede that you are a strong, smart, fully-grown woman who is capable of taking care of herself. But my mother would have my head on a platter if I didn't at least make sure you got home safely, so do me a favor and knock it off already."

Bailey snorts, but apparently decides to accept my answer this time. I can tell she's still pissed; she hasn't actually looked at me since we left the gala. And that's pretty fucked up, considering this whole mess is Cooper Lawson's fault. I mention that as the cab driver navigates us into traffic.

"You're kidding me, right?" Bailey finally whirls around to face me. "Andrew Hicks, you all but lifted your leg and pissed on me right there in the middle of the ballroom."

The driver's bulging eyes meet mine in the rearview mirror.

"He was deliberately provoking me," I say.

"That's your excuse?" says Bailey. "Really? 'He started it'?"

"Well, he did." Bailey laughs in disbelief. "And for somebody you barely knew so many years ago, you're awfully quick to defend him," I say. This has been bugging me all night. Just how well did they know each other?

Not that it's any of my business. Goddamn it.

The rest of the ride is silent. Bailey's fuming, and I can't even blame her. I'm not exactly pleased with myself, even if I managed to hold it together there at the very end. Instead of beating the crap out of our new competition host, I mean.

And if I'm still half-hard from whatever the hell happened back there... chalk it up to adrenaline and all that energy needing somewhere to go. Because there's sure as hell no other explanation.

The driver pulls up to Bailey's apartment building and she gets out without a word. Figuring I deserve that much, I pay the man and wave him off. We're not done talking about this. If I have to, I can walk home from here.

Since she doesn't lock the door behind her, I follow her inside. Bailey pours herself another glass of wine and points to the cabinet where she keeps her liquor, so I help myself. She sprawls out on one end of the sofa, kicking off her shoes and moaning as she rubs her feet.

"Fucking heels," she says. Normally I'd crack a joke about the view being worth her pain, but I doubt Bailey's in the mood to be teased. And maybe I'm not so happy with the way the night played out either. After all, she was my date. What was she doing flirting with *him* half the night?

"I can practically smell the smoke coming out of your ears," Bailey says after a minute, head laid back, eyes closed. "Ask me already."

"Just how well do you know Cooper Lawson?" I ask. I'm hedging —it's not the question I really want to ask and she knows it.

Bailey sighs. "Coop and I were assigned lab partners freshman year. Intro to Chemistry."

"I met you that same semester. We were hanging out all the time. How is it possible I didn't know him, too?"

Bailey shrugs. "You were already in the higher level sciences by then. And it's not exactly a small school." She sips her wine and studies the glass. "Plus, he looks a lot different than he used to. I barely recognized him tonight."

How so?

Another question I'm not ready to ask.

"Just lab partners, then?" I say instead. I wait for her to tell me it's none of my fucking business. Maybe I'm even hoping she will, rather than answer my chickenshit question.

Bailey rolls her head around to look at me. "All year," she says. Just as my lungs start working again, she finishes the thought. "Until the week of finals."

I can't do this. It's none of my business. I have absolutely no right to ask her for details, let alone to feel jealous over something that happened so long ago.

"He asked me out," Bailey continues. "We went to celebrate after our final exam. One thing led to another." She shrugs again, not meeting my eyes. "You know how it goes."

I force my teeth to unclench.

"And then what?" I ask.

Bailey shrugs again, but this time there's color in her cheeks. "Then nothing," she says. "Summer break happened. I went home and that was the end of it."

That was the same summer break I introduced Bailey to my brother Alan.

"You didn't keep in touch?"

She looks uncomfortable. "I saw Coop around campus a few times," she says, and there's sincere regret in her voice. "But by then I was already with Alan. Didn't seem fair to try to be friends, and I was too far gone over him by then to think much about anybody else anyway."

The silence hangs between us, not as easy as it ought to be between two old friends talking about their college exploits.

"Well," I say at last, polishing off my whiskey. "That certainly explains some of the hostility tonight."

"Does it?" asks Bailey, her gaze going sharp. "Because Cooper wasn't the only one who got hostile. Care to explain yourself?"

"I don't know what you're talking about." Liar.

"I already mentioned the leg-lifting," she says. "Don't make me say it again."

"You're just mad because I kissed you," I say. Immediately, I know it's the wrong thing to say. Not to mention kind of dumb, because she's the one who kissed me. And because I hadn't ever planned on talking about it. Ever.

"Is that what happened?" says Bailey, coming to her feet. "Because as I remember it, *I* kissed *you*. And you're welcome, jackass. By the way."

"What?"

"I saved your ass from Mila the bitch, that's what," she says. "You owe me. Big time."

Kissing me was that big of a favor, was it? I choke it down, but goddamn, I'm tempted to shout it.

Because to me, kissing Bailey had felt like coming home. Like I was finally doing something right with my life. Like for once, every part of me was exactly where I needed to be doing exactly what I needed to be doing.

Say what you want about Cooper Lawson, but his level of fuck-it is something I could use right about now. If I had half his attitude, maybe I'd be kissing Bailey again instead of arguing with her.

Not that I need to be kissing my best friend. Not that I want to. Because we are friends, just friends. And if in some alternate universe we somehow ended up being more than friends, my family would freak right the fuck out because she almost married my brother once.

Alan would flip his shit.

Also, I don't want her like that. Obviously.

Apparently I've been stewing in my own head too long, because Bailey waves a hand at me.

"Whatever," she says tiredly. "It didn't mean anything. And you're welcome. I'm exhausted. Crash on the couch if you want. More booze in the cabinet. I'm going to bed."

Before I can decide what I'm supposed to say to that—it meant something to me, goddamn it—she's gone, her bedroom door closing with a firm click.

6

COOPER

Monday morning is brisk, almost cold, and I'm damn grateful for it. It'll keep me from sweating out my nerves. This is the first time since signing my contract with Sizzle that I've been asked to attend a meeting with the higher-ups in their corporate office. Since they called the meeting over the weekend, I can only assume it means I'm in trouble for something.

That little scene with Drew Hicks at the kickoff gala might have something to do with it. Just a guess.

Which means this shitty day is all his fault, right down to the coffee staining my tie and the pain from stubbing my toe getting ready this morning.

My livelihood puts me in front of a camera on the reg, so I've got no problem with dressing accordingly. Most days. This morning, though, not a damn thing looks right or feels right, and since I'm feeling pissy, that's Hicks's fault too.

I'm fucking nervous, and I hate feeling nervous. They can't fire me at this point—I haven't done anything wrong, for one thing. And good luck finding another host when the competition starts in less than forty-eight hours. So I'm pretty sure my job isn't in danger.

Still. I have the distinct feeling of being sent to the principal's office for acting up in class.

45

He started it.

Sizzle headquarters takes up the top ten floors of one of the tallest buildings downtown. The lower floors are mostly studios and test kitchens, plus wardrobe and makeup and equipment storage. I've only had to go upstairs a handful of times during the interview process, and the trip is as daunting today as it was then, complete with the upscale yet subdued decor. Everything is gray and taupe and beige and other not-quite-real colors.

Not my style at all, but it has the desired effect, I guess. The place looks appropriately professional and high-end and sterile.

The elevator chime echoes in the marble foyer. The suits must have already clocked in, since I'm the only one waiting for a ride. Stepping inside, I hit the button for the nineteenth floor and breathe deeply, hoping whatever's about to go down happens fast and doesn't end with me unemployed.

A hand catches the sliding doors just before they close and in walks Dickbag Drew Hicks himself.

He does a double take at me as he steps into the elevator, his expression going flat as he focuses on the numbers over the door.

"Lawson," he says.

"Hicks."

"Nice weather we're having," he says blandly, making me snort. "What?"

I roll my eyes and he finally climbs off his damn high horse long enough to catch me in the act.

"We're making small talk now?" I ask.

"Got something better to do?" he says.

"Only anything in the universe." Fourteen more floors. I swear to God, this is the slowest elevator on the planet.

You'd think in a building this size the elevators would be spacious, but there's only a couple of feet between me and Hicks. I can smell his scent from here—something earthy that makes my mouth water, goddamn him—and it puts an itch between my shoulder blades. I shift back, pressing against the handrail.

"Whatever," says Drew. "I'm just making conversation." It's the closest I've heard him get to surly, except when he was marking his territory around Bailey. The itch between my shoulder blades grows.

He just takes up so damn much space. Not physically—with his presence. Ugh. Why can't he just stand there like a normal person? He's not doing anything in particular, just leaning against the rail across from me, arms crossed, tapping his fingers on his arm like he can't wait to get out of here either.

Why that irritates me further, I have no idea. God knows, I don't want to be locked in here with him any longer than I have to be.

"You can take your conversation and shove it," I say, the cap popping on my frustration. I realize belatedly that this is the first time we've ever been alone and the thought makes it hard to breathe, which confuses me and pisses me off even more.

It's all his fault, all of it.

"This is all your fault," I say, stepping forward. A second step takes me squarely into his personal space and Hicks stands up to his full height. He's only a couple of inches taller than me, but broader and thicker and clearly aware of it.

Hell with that. You don't scare me.

"What the hell are you talking about?"

"You're really going to tell me you don't know what this meeting's about?" I say, sneering.

"Pretty sure that scene you caused Friday night has something to do with it," he says, leaning forward. If he's trying to intimidate me, he's failing. Miserably.

"That I caused?" I poke him in the chest. "You're the one who decided to go all caveman over Bailey—"

"Don't talk to me about Bailey," he says, his voice going low.

My stomach gets that weird weightless sensation when I realize Hicks is close enough I can feel his breath on my face, the heat coming off his body. I think he picks up on it at the same time and for one weird moment his gaze drops inexplicably to my mouth.

Like it did at the gala. I thought I must have imagined it.

It takes me a beat too long to realize the elevator is slowing to a stop. The chime announcing our arrival makes me jerk back a step.

"You don't get to tell me what I can and cannot do," I say, keeping my voice down as I step out into a small, mercifully empty foyer.

A firm grip on my arm stops me before I can walk too far. I pull away, but Hicks doesn't let go until I turn around.

"What?"

"What is your problem?" he asks. "You have been nothing but antagonistic toward me from the day we met."

"My problem is that I'm late for a meeting that wouldn't even be happening if it weren't for you causing a scene in a room full of reporters." That's not the only problem, but it's as true as any of the others. Hick's mouth tightens.

"As I recall, I wasn't the only person involved," he says, his voice hard.

Whatever brilliant, scathing reply I'm about to make is lost when Bob Greeley, an executive producer with Sizzle and the man in charge of the cooking competition, comes around the corner.

"Ah, there you both are!" he says. Greeley has the relentless, overly jovial manner of a lifelong salesman. Ten bucks says that's where he started before getting promoted to VP of Whatever He Does.

Greeley waves us down the hall. "Come on. Now that you're here, we can get started."

Ignoring Drew Hicks with every last cell in my body, I follow Greeley down the long hall to the conference room. It's another expanse of gleaming professionalism—the long mahogany table surrounded by over a dozen empty chairs. There are a handful of other people already seated, tapping away at laptops, nodding absently as we take our seats. I make a point of putting an extra seat between Hicks and me. His quiet snort tells me the move isn't lost on him.

"Let's get started," says Greeley. More nodding from the... assistants? Interns? I recognize at least one other producer, Kenna Burch, plus Hicks's boss, Ty Wilkes, but that's it. "Ty?"

"Right," says Wilkes, laying a hand on the conference table. "We'll keep this brief. As you all know, our first local cooking competition kicks off in three days. Cooper here," he says, pointing to me, "is our host."

"Glad to have you on board, Cooper," says Greeley.

"Thank you."

"It won't be news to anybody that part of the reason you were chosen as host is because you have a dedicated online following," says Ty.

More nodding from the room at large. I've built a pretty extensive audience the last several years, first with blogging, then with various social media platforms. Things really took off after I started making videos. I'm sure my experience is why Sizzle offered me the hosting gig—well, that, plus getting access to my audience.

"Which brings me to why we're here," says Ty. "The traditional media outlets are desperate for anything that'll get them attention. Anything that might go viral gets a mention, and considering your name already draws a good amount of traffic online—" Ty lets the thought hang.

"Let's just say we'd like to be careful about the type of attention you draw," says Greeley.

"Which means no more scenes like the one at the gala the other night," says Kenna.

"I thought there was 'no such thing as bad publicity,'" I say, defensive despite my best effort to sound innocent.

"Yes, well," says Greeley, blustering. "Given the current political climate, the board feels it necessary to maintain a certain level of decorum. Keeping things family friendly, you know."

I can just imagine. Sizzle is owned by a middle-grade media company with delusions of playing in the big leagues, and Sizzle's the most popular channel in their network. If they're playing the political angle, this meeting makes total sense.

Except it sounds like I'm not going to get my knuckles smacked for bad behavior. So why are we here?

"I appreciate being kept in the loop," says Hicks, radiating wholesome golden boy from every pore. Give me a fucking break. "What do you need from me?"

Ty Wilkes turns to Hicks with a pointed look. "You're here to help," says Wilkes. "I understand Cooper had some... challenges during your class this summer."

I absolutely one fucking hundred percent refuse to blush, digging my nails into my palm to distract myself.

So I had some trouble keeping up with the class. Sue me. It wasn't part of my contract—signing up for that cooking class was totally voluntary, my own dime on my own time. It was a chance to scope out how Sizzle worked and see if I could glom on to any useful skills in the meantime.

The fact that Drew Hicks taught the class had absolutely nothing to do with it. If anything, I thought watching him try to pull the stick out of his ass to talk to mere mortals once a week had been worth the time spent. And yeah, maybe I got a charge out of terrorizing him a little, and sometimes maybe I played like I was worse at cooking than I really am. Big deal. My pride got a little dinged up but nobody got hurt.

In retrospect, it probably wasn't my smartest move.

Hicks glances my way and I brace myself for the coming humiliation.

"No more than any other students I've had," he says blandly. I blink three or four times, losing track of who speaks next.

Excuse me? What the hell is he up to?

"—so the board has suggested we have a Sizzle employee tag along to help Cooper through the process. Considering he's a contractor, it's the least we can do."

Hold up.

"I don't need a babysitter," I say.

Greeley holds up a hand. "No, of course not. That's not what this is about."

"It's about making sure this competition runs as smoothly as possible," adds Kenna. She gives me a small, kind smile. Try as I might, I can't find any sarcasm or condescension there.

Then the other shoe drops.

"Wait," I say. "You're putting me with Hicks?"

"I don't think—" Hicks is pushing back in his chair but Wilkes holds up a hand, stalling us both.

"Drew is one of our most reliable employees," says Wilkes to me. He looks at Drew, his expression hardening. "And I know he'll do whatever it takes to make this competition a success."

"This was your idea," Hicks says. It's not a question, but Wilkes nods. The air is thick with tension, and I think it's all sitting in the empty seat between Hicks and me.

Unbe-fucking-lievable.

"The two of you caught a fair amount of attention the other night on the dance floor with that blond woman," says Wilkes.

"There's a viral GIF and everything," adds Kenna. I think I'm finally catching on.

"So you stick us together to control the narrative," I say. My stomach feels hot for some reason. Hicks's shoulders are damn near covering his ears, he's so tense.

"I'm not sure I'm the right person for this assignment," he says. Wilkes pins him in place with a look.

"I am," says Wilkes.

"As am I," says Greeley, who has been watching all of us with interest. His eyes keep bouncing between Hicks and me, like he's trying to do invisible math.

"So what are we supposed to do?" I ask, getting restless. "Fight on camera?" My brain's already conjured up an adolescent fantasy of besting Drew Hicks in an argument while Bailey looks on, wide-eyed and awed and grateful. I shift in the chair to make a little more room for my dick, because the thought of a grateful Bailey while I dominate the hell out of that asshole turns me on.

Not that kind of dominate, though. Jesus, what is wrong with me?

"Not in so many words," says Greeley. "This isn't that kind of reality TV. But if the press happens to stick around because they think something like that confrontation might happen again, well..."

I get it. I don't like it, but I get it, so I nod. Greeley smiles and focuses on Hicks, who appears to be frozen in his seat.

I've got a pretty good idea Wilkes's golden boy is none too happy about this arrangement. I can't say I'm excited about it, but Hicks's obvious consternation tickles some dark place in me that likes to see him squirm. Let him get a taste of how it feels being on the spot for once.

Greeley ticks off orders at the interns before dismissing everybody. I do my best to be polite, shaking hands and smiling as they leave, waving at Kenna as she heads out. I'm pushing my chair back when I hear my name.

"Can you stick around a minute?" Wilkes says. It's just me and him and Greeley left in the conference room.

And Hicks, of course. He hasn't moved a muscle since their little announcement. I think I'd be offended, except his obvious discomfort is pretty damn amusing.

"Drew," says Wilkes, waiting for him to look up from the table. "Is this going to be a problem?"

"No, sir," says Hicks softly. There's steel in his voice.

"Good," says Wilkes. "Because we cannot afford to have this competition derailed by some personal bullshit."

Hicks doesn't say anything.

"So what exactly do you need from us?" I ask. The "us" feels weird on my tongue. Weighty.

"Drew here will stick close to you for the duration of the competition," says Greeley, piling up papers into a briefcase. "Inasmuch as your schedules allow, anyway. Doesn't need to be on camera necessarily, but as long as you're on-site I expect you to stick together. Don't go looking for attention."

They want us practically holding hands. Jesus. But Greeley literally signs my checks for the next few weeks, so I suck it up and nod. Greeley shakes my hand, then Hicks's after he finally rises from his seat. "I'm in meetings the rest of the day, so if you'll all excuse me. Ty here will be your point man if anything comes up," says Greeley. He nods at Wilkes. "I appreciate your cooperation, gentlemen." Picking up the briefcase, he's out the door.

Hicks still has barely spoken, and Wilkes doesn't look too happy about that fact. Folding his arms across his chest, he says, "Last chance, Drew. If we're going to have a problem, now's the time to say so."

"I can handle it," he says. I snort, and he finally looks at me.

Golden Boy's got laser vision when he wants to. The heat in my stomach ticks up a notch.

"Get it out of your system now," says Hicks. "I don't want to have to deal with this crap all week. Some of us have work to do."

"You think I'm here for fun?" Asshole.

"I'm not sure what you're doing here at all," he snaps.

"Running circles around your ass, apparently."

"Oh, I'd like to see you try."

A bang cuts me off as Wilkes slams his hand down on the conference table.

"Enough," he says, pinching the bridge of his nose. "You two can take your weird foreplay somewhere else. Do your best to keep it off camera. Or don't—I don't care either way. But in case Greeley didn't make it clear, for the duration of this competition, working together is part of your job. Both of your jobs." Wilkes fixes us each with a hard look and strides out of the room.

That word, *foreplay*, puts the itch right back between my shoulder blades, making me stand up straighter. Time to go.

I shut my damn mouth because foreplay? Really? Why'd he have to say it like that? And don't make a sound when Hicks and I get stuck on the same elevator down to the lobby.

7

BAILEY

A FEW DAYS LATER...

Parking at the arena is such a clusterfuck that I end up taking a shuttle to the entrance. The crowd isn't helping my nerves one bit, that's for sure.

After the gala Friday night I spent the weekend thinking about what Kenna had said, about signing up for the cooking competition, turning over the possibility again and again. I completed the forms with wine-soaked enthusiasm just before registration closed late Sunday night. Posing as Drew's fake girlfriend was no reason to stop me from doing something I genuinely wanted to do, after all.

My boss doesn't share my enthusiasm. But since I never go on vacation—hell, I haven't taken off more than a day or two in the last three years—there's nothing he can do about it.

As for Drew... I wouldn't say I'm avoiding him, exactly, but I haven't seen him since he left my apartment that night. And just because I haven't responded to any of his texts since then doesn't mean I'm avoiding him.

Sure thing, girl. Whatever you want to tell yourself.

It's just that if he'd stayed on my couch any longer Friday night, I was either going to hit him or kiss him again. And considering he's my best friend, neither seemed like a good idea.

The check-in line isn't nearly as long as I expected, considering the crowd. I guess most of these people are here just as spectators, which makes sense. They've got vendors and sponsors set up along the walkways like some kind of damn carnival.

If last week hadn't gone all weird, I'd probably be here as a spectator too, if for no other reason than to support all of Drew's hard work. He's logged plenty of overtime the last couple of months getting this competition set up.

Naturally, my interest in being here has nothing whatsoever to do with the possibility of seeing Cooper again. Even if I did see him, he's surely busy working. Considering he's the host, he'll likely have cameras on him constantly.

I remind myself of that as I wait in line to check in. Cooper and Drew are both here to work, and considering they're both in high demand today, I'm not likely to see either one of them.

Which is fine. Fine.

And if I've woken up every day since needy and hot from dreaming about them—either one, both of them, all of us together... Jesus, knock it off already—that's my business.

The line shuffles forward slowly, giving me plenty of time to school my thoughts. Fantasizing about two men is one thing. Obsessing is another, especially when it involves two people I know in real life. Though I have to admit, it's a nice change of mental scenery from being pissed at my ex. Torturing my celibate self with slightly guilty fantasies of Drew and Coop is a vast improvement, if you don't count the masochistic element. Because there is zero chance it would ever happen. None.

Damn it.

It's silly to waste time regretting something that's never going to happen, and besides, I'm here for growth. It's high time I did something just for me. Something less destructive than, say, cutting my bangs with kitchen shears. Lord knows I do not have the bone structure to pull that off again. What was I thinking? Luckily, my hairdresser was able to squeeze me in to get that fixed. If only all my problems got fixed so easily.

According to the Sizzle competition website, the competition was capped at two hundred participants. Realistically, the chances of me getting to the next round, let alone the finals, are slim to none but it doesn't matter. I'm here because I want to be, and nobody's going to bring me down. This is fun, goddammit.

The person in front of me walks away with their paperwork in hand so I step up to the table.

"Hi, I'm Bailey Ross. I'm here to check in."

"Ross, Ross." The brunette shuffles through the box of files on the table, withdrawing a folder and handing it over. "Here you... Shit."

I look up and realize I'm standing face-to-face with Drew's bitchy coworker, Mila.

"Ah," I say eloquently, clearing my throat. "Hi."

"You. You're competing?"

"Looks like it," I say, channeling all the fake politeness I can manage. My mother would be so proud of me right now. "Nice to see you again, Mila."

She snorts, dropping the file on the table before I can get a grip on it.

"Hardly," she says, crossing her arms. "I can't believe they let you sign up."

The producer I went to college with—the one I met at the gala— walks up around the table, scribbling notes on a clipboard, a frazzled-looking younger man hurrying to keep up behind her.

"There a problem here, Mila?" she asks, then looks at me and smiles wide. "Bailey! You're here. I take it you signed up after all?"

"Looks like," I say, smiling at Kenna Burch.

"Ms. Burch," says Mila, turning her back to me to address Kenna. "This... this woman isn't eligible to compete. She's Drew Hicks's girlfriend!"

"Sure she can," says Kenna. "The rules only forbid immediate family members."

"Do you really think she should be allowed—"

"I certainly do," says Kenna cheerfully. "I'm the one who told her to sign up in the first place."

Mila doesn't know what to make of that, her mouth gaping wide.

"Good luck today, Bailey!" Kenna makes another mark on her

clipboard and waves as she walks off. I grab my folder off the table and make a beeline out of there.

"Jeez, what crawled up her butt?" comes a voice at my elbow.

I turn to look. A statuesque redhead I recognize from the registration line falls into step beside me as I follow the signs for the competition floor.

"Nothing good," I say, shaking my head. "I'm Bailey."

"Evie Reynolds," the Amazon says, offering her hand. "You pick a workstation yet, Bailey?" I shake my head. "Come on," she says, tipping her head in the direction of the stage.

The competition's been set up with small groups of five workstations each, each arranged around a set of shelves containing ingredients and equipment. Stations don't appear to be preassigned, but I guess Evie got here early enough to choose one up close to the action.

She leads me all the way up near the front, almost to the stage itself.

"That's mine," she says, pointing at a station covered in pink glitter. Neither of the stations alongside hers appear to be claimed, so I set my folder down, claiming the one next to Evie's.

"Seriously though," says Evie as she dusts off her hands, "what's that chick's problem? You owe her money or something?"

"It's not that," I say, laughing. "She kind of has a thing for this guy I'm, um, seeing."

"Ah," Evie says, a knowing look coming over her face. "Say no more. Not a great way to start the competition though."

"Yeah, probably not," I say. A thought occurs to me. Shit. "Oh, God. What if she's one of the judges?"

"Nah," says Evie, holding up a hand to block the sun from her eyes as she looks up at the stage. She points to the far end. "See the table there at the end? Those seats for are the judges. If the bitch isn't up there already, you're in the clear."

Sure enough, all four seats at the table are occupied, the judges chatting and smiling, no Mila in sight.

"Lucky break," I say, laughing nervously. Evie gives me a warm smile.

"First time competing?" she asks.

58

"Isn't it everybody's?" I ask. It's the first year the network's held any kind of competition as far as I know. Evie shakes her head.

"It's Sizzle's first, maybe," she says. "But a lot of these people here have competed in cooking shows and demos locally for a long time."

"Have you competed before?" I ask her. Evie nods.

Double shit.

"Don't sweat it," says Evie. "It's supposed to be fun, isn't it?"

"Isn't that what the losers always say?" I say before I can think better of it. Evie snorts and I slap a hand over my mouth. "That was rude of me, I'm sorry."

"Girl," says Evie, cracking up. "We're gonna get along just fine."

"Contestants! Choose your stations quickly, please," comes a familiar voice over the loudspeaker. "We'll begin the first round in approximately fifteen minutes. Again, please choose your stations quickly."

I look up at the stage and there's Drew, front and center, holding a microphone. He secures the mic back into its stand and sets his hands on his hips, scanning the crowd. Looking for what, I'm not sure.

God, he looks good. It's not like I didn't know that. It's not like it's news to me that he's good-looking. Hell, I wanted him when I first met him, did I not? But now there's all this history... damn near ten years of being friends. All that water under the bridge of our friendship. I can't let one fake kiss as his fake girlfriend on one fake date ruin that, can I?

I told him that kiss didn't mean anything. I had to, didn't I? He matters too much. I don't know what the hell would I do without him, and since the surest way for me to get rid of a man is to get involved with him, that means Drew is off-limits.

Off. Limits.

Just then he catches sight of me. Drew's arms drop to his sides and I watch his chest rise as he sucks in a breath, straining his T-shirt at its seams.

"Hot damn," breathes Evie. "Friend of yours?"

"The best," I say, and leave it at that.

I shake my head and turn back to my table, forcing myself to focus on the layout. The first round requires cooking with a surprise ingredient. I tried to focus on recalling every TV cooking competition I've ever seen, mentally cataloging all the weird surprise ingredients I can remember from those shows. Mostly, though, I'm ignoring Drew for all I'm worth. Maybe it's shitty of me to have blown him off all week, but really. A girl can only take so much rejection, even if it comes from a well-meaning friend.

Besides, technically I'm the one who kicked him out, so if anybody should be feeling rejected, it's Drew. Right? Which makes no sense, and dwelling on it only makes me more tense.

Time to focus, girl.

The next time I look up at the stage Drew's leaning casually over the judges' table, but this time I can spot Cooper just off to one side, someone pinning a microphone to the lapel of the shirt.

Speaking of good-looking men. Lord, have mercy.

Coop's got that hot hipster thing down to a T—the tailored button-down shirt, sleeves rolled up to show off the tattoos creeping across his forearms, perfectly fitted jeans. He was cute in college, handsome in a nerdy kind of way. Now he's flat-out hot.

I'm more than a little weirded out that my body's having such a strong reaction to Cooper only moments after salivating over Drew, but I'm a grown, unattached, hetero woman. I have eyes in my head and a functioning sex drive. It would be weirder if I *didn't* notice them both. Probably.

Evie gets me out of my head by dragging me over to the supply station and we speculate on the surprise ingredient, trying to come up with the wildest competition scenes we can recall, from Japanese seaweed to obscure French mushrooms. Before long, a noise from the stage calls us back to our stations.

"Ladies and gentlemen, welcome to Sizzle TV's very first cooking competition," Drew's voice booms over the loudspeaker, momentarily drowned out by raucous applause. He waves down the crowd from his spot at the center of the stage. When the noise dies off, he starts again. "Ladies and gentlemen, welcome. You're here to witness our first ever amateur cooking competition. We'll get started in just a moment, but before we do, I'd like to introduce you to your host. He's curator of several blogs and vlogs, not to mention an enormously popular video channel on YouTube. Please welcome Cooper Lawson."

Cooper takes the stage, smiling and waving. I've never seen him like this before—completely at ease, absolutely hamming it up, even blowing kisses at the audience, many of whom are screaming his name.

He looks like a total rock star, a far cry from the skinny lab partner I knew ten years ago.

Coop takes the mic from Drew. I doubt anybody in this whole crowd besides me notices the smug challenge on his face as Coop extends a hand for Drew to shake. Drew doesn't fall for it, though. Instead, he pulls Coop in for a hug, clapping him on the back hard enough my own shoulders twitch in sympathy.

Coop takes it in stride though, laughing and taking the microphone.

"Thanks, Drew," Coop says, turning to the crowd. "How's everybody doing today?"

He spends the next several minutes winding up the crowd. I have to give him credit; he knows exactly how to play an audience. Inside of five minutes, the crowd is near to frothing with enthusiasm.

"Now that we've got the introductions out of the way," says Cooper, "contestants, I need you at your stations. Everybody ready?" A resounding "Yes!" echoes up from the competition floor.

"Great," says Cooper. He reaches into his back pocket and pulls out an envelope. "I have here in my hand today's secret competition ingredient. You've all been advised of the rules, but just as a reminder: whatever you choose to make has to be an edible dish. It has to be of your own concoction, so no pre-written recipes allowed. No cell phone use, no crib sheets." Cooper wags a finger, drawing laughter from the crowd. "And, of course, you must actually use the secret ingredient in whatever you choose to fix." Coop nods at somebody standing offstage.

"All right, folks. Everybody ready?"

"Here we go," Evie mutters to me.

"This secret ingredient is..." Cooper opens the envelope with a flourish. "Green tea leaves."

THE NEXT TWENTY-FIVE minutes are a blur. I'm too busy scrambling to find what I need to register much from the people around me, except the insane amount of noise produced by the chaos.

Evie and I bump into each other repeatedly, darting to and from the supply shelves. She's a good sport, unlike the rest of our group. Sizzle has staff manning every set of supply shelves, but there's no way to ward off the elbows trying to push me out of the way.

I don't let it get me down. Between the adrenaline rush I get every time I look at that massive countdown clock on the big screen and the stress of focusing on the task at hand, I don't notice much of anything else until the vegan vegetable soup I pull together finally starts to taste the way I want.

Green tea isn't only for drinking, but I don't think very many people here know that, considering the number of blenders I hear running, and the number of people fighting over espresso machines.

The buzzer sounds a few seconds after I take one last satisfied taste of my dish, prompting groans from all over the competition floor and cheers from the audience at large.

"And that's it, folks!" says Cooper, striding to the center of the stage. The applause is deafening as staffers move in to make sure everybody has stepped away from their workstations. Evie and I shake hands with the rest of the people from our group.

"All right, everybody," says Cooper, waiting for the noise to die down. "Now as you might expect, with two hundred entries to judge, this is gonna take a few minutes. Before we get to that, the judges have asked me to remind you of the rules. Y'all remember what they are?"

The crowd shouts affirmatively.

"That's right," says Cooper. "Rule number one: must be an edible dish. Those of you who produced a beverage of any kind, will you please step out into the aisles."

I was right about all those blenders. More than half the competitors shuffle to the wide aisles between the workstations.

Cooper waves them forward, drawing them toward the stage.

"Folks, I'm sorry to tell you that based on rules of the competition, if your entry is a beverage of any kind, at this point you have been disqualified." Sighs and jeers and shocked cries sound from the crowd.

Cooper shakes his head. "Rule number one, remember? Has to be an edible dish. No beverages will be submitted for judging."

"Damn, that's harsh," says Evie. I nod. Harsh, but smart. How else were they going to get through all these people in one day?

"Thank you for coming out," says Cooper as the dismissed contestants make their way out into the crowd. "Y'all can just make your way out up the stands." Low, pulsing music begins playing, reminding me of those celebrity awards shows when somebody's been talking onstage too long.

"As for the rest of you," says Cooper as the disqualified contestants make their way up into the audience, "congratulations! You've officially passed to round two." The crowd's applause is deafening.

It looks like maybe fifty or sixty people made it past the first round, including Evie and me. It'll be nice to have a familiar face nearby for round two tomorrow, especially since we don't know the details of the next challenge yet.

We've been instructed to leave cleanup for the staff, so Evie and I head for the winner's tent with the rest of the round one competitors. I try to keep an eye out for Cooper or Drew, but no luck.

"What gives?" asks Evie as we line up to get inside. "You made it to the second round. You're supposed to be smiling."

"It's kind of a letdown, isn't it?" I ask. "All that work and nobody's going to even try the food."

"The judges will try it," says Evie. "Didn't you see that part? Anybody who gets through round one gets scored on their dish. The score will count toward your final tally. Highest scores at the end of the weekend make it to the final five."

"Must have missed that part," I say. "Shame they can't just feed it to all these people."

"Well, how else are they supposed to make any money off this circus?" she says, laughing until I laugh too.

"You're right," I say, thinking of all those vendors selling food outside the arena. "I'm parched. Let's go get a beer."

"Hey, Ross."

I turn. Cooper's standing right behind me. I throw my arms around him for a hug before I think twice.

"You," I say, smacking a noisy kiss on his cheek, "were amazing up there!"

Coop laughs, squeezing me tight before setting me back on my feet.

"Thanks," he says. "Apparently you're not so bad yourself, making it past the first round. Veggie soup, huh? You'll have to make it for me sometime."

"Anytime," I say. "Coop, this is—"

"Evie," she says, thrusting a hand forward. "I'm a big fan."

I swear to God, Cooper blushes. Blushes.

"Thanks," he says.

"I'm outta here, Beezy," says Evie. "I'll track you down tomorrow. Nice to meet you, Cooper." Evie blows me a kiss and wanders off in the direction of the bar.

"You want to grab a drink somewhere else?" says Cooper.

Hell, yes, I do. Coop's already drawing attention among the other contestants, and I've somehow managed to avoid Drew this long. Knowing that my luck won't last, I nod, following Cooper out of the tent.

8

DREW

Hugging Cooper Lawson was a mistake.

I blame stage fright, aka the main reason I'm content to stay backstage most of the time.

I figured he'd protest, despite the fact that we were onstage in front of several thousand people, or make a big joke out of it, but the guy took it in stride. Which, frankly, shocked the hell out of me. Pains me to admit it, but Cooper's pretty damn good at his job.

Doesn't mean I have to like it.

I sure as hell don't like that I've been walking around half-hard ever since. Thankfully, everybody's too busy taking pictures of the pseudo-celebrities here for promotion today to notice my condition.

I'm not completely oblivious. I know what this is. I've been attracted to both men and women since... well, since I was old enough to know that was even an option. Just goes to show you when it comes to good judgment, penises don't have any.

Cooper's an easy scapegoat for my shitty mood, but it started even before that center-stage hug. Bailey's been avoiding me, but I've been kind of avoiding her right back and it chafes. That's not who I am. If there's a problem, you own it. That's just the way I see it.

Hard to take responsibility for something when the other person involved won't even call you back, though. Or answer a text. Or say hi when she sees you up onstage.

There are a couple of possible explanations for why Bailey's avoiding me, but it's obvious to me she's freaking out about that kiss. I broke all kinds of rules with that one, and if she had any idea how much I was into it, she'd disown me for sure.

Who am I kidding? She's Bailey. She knows me better than anybody. And anybody with sight could see how much I liked kissing her. Possibly from space.

I have to talk to her. Just because I liked kissing her doesn't mean things have to change.

"Hey, handsome." I look up from the checklist I've been pretending to read for the past five minutes and see Mila from work heading my way, tapping a clipboard against her leg. "Helluva show."

"Hey, Mila."

"You did a great job up there," she says, wrapping a sharply mani-cured hand around my bicep and giving a small squeeze. "I don't know why they didn't have you host. That fool Cooper has nothing on you."

"I thought he did a great job," I say, surprised to hear the words coming from my own mouth. And I mean them.

"You're defending him?" asks Mila in disbelief. "I thought you guys hated each other."

"He's not so bad once you get to know him," I say, lying through my teeth. It's not outside the realm of possibility that Cooper might not be so bad, but I hardly know the man. No backtracking now, though. And Mila doesn't seem to care either way.

"Well," she says. "I'd still rather watch you any day of the week." She squeezes my arm again.

"Thanks," I say, disengaging before I get mauled by her nails. "Are you working the afterparty?"

"I wish. They had me at registration," says Mila, shaking her head. "Now I'm just processing paperwork." Which means she's supposed to be back at the office by now.

"Well, I won't keep you," I say as cheerfully as I can.

"Oh, it's no trouble. I'd rather stay and talk to you," she titters.

66

This is getting out of hand. Maybe Bailey's right—maybe it's time I mention this to Tyler, or somebody else at the office.

But really, what could I say? She asked me out too many times? It's not like she's done anything wrong or hurtful. And rejection is never fun for anybody.

With that in mind, I lower my voice.

"Mila," I say, glancing around to check for eavesdroppers. "I told you. I'm seeing someone."

"Hmm," says Mila, her lips twisting for a second. "Yeah, I saw your girl. She came through my check-in line earlier."

Seeing Bailey in the crowd of competitors earlier had shocked the hell out of me. Last I heard, she wasn't planning on signing up, but I guess Kenna must have talked her into it. I didn't get to see her compete, but since she hadn't been among the herd of people who got the boot for making a drink, I knew she'd be back for round two tomorrow.

"Anyway," Mila says. "I saw her over at the beer garden. With Cooper." Her thoughts on that little tidbit come through loud and clear in her tone.

"Thanks," I say, already walking away. "See you back at the office."

She calls out something I don't catch, as I'm too busy making my way through the various blue-shirted staff members backstage, trying to get to the winners tent.

I should have known better. I'm supposed to stick to Cooper like goddamn glue. He sneaked away after we dismissed the contestants. I figured it was no big deal, since the rest of the day is mostly getting set up for tomorrow. They didn't need us on camera, so when he crept off backstage, I let him.

Evidently he made a beeline for Bailey.

The heat in my stomach twists, confusing the hell out of me. I'm not supposed to be jealous of Bailey, she's my friend, not my girl, but if she were... shouldn't I be more jealous of them spending time together?

Good thing I'm not jealous. Not at all.

Satisfied with that much, though my thoughts clearly make no sense whatsoever, I make my way around backstage. I pass a group of my cooking school students and get pulled into the conversation before I can slide by unnoticed.

"Drew!" I'm caught in a fierce hug before I can identify who it is I'm talking to. I lean back to see one of the most regular students in my classes. If I'm honest, she's one of my favorites.

"Mrs. Weaver," I say, finally hugging her back. "Good to see you again. Did you compete today?"

"I did," she said, shaking her finger at me. "Those sneaky producers know what they're doing, eliminating more than half the competition in the first round."

"You made a smoothie, didn't you?" I ask with a grin.

"Of course I did," says Mrs. Weaver. "It was the only reasonable thing to do. Who knew you could actually cook with tea?"

"I know what you mean," I say. "But wait. If you didn't get past the first round, how did you get backstage just now? Security's not supposed to let you back here."

"Pish tosh," she says, waving a hand. "I met that nice Mr. Greeley during registration and told him all about how much I love your classes at the studio. We'd barely started talking before he gave me this pass." She indicates the All-Access tag draped around her neck. I can just imagine my boss's reaction in the face of all of Mrs. Weaver's... enthusiasm. She can be persuasive when she wants something.

"As long as you've got a pass, you're good to go," I say. "I hate to run, but I have to be somewhere. Will you be back to watch the rest of the competition this weekend?"

"Wouldn't miss it," says Mrs. Weaver. "Before you take off, I wanted to ask you why you're leaving."

"Excuse me?"

"One of the ladies at registration said you're leaving Sizzle. Said you've decided to pursue opportunities somewhere else," says Mrs. Weaver, putting air quotes around it and looking disappointed. "Imagine my surprise, since I just signed up for your next session."

"Mrs. Weaver, I don't know why they told you that, but I promise you I'm not going anywhere."

"Promise?"

"Promise." I hug her again.

"That's a relief," says Mrs. Weaver. "I already paid up-front." I laugh because she wants me to, and she waves me off, already calling out to talk to somebody else.

What the hell was that about? There were only six people assigned to work that registration table. I know, because I assigned them myself. As I make my way back to the winners tent, one name sticks out.

Mila Hague.

Why would she make that up? I can't think of any reason she'd have to lie about me, least of all to one of my cooking class students. And a well-known student at that; Mrs. Weaver's been attending classes since before I started teaching them. Practically everyone at the network knows who she is.

Whatever Mila's motivation was, I don't have time for it now. I have to find Bailey. If she's really with Cooper, I'll... I don't know what I'll do but it won't be good. My neck prickles at the thought of another scene like the one at the gala, the three of us going at it again. Not that I'd want that.

Maybe in a world without consequence. Not to mention common sense, or self-preservation, or any rhyme or reason. So if you deconstruct reality completely, then I could see it happening.

Bailey and me. Or Cooper.

And Cooper.

But that's never going to happen in this universe or the next, so I shake the insane thought from my head, furious with myself for thinking about it at all.

The winners' tent is small by design. It's meant to keep the competitors corralled to one space so they don't get in the way of the staff the rest of the weekend, a security measure more than anything else. Not to mention keeping the heat in against the rapidly cooling weather. Even so, there's a line out the door of the tent. The music's loud, the atmosphere festive.

At first glance, I don't see Bailey or Cooper anywhere. The statuesque redhead woman I vaguely remember standing next to Bailey before the competition is chatting with a group of people near the corner, so I head that way first.

The blonde catches sight of me as I approach the group. "You looking for Bailey?" she shouts over the noise.

I nod.

"Just missed her," says the blonde. She jerks a thumb over her shoulder to the back entry and I catch sight of Cooper's spiky dark hair, his arm around Bailey's waist as they shuffle their way through the crowd.

So Mila was telling the truth, at least about that part.

I nod my thanks to the blonde and sneak out back the way I came before I get stopped by anybody else.

So Bailey's leaving with Cooper. It doesn't matter. It shouldn't matter.

It can't matter. She's my friend, and while I might tease her about her questionable taste in men, she makes her own decisions.

Hell, who are we kidding? As far as I can tell, with the obvious exception of my brother, Bailey and I have practically the same taste in men. And isn't that just a bitch?

I'm sure I'll laugh about it someday. In the meantime, I have a job to do.

9

COOPER

Bailey points me to a dive bar a few blocks away from the arena. It doesn't look like much from the outside, the open sign on the door flickering every now and then as though it could give out any moment. The crowd inside is low-key, and I don't immediately recognize anybody from Sizzle. Taking it as a good sign, I follow Bailey when she chooses a booth in the back.

"Feels a little weird," says Bailey. She waits until I sit down to finish the thought. "A cooking show competition where nobody eats anything."

"Speak for yourself," I say, snagging a menu from the back of the table. "I had to taste half those damn smoothies before they got discarded."

"Guess that's what you get for being so popular," teases Bailey. She gives me a grin that makes my heart hurt in my chest, looking so much like my nineteen-year-old lab partner that for a moment I'm transported back to the one night I had her alone.

I shake my head, coming back to the present.

"It won't last," I say. "It's good for the competition, but my contract with Sizzle was only for the live competition, plus the final rounds next week."

"Much to the dismay of your new fans," says Bailey, eyeing the menu. "Pretty sure you found some new ones today, too."

"Can't hurt," I say. "That's the nature of the business. I need all the eyeballs I can get." Weirdo. "I mean—"

"I know what you mean," says Bailey, laughing. "How'd you get into the whole blogosphere thing, anyway? Though I hear you're mostly doing videos now."

"Same way as anybody else, I guess," I say looking around for a server. "I started posting pictures of every meal I had that I liked, and after a while people started responding. It was easy to go from photos with captions to making videos. After a few months, I had companies emailing me about sponsorship."

"Why do I suspect that's not the 'same as anybody else' at all?" says Bailey, arching a brow.

I grin. "You may be right. You want a beer?"

"I'll have whatever you're having," she says. I head up to order our drinks, leaving her to scour the menu.

The bar top is almost empty when I get up there, resting on my elbows on the edge as I wait for the bartender to come back from the kitchen. An attractive dark-haired man to my left clears his throat. Twice.

"Can I get you something?" he asks. I turn my head, bracing for confrontation, but the grin on the guy's face is warm, bordering on flirtatious. I feel my own lips quirk but shake my head, turning down whatever he's offering.

"Just waiting on a beer," I say. If I'd come here alone, I might have taken a seat just to see what else he had in mind. The guy's built, no two ways about it. I don't usually go in for that much muscle but he's good-looking too, almost pretty.

The image of another muscular man who is absolutely, positively not my type whatsoever comes to mind, but I ignore it because Bailey's waiting for me, and if this turns into a second chance with her, I'm not blowing it. Not for pretty boy here at the bar and sure as hell not for some know-it-all Captain America knockoff.

"My bad, man," says Pretty Boy, shifting in his chair and averting his eyes.

"Not a problem," I say. "Any other day, maybe, but I'm here with a friend."

"Yeah?" He grins at me again.

I grin back. "Yeah."

The bartender comes back and takes our order, and I make my way back to Bailey with drinks in hand. Can't say I expected to get hit on by another dude in a place like this, but I guess you never know.

"What was that all about?" Bailey asks.

I can't remember if I ever said anything to Bailey about dating guys back when we were in college. I might have. College was a lot easier, in a way; you could explain any damn thing away as a phase. Not so much anymore, and turned out it wasn't "just a phase" for me anyway. It might repulse her; it wouldn't be the first time I'd gotten that response from a woman I came out to. Better to find out now.

Just the thought of Bailey rejecting me has my gut churning, but it's better to know up front. So I tell her the truth.

"The guy at the bar was hitting on me," I tell her, setting the drinks down and keeping my voice low. I slide into the booth to sit next to Bailey, letting the words hang in the air, waiting for her reaction. Bailey keeps glancing back and forth between the table and my face, like she can't decide if she should ask the obvious question.

"Ask me."

She opens her mouth once, closes it. Then shakes her head. "It's none of my business," she says. I give her a break, if only to get this part over with.

"He wouldn't be the first guy I've taken home from a bar," I say quietly. "But hooking up when I'm out with an old friend seems pretty tasteless, even for me."

Bailey's eyes go a little unfocused. She won't look at me. What does that mean?

"Are you gay?" she asks, matching my tone.

"Bi," I say. "Or pan, or something like that. I mostly think of it as open-minded." I nudge Bailey with my elbow, trying for a grin. She's still not looking at me, though. The churning in my gut gets exponentially worse.

After a long pause, I can't wait anymore. "Look, I shouldn't have said anything—"

Bailey lays a hand on my arm and finally turns to look at me.

"No," she says. "No. It's not that at all. You just surprised me." The churning begins to recede enough that I'm distracted by Bailey biting her lip. After a moment, she meets my gaze again. "In the spirit of sharing, I have a confession to make, too."

This should be good.

"Do tell," I say, my eyebrows raised, not totally appeased by her answer but willing to play along. "I'm an excellent secret-keeper."

I'm still trying to get a smile out of her, but she nods soberly and actually checks over her shoulder as though someone might be hiding behind the booth listening to us. Not likely, considering we're at the back corner of a nearly empty bar on a chilly Thursday afternoon.

"The other night, at the gala," she says slowly. "The thing is, I was there with Drew, but we're not actually together."

Huh.

"Not together," I say. "Meaning..."

"Meaning, he asked me to pose as his girlfriend, so I did."

"Why a girlfriend?" I ask. "Why not just go as his date? I assume there's a reason."

"You remember Mila," says Bailey. I nod; it would be awhile before I forgot those nails. The scabs were still healing. "She's been giving Drew a hard time at work, asking him out and not taking no for an answer. He asked me to pose as his girlfriend to head her off."

"Isn't that sexual harassment?"

"That's what I said!" She shakes her head again. "Drew swears it's not a big deal, but asked me to pretend to be his girlfriend just to help the night go a little more smoothly."

I snort. "How'd that work out for him?"

Bailey laughs weakly.

"I have to admit, I'm surprised," I say speculatively. "Why didn't Drew just bring an actual date? Aside from the obvious fact that you're the most beautiful woman in the city."

Bailey rolls her eyes and smacks my arm playfully.

"I asked him that too," she says, shrugging. "Drew's never had a problem getting a date, male or female." Before the last word is out of her mouth, Bailey slaps a hand over her lips.

"Male or female," I say slowly.

Oh.

"Shit," whispers Bailey.

So Andrew swings both ways. That's... interesting.

Not that it's all that interesting to me. Just interesting in the abstract. Go team queer, and all. My pulse trips, though that could easily be explained by proximity to Bailey. I can feel the heat where our thighs are pressed together in the booth. I thought I'd kept a polite distance when I first sat down, but she's close enough I can hear her whisper.

"I shouldn't have said that," she says.

"Don't worry about it, Ross," I say, wrapping an arm around her shoulder for a half-hug. "Your fake boyfriend and I might not have much to say to each other, but I got no problem keeping secrets. I won't say anything."

"It's not a secret, exactly," she says, looking miserable. "Drew's been out since college. But please don't say anything. I shouldn't have."

"I won't." A beat passes. I shouldn't push my luck with her, but I've never been good at restraining myself with Bailey. "How is it that you and Hicks never got together? For real, I mean."

"Hah." Her laugh is forced, but I let it slide because she's still tucked under my arm, leaning into me. "I met Drew the same year I met you." Bailey takes a deep breath, tensing up all over again. "Later that summer, Drew introduced me to his brother, Alan."

I vaguely remember Bailey having a boyfriend named Alan in college.

Then it registers. Alan was the guy she got engaged to a few months after she and I spent the night together.

I'd spent a sizable amount of energy hating that guy sophomore year, though I'd never seen him before in my life. Bailey's clearly uncomfortable bringing it up with me, and that's the last thing I want, so I focus on Drew instead.

"I guess that would be awkward," I say. "Dating brothers and all."

"Alan wouldn't take it well," Bailey says. "And Drew's parents would freak." Her tone makes it clear she's downplaying just how bad the fallout would be.

"If that's the only reason he's not asking you out, Drew Hicks has even less of a functioning brain than I gave him credit for," I say. Family's important to some people, sure, I get that, but come on.

Bailey still looks miserable, whether it's because we're talking about her ex or for outing Drew, I can't tell. I'm not ready to drop the subject yet, but maybe I can distract her.

"What happened with the fiancé?" I ask. "The other Hicks dickbag."

Bailey downs half her beer before she answers.

"He called it off a few months after we got engaged," she said, eyeing her glass. "Said we weren't a good fit."

"Cheating?"

Bailey shakes her head. "Not that I ever found out about. I suspected, though." She's quiet again, and I'm about to change the subject altogether when she speaks again. "He didn't respect me, you know? It took me a long time to figure it out. Too long."

I don't know how anybody dates someone they didn't respect, let alone propose marriage. But then, I can't imagine getting married at all.

"My fatal flaw, I guess," says Bailey. "You'd think by my third fiancé I'd have learned better."

Hold up. I pause, my glass suspended in midair.

"Third engagement?"

Bailey looks mortified, her eyes pinned to the glass in her hand. She downs the rest of her drink and I'm quick to refill it from the pitcher on the table.

"Alan was the first," she says. "Stephen came along a couple of years later. He was definitely cheating. And Peter... well, we just broke up."

"Define just," I say.

"He left about a month ago."

Jesus. I try my best to hide my shock, because Bailey's holding herself so stiffly I'm afraid she might break if I so much as look at her sideways right now.

"Bet you're glad you knocked on this door," Bailey says, her self-deprecating laugh shaky and thin. I squeeze her shoulders hard then pull back to look her in the eye.

"A string of jackasses is nothing but bad luck," I tell her. "And maybe some questionable judgment." I smile, letting her know it's a tease, not a criticism.

It makes Bailey laugh, though she still sounds on the verge of tears.

"Guess I should've stuck with you, huh?" she says, nudging me with her elbow.

"You said it, not me." That's exactly what I'm getting at.

Bailey turns her hand under mine, lacing our fingers together and squeezing.

"I wish I had." She looks up at me through her lashes, a blush staining her cheeks. Bailey leans in closer, whispering again. "I can't tell you how many times I wished for that."

Need surges in my veins. I bring our linked fingers to my mouth, pressing a kiss to her fingertips. Bailey's breath hitches. I can feel her hand tremble in mine.

"Cooper?"

I don't want to lose this, not again. Fate dropped Bailey in my lap for the second time. I'm not letting her get away again.

10

BAILEY

"Bailey, look at me," says Cooper. His fingers tighten around mine. It takes me a minute to get there, but I finally meet his gaze. "There's nothing wrong with you. You had a run of bad luck with some assholes who couldn't appreciate you. It happens to people all the time."

I close my eyes, basking in his conviction even if I can't believe his words. I know it's my own fault.

"There's not a man in town, hell, probably not a man alive, who wouldn't beg on his knees for the chance to be with you."

"Cooper, stop."

"I will not stop," he says, bringing his face close to mine. His breath is warm against my cheek. He waits until I look at him again before he speaks. "You're smart, generous, kind. You make the best chocolate butter cookies I've ever had in my life."

I laugh, remembering the cookie experiment I'd made for his birthday a few weeks after we'd met.

"I can't believe you remember those."

"Remember them? They changed my life." His eyes glitter in the dim light of the bar. It's slightly more crowded now, the noise of the other patrons drowning out the sound of my heart pounding in my own ears.

I take a deep breath and pull my hand from Cooper's, laying it on his leg and squeezing gently.

"Thank you," I say. "That means a lot, coming from you."

Cooper swears under his breath. "You don't have to thank me. For God's sake. Do you have any idea what you do to me?"

Without warning, Cooper shifts his hip a couple of inches to the left and where my hand had been patting his muscular thigh, it now covers the swollen head of his erection.

Oh, God.

"You fuck me up, Ross," mutters Cooper, leaning closer to whisper in my ear. "Sweet Christ, you fuck me up. You always did."

My fingers squeeze without any conscious direction on my part, and Cooper sucks in a breath.

"Coop, we can't," I stammer.

"Can't what?" he asks, rocking his hips under my hand, forcing the friction he wants. My breath catches in my throat.

"Those people—"

"Are all busy getting their drink on," he murmurs. Above the table he looks like any other attentive lover, flirty and close. The heavy wooden table hides my hand, his movements, and the thrill of getting away with this makes me hotter than hell.

"You like this," Coop says, surprised. I nod, bringing a smirk to his face. "God, me too. So little Bailey Ross likes to get her freak on in public. Who knew?"

My face is so hot, I must match the neon in the windows by now. It doesn't deter Coop, though.

He twists to face me, holding my wrist to keep my hand where he wants it, stroking his fingers along the hem of my skirt with his other hand.

"Tell me to stop," he says quietly. His thumb traces back and forth, back and forth, over the fabric covering my legs. "Say it."

"No." It's barely even a word, nothing but a puff of air I can't even hear myself. Cooper hears it somehow, his nostrils flaring, eyes going dark.

"Here's what's going to happen," says Cooper. His thumb is burning a track across the top of my thigh. If he doesn't touch me soon, I'm going to scream, and not in a good way. "You're going to pull your skirt up and spread those pretty legs for me. Then I'm going to make you come."

"Here? Now?"

"Right here, right now," says Cooper, raking his teeth over my earlobe. "What's it going to be, Ross? You going to let me make you come right here, in front of all these people?"

I shudder hard, almost climaxing on the spot. Cooper raises his eyebrows.

"You really like that." His grin turns wicked. "Looks like something else we have in common." I can't tell if he means the dirty talk or the fooling around in public, but it's working for me all across the board.

Cooper dips his chin, indicating I should get on with it.

Backed into the corner of the booth like I am, it'd be almost impossible for anybody to see what we're getting up to. That, plus Cooper's broad shoulders blocking me from sight and the dimness of the bar... it buys a lot of leeway if somebody was inclined to be discreetly indiscreet.

I know I swore off men, but this doesn't count. Technically. It's Cooper.

I pull my hand from his lap and tug the fabric of my skirt up, shifting side to side to inch it up to the tops of my thighs. His breath against my cheek makes me shiver.

"Good girl," he whispers. His thick palm covers my knee, pulling it toward his body. "Open up."

I keep my hands fisted in my clothes to try to stop them shaking. I don't dare look over his shoulder in case somebody is watching.

Which makes no sense. This whole damn situation is crazy to begin with. Sense stopped being a factor about the time I laid eyes on Cooper at the gala last week.

"Anybody ever watch you get off, Bailey?" Cooper asks, kissing my neck between his words. His hand begins a slow slide up between my legs and I stop breathing, anticipating his next move. It's all I can do to shake my head in answer. I'm beyond words now, so aroused I might come just from hearing him speak to me like this.

"They'd kill to see you like this, everybody in this room," he says, his fingers finally, finally grazing the seam of my thong. "Look at you. You're fucking gorgeous, baby. You're burning me up."

His fingertips are stroking softly, barely any pressure at all, but they're exactly where I need them, making me desperate for more. Need coils tight in my belly, urging me to press into Cooper's hand, to make him do what I want. But more than getting off, I want him to be the one who makes it happen, to make me. So I wait.

"I'm dying," I whisper. "Touch me, Cooper."

With a growl, Cooper captures my mouth, silencing the cry that comes automatically as he slides his fingers against my clit, just so. The pressure is perfect, perfect, perfect, and a choking heartbeat later I'm coming before he ever touches my bare flesh.

"Yes," he growls, holding me tight as I shiver and melt and die in the corner of the booth. "Jesus. Jesus Christ, Bailey."

I KNOW I'M DREAMING, but it doesn't stop the adrenaline rush. I'm standing in a parking lot watching Cooper and Drew play tug-of-war over something I can't see. I know there's somewhere else I need to be, but I'm riveted to the spot, unable to look away.

Coming awake with a panicked start, I bolt upright out of bed, sure I've overslept my alarm. The clock on my phone tells me I still have three minutes, though, and I collapse back on the bed with a groan.

Drew and Cooper playing tug-of-war while I watch. Really? I don't usually buy into the whole dream analysis stuff, but as subconscious messages go, that one's not subtle.

I pull the pillow over my head, groaning again. Leaving the bar yesterday was an exercise in awkwardness, to say the least. By the time my brain stopped shaking from the orgasm he forced out of me, my body was ready to go. His place, my place—even the bar bathroom would've worked.

In the end, I went home alone. It's not fair to Cooper, not when Drew's face keeps coming to my mind. And I swore off men for a reason. New leaf, new Bailey, that's me. I'm done being rejected, passed over, done being somebody's last priority. Time to focus on me.

It's that thought that gets me out of bed and into the shower. Today's competition round is meant to be another surprise, though we've been told it's not a surprise ingredient this time. I tap out a text to Evie as the water heats. By the time I'm clean, I'm resolved to avoid Cooper and Drew both.

A smaller crowd of contestants might make that goal a challenge, but they'll both be working. Shouldn't be that hard.

I have other things to focus on, besides the fact that the men I want don't seem to want me back.

Cooper definitely wants you back, girl.

Cooper says he wants me, but physical attraction happens all the time. It doesn't mean anything. And I'm done coming in last place with men.

Time to go kick ass at this competition, meet up with my new friend Evie, and enjoy the hell out of what's left of my time off work this week. God only knows when I'll get the chance to do something like this again.

Come to think of it, that changes today too.

By the time I get to the competitors' tent, I'm in full kick-ass mode. Evie flags me down from the bar where blue-shirted staff members are dishing up coffee and mimosas.

"Didn't know what you drank so I got both," says Evie, pointing at a mug of coffee and a champagne flute on the bar.

"Coffee, please," I say.

"Ah," says Evie. "Game face?"

"That's right," I say. "I'm here to kick ass and chew bubblegum and I'm all out of bubblegum."

"Is that a movie quote? I bet it's a movie quote. I'm not going to ask you which one, I seriously suck at that game." She toasts my mug with her glass. "You ready for today?"

"Ready as I'll ever be," I say, letting the reference to *They Live* slide as I survey the room over the rim of my coffee cup. "How much time do we have?"

"Not much," says Evie. "In fact, we should probably—"

A familiar voice comes over the loudspeaker, cutting her off.

"Attention, contestants," says Drew's disembodied voice. "Please report to the competition floor. We'll begin setting up for round two shortly."

Evie turns to me with a grin. "That's our cue." She drains her drink and hands it to the bartender with a flourish.

I follow her out of the tent. We've just about reached the competition floor and I'm thinking I'm home free when I hear someone call my name. Evie stops with me, as we turn to look at the three men standing next to the stairs leading backstage.

"You go on ahead," I tell Evie weakly. "I'll be there in a minute." The concern on her face is clear, but she nods and walks away.

I turn back slowly, making my way closer to the men, acutely aware of every inch disappearing between us.

"Hey, Drew, Cooper," I say.

Deep breath, deep breath. Do not pass out.

"Hello, Alan."

11

DREW

I pinch the bridge of my nose and get a chokehold on my temper. "You were explicitly instructed to stay away from the competition setup."

"I didn't touch anything," says Cooper, flagrant insubordination in his eyes. "All I did was move the shelf. It looks better there."

I swear, the man goes out of his way to disobey any instruction I give him. It's a miracle we survived each other all those weeks in class.

"And in the process of moving the shelf that was set up by staff members two days ago, you managed to disengage the gas line to the stovetop." My watch beeps, and I realize we have to be on stage soon. Lecturing Cooper isn't helping matters, in any case. "We don't have time for this. Round two starts in less than ten minutes. Don't they need you in makeup or something?"

Cooper sneers. "You tell me, boss."

The effect that tone has on my body is immediate and intense. Inexplicable heat coils in my gut. I ignore it.

Despite my current frustration, Cooper's been surprisingly compliant the last few days. The audience absolutely adores him. Doesn't matter what nonsense he spews, they eat it up.

"What's got your panties in a bunch, anyway?" Cooper asks. I'm checking my watch again when he asks, trying to get my body back under control and answer him without thinking it through.

"I saw you leave with Bailey last night," I say. Cooper's eyebrows shoot up and I swear under my breath.

We really don't have time for this. This whole competition has been my pet project for months, entrusted to me because Tyler thinks I might be ready to take on more work as a producer. If something goes wrong because I'm distracted by some dark, hot, hipster smart-ass, there's going to be hell to pay.

Hell for *him* to pay.

"Jealous, huh? Can't say I blame you," says Cooper. His sneer melts into a cocky grin. "If I had a girl like Bailey—"

"Well, you don't," I snap. Which is total bullshit, since for all I know, he might have Bailey. Especially if she told him the truth about our nonexistent relationship.

"There he is!" a chirpy female voice exclaims. Cooper and I turn to see an intern heading straight for the stairs where Cooper and I've been arguing for the last five minutes. Trailing in her wake is my brother Alan. The intern takes off without another word.

"Pretty nice setup you've got here, Andy," he says.

"Thanks," I say through my teeth. "What are you doing here, Alan?"

"Since you're not answering my calls or messages, figured I'd track you down."

"We have to be on stage in five minutes."

"This won't take long," says my brother. He eyes Cooper openly. "Who's this?"

Cooper extends a hand, a flirtatious smile on his face. Why that smile gets under my skin, I couldn't say. Smarmy bastard.

"I'm Cooper Lawson," he says. "I'm hosting the competition. You must be Alan." Cooper doesn't meet my startled gaze, his attention completely focused on my brother. "I've heard so much about you."

My brother looks puzzled, and I can't blame him. How the hell... Oh. Bailey.

I choke down the resentment that thought brings.

"What did you want to talk to me about, Alan?" I ask.

"Mom told me you'd be down here all weekend. She and Dad wanted to make sure you're bringing your new girlfriend to their anniversary party. It's only a few weeks away, you know."

"I know. What do you mean, girlfriend?" Out of the corner of my eye I see Cooper tense.

"Well, they said date, but that intern mentioned you brought your girlfriend to a company party last week. Apparently she made quite the impression."

I don't dare look over at Cooper right now.

"Hey," says Alan, looking over my shoulder. "Is that...? Bailey!"

Well, shit.

Bailey stops, her eyes going wide. She says something to the tall red-haired woman I saw her with yesterday, presumably sending her on her way because Bailey comes toward us alone.

"Hey, Drew. Cooper," says Bailey. She swallows. "Hello, Alan."

Bailey doesn't meet my eyes as my brother leans over to kiss her cheek. Help comes from where I least expect it, in the form of Cooper waving us up the stairs to head backstage.

"I appreciate a good reunion scene as much as anybody," he says. "But maybe we should take this conversation somewhere else."

Backstage is mercifully free of onlookers, at least in the alcove we find just past the top of stairs. That won't last long. Cooper and I are expected out front any minute now, and Bailey's due on the competition floor.

"How have you been?" Alan asks her.

"Good," says Bailey. When she finally looks my way, her eyes widen. It's almost funny how awkward this is. Except if Alan finds out, he'd go ballistic.

"Good," says Alan absently. "Did you get your invitation? I know Mom is looking forward to seeing you."

"I sent my RSVP last week," says Bailey. "I wouldn't miss it for anything."

Another long beat passes. I can practically hear the clock ticking.

"This has been fun, Alan," I say dryly. "But we've really got to go."

"Yeah, okay," he says. "I won't keep you much longer. Seriously though, about your girlfriend—"

Bailey's gasp is audible. Cooper and I rush to cover it at the same time.

"It's not—" I stammer, cutting off with a huff as Cooper elbows me hard.

"That's what happens when you listen to gossip," says Cooper coolly. He waits until Alan looks at him. "I'm not a girl."

"Excuse me?" Alan asks, clearly confused.

You took the words right out of my mouth, big brother.

Cooper steps close and slides an arm around my waist, pulling until our hips bump together. My brain stutters to a halt.

"Unless you've got a girlfriend you forgot to tell me about," Cooper says to me with a teasing grin. I have no idea what he's talking about, but I lose the thread completely when he leans up and touches his mouth to mine.

His mouth is softer than it looks, and sweeter than anyone so bitter has a right to be.

Cooper Lawson is kissing me.

The rest of the world just stops. The only feedback coming through is all him—the hint of his breath on my cheek, the scratch of stubble on his chin, the absolute, deafening silence around us.

The kiss is infuriatingly, mercifully brief. Before he lets me go, he catches my lip between his teeth and nips there. The sudden small shock of pain is enough to bring back the rest of the world in a rush.

I catch his arm before he can pull away.

"Uh," says Bailey. Alan rolls his eyes.

"You could have just said so," he says. "Nobody cares if you've got a boyfriend, Andy, you know that."

"Right," I say. Cooper tries to step away, but I can't let him. Not until the situation in my jeans resolves itself. Alan shakes his head at me.

"Mom and Dad just want to know if you're getting serious, that's all," says Alan. It's the same "when are you going to settle down" routine I get from everybody in my family the last few years. "We all do. We worry about you, Andy."

"I'm perfectly capable of taking care of myself," I say, barely hearing him at all. It takes all my concentration to get the words out.

Cooper Lawson kissed me and made me hard. My brain is trying to implode.

"Be that as it may," says Alan, condescending in a way only an older brother can be. "You didn't answer my question."

"You didn't ask a question."

"Is it serious?" Alan asks. I feel my face heat. Cooper takes the lead before I can come up with a response.

"Of course, it's serious," he tells Alan. "Drew's been after me for months."

Bailey's eyes can't get any wider and her face is at least as flushed as mine must be. She bites her lip, and I can't tell if she's trying not to laugh or trying not to cry.

"It's true," she chimes in. "They've been circling each other for ages."

I guess in a way it is true, but jeez, did she have to make it sound so suggestive? Bailey just shrugs when I glare at her.

This time instead of trying to pull away Cooper backs up closer to me, pulling my arm around his front. I try to keep a polite distance between us, but he parks his ass right on top of my dick. Pulling back now would give us away. I grit my teeth and brace myself for the humiliation waiting for me when Alan finally leaves.

"Glad I got a chance to meet you," says Alan, extending his hand to Cooper to shake. "Should I tell Mom—?"

"Tell her I'll call her in a few days," I say. Alan puts his hands up in surrender.

"Don't forget," he warns. "You know how important this party is to them."

"I won't."

Alan nods at Bailey and heads back down the stairs.

The instant my brother is out of sight, I pull my hand away from Cooper's waist.

"Well, now," drawls Cooper. "That was illuminating." He turns around slowly, all sorts of questions in his eyes.

"Thanks for covering for us, Cooper," says Bailey in a quiet voice.

"Don't thank me, Ross," he says. There's an edge in his tone. "You'd better get down to the floor."

Pulling aside the heavy stage curtain next to us, I check the countdown clock running on the Jumbotron overhead. We've got about twenty seconds to get up on stage. Bailey takes off down the stairs at a jog, disappearing from sight.

Cooper doesn't move.

12

COOPER

The headset looped around Drew's neck crackles with static a moment before I hear Kenna Burch's voice coming through the speakers.

"Somebody... in the control room..." she says. "On standby..."

Drew pulls the microphone to his mouth and hits a button on the receiver.

"Do you need me?" he asks. After a second he shakes his head and the speaker goes silent once more. "Five to seven minutes, she said. Some kind of technical delay in the sound booth."

Unexpected delays are never good in this business, but I'm glad for the chance to get my head back on straight. So to speak. Not that I'd ever admit it out loud.

"Alan seems nice," I say. Drew looks over at me and snorts disbelievingly. "What?"

"Liar," he says. He's standing too goddamn close but there's not a lot of room to move around back here without bumping into the stage curtains, or worse, other people. Or worse still, bumping into each other. And I've got one particularly hard reason not to be bumping into anybody just now, least of all Drew.

It's his own goddamn fault. Though at the moment I can't exactly remember why.

"So your brother's not nice?" I ask. Maybe if he's too busy talking he won't notice.

"Alan is..." Drew scrubs a hand over his face. "He's Alan. An older brother, through and through. He's a little uptight, but he's not a bad guy."

It's my turn to snort.

"Now what?" Drew asks.

"Guess it runs in the family," I say. "Being uptight." I watch, fascinated, as Drew's face goes tense and hot.

"Not so uptight that I'll stop you from telling my family that you're my boyfriend," Drew mutters, glancing around. I can hear people shuffling around a few feet away, but I can't see anyone. This corner of the backstage waiting space is lit only by the faint blue-green light coming from a storage closet behind Drew. Most of his face is shadowed and I can't discern his expression but he sure sounds annoyed.

"Yeah, you're welcome."

"Excuse me?" he asks.

"Bailey told me about dating your big bro," I say. "How he'd freak out if he found out you two were an item. I obviously did you a favor back there."

Drew snorts. "Some favor." I just know he's thinking about that kiss when he says it, and it pisses me right the hell off.

"Kissing me was just a bonus," I say, poking him in the chest, unable to stop myself from getting up in his face. "No need to thank me for that, either."

Drew looks down at my finger, still jabbed into the dense muscle of his pecs. When he looks back up at me, the air between us disappears and suddenly I don't have to guess what he's thinking anymore.

"Back off." He says it quietly, slowly. It's a command, not a request, delivered in a tone I've never heard him use before. Every inch of my body responds to the challenge, and as much as I might try to tell myself it's pride, my thickening cock says otherwise.

"Or what?" I push against his chest just a little bit harder. It's a dare, and he knows it. We both have to be onstage and presentable, doing our very public-facing jobs in a matter of moments. Drew's not going to hit me. Maybe I'd have feared that from him back in college —big, thickheaded jock that I thought he was. Not anymore; I know him better now. That's just not who he is.

I never see him move, but suddenly Drew's right in my face, leaning into my finger on his chest. He moves slowly, never taking his eyes off me, his hand coming up to wrap around mine. I hate him for the way it makes me shake. God, do I hate him.

"Or else."

I've lost my place in the conversation, but it's too late to back down now. I couldn't pull myself away if I tried.

It was the same with Bailey at the bar yesterday. Like she belonged in my hands.

Fucking Drew Hicks.

He sees something in my face, I guess, and it sets him off. The hand wrapped around mine closes tightly, yanking me forward even as Drew steps and twists, so I stumble past him into that small, mostly empty storage closet, bracing myself against the wall under the weird blue-green light as Drew pulls the door shut behind him.

"What the hell are you doing?" I ask, humiliated beyond belief when my voice cracks.

"Making sure nobody can see us. What do you think I'm doing?"

Drew steps closer, crowding my space. I pull back hard, pressing my hands to the wall behind me.

Unbelievably, I hear him laughing softly and my temper hits the red zone.

"You don't actually think that I'm going to hit you," he says, sounding supremely confident. The dim light casts shadows across his face, letting me see that the humor I hear in his voice hasn't reached his eyes.

"Wouldn't put it past you." The words come out solid this time, thank Christ.

"Hmm," Drew murmurs, stepping still closer. Another fraction of an inch and we'll be touching. "I bet you wouldn't. But I'm not going to make it that easy for you."

"Easy?" I splutter.

"That's right." Drew's hand comes up, circling my throat, and my heart stops beating altogether. He doesn't squeeze, doesn't exert any pressure whatsoever, but he pins me in place with his grip all the same.

"It'd be easier if I took a swing right now, I bet," he murmurs, his eyes on his claim over my throat. "Give you a real reason to fight back for once. I must just frustrate the hell out of you, Cooper."

"Fuck off, Hicks," I say. There's no way he can miss how hard I'm trembling, but to hell with him if he thinks I'm going to admit it.

"Close enough," says Drew. His fingers tighten ever so slightly around my neck as he plants his other hand on the wall over my head, bends down, and kisses me.

For the second time in ten minutes, I lose my goddamn mind.

No shocked passive participation this time, Drew teases my mouth open, drawing me out with his tongue. At the first touch of that tongue on mine, a choked moan—it might have been mine, but I'll never admit it—has him pulling back to look me in the eyes. Whatever he sees there makes his breath catch, and in the next second his body is tight against mine, pressing me back into the wall.

My hands come up to slide under the back of his shirt before I can stop them, my fingers tracing the groove of the muscle there, digging in when Drew wraps his lips around my tongue and sucks. I pull away just far enough to catch my breath.

"We can't—" Don't ask me what the hell I was going to say; I don't have a damn clue. Right now there's nothing in the world I can't do, so long as he keeps touching me. But Drew gets it.

"I know," he says, kissing the side of my neck with such enthusiasm my knees get weak. "Jesus, Cooper."

Drew rocks his hips into mine, lining up our erections to rub off on each other.

"Fuck."

"Later." He gasps, biting down on my shoulder through my shirt. I slide my hands over his hips, gripping the insane bubble of his ass hard enough to have his head jerking up to look at me. Drew grabs my wrists and pins them to the wall beside my head. The move runs through me like a shock, stiffening my spine. Among other things.

"You like that," he says, his eyes taking in every detail.

It's too much. All of it. Whatever he sees when he looks at me, it's too much.

"No," I say, denying him despite all evidence to the contrary.

Tension creeps into his features, but before he can call me out for lying—again—the headset we've somehow knocked to the floor gives another burst of static. Drew's hands come off my body immediately, like he's been caught doing something wrong. It infuriates me all over again.

"Get the hell off me," I say, bracing my weight against the wall and shoving him hard, mortified by how breathy my voice sounds. Fucker barely sways but he takes a calm step back.

Drew picks up his headset, setting himself to rights. I try not to watch him adjusting the thick mound behind his fly, and fail.

That's twice today Drew Hicks got hard for me. I want to smack myself for how deeply that thrills me. He's not mine to be thrilling over, not at all.

"And stay away from me," I add, a little too late to make it convincing, I guess, given Drew's only response is to glance down at my erection as he raises one eloquent brow. "Don't you have a girl-friend to see to? What would Bailey say if she could see you right now?"

Unbelievably, Drew laughs.

"She'd probably ask to film us. Or at least watch," he says, heat flashing in his eyes. Noticing my glare, he rolls his eyes. Nobody takes me all that seriously, but it rankles coming from him.

"Your girlfriend—"

"Is not Bailey," he says, fiddling with the headset and receiver again. "And I'm pretty sure you know that, considering you left with her yesterday."

I didn't know it when we left together last night, but I don't mention that part. My intentions at the time were pure. More or less. And since Bailey's only posing as his girlfriend, it doesn't matter anyway.

"Doesn't explain why you're kissing me in a closet," I say, still glaring.

"Is every damn thing suspicious to you?" Drew asks, finally looking right at me.

"I'll leave aside the very obvious jokes about being stuck in a closet with you. At the risk of sounding like a teenager, you started it," I say. God, he's annoying. "And by the way, you're welcome, asshole," I add.

"I didn't ask you to lie," says Drew, his temper coming back. "Neither did Bailey, I bet. Speaking of which," he says, his eyes shrewd. "She must have mentioned I'm bi. Why else would you assume it's okay to kiss me?"

I'm going to kill him.

"Maybe because you've been eye-fucking me since I signed up for your class last summer." The jab lands. Drew clenches his teeth hard enough I can see it, even in the eerie light. Good.

"Bullshit."

"Really?" I'm back in his face before I think twice, my hand coming up to cup his still-hard cock, squeezing him through his jeans. His nostrils flare, the rest of Drew's body going taut and still.

"Does it ever occur to you to let somebody else have the last word?" he asks, his voice low and thick.

"Never." Having Drew Hicks at my mercy is a heady feeling, addictive in the ways all bad things are. So I'm grateful when static pops through the speakers on his headset and I hear our names being called up to the stage.

I'm grateful. Really.

Really.

Drew takes a deep breath. He grips my wrist, removing my hand from his cock.

"We've got about thirty seconds to get to the curtain," he mutters, releasing me to adjust himself. I do the same. Drew's staring a hole through the door when he speaks a beat later.

"You realize you just committed us to going to my parents' anniversary party together."

That gets my attention enough I can finally look away from his hands where they're still adjusting his fly.

"Seriously?"

"Alan very likely called to tell my family about you before he even got back to his car," says Drew, his expression blank once again but for the faint sneer he aims my way. "They'll be expecting to meet this boyfriend I neglected to tell them about, especially since you had Bailey as a witness."

"What's she got to do with it?" I ask. Though I'm feeling a twinge at just what Bailey must be thinking after that little scene with her ex-fiancé. Considering I was kissing her just last night... in my experience most women wouldn't take too kindly to seeing a guy kiss someone else inside of twenty-four hours.

"We'll deal with this later," says Drew, shaking his head. Opening the door, he stalks out, heading to the stage.

"Great," I call out to his back. "Can't wait."

13

BAILEY

The bathroom mirror is obscured by steam, but that doesn't stop me from staring at it.

Round two was deceptively simple—just completing the dish in the required amount of time, no surprise ingredient or anything. It was tight, but I managed. The only people who got eliminated yesterday were the ones who didn't actually finish. The rest of us got scores, but we won't find out what they are until the finalists are announced on Sunday.

Round three today kicked my ass. Suffice it to say, I'm not holding my breath about being a finalist.

Which is honestly fine with me. I didn't sign up for this to win the cooking show gig or a contract with Sizzle or sign a book deal, or any of the other sparkly things I've heard other competitors talk about the last few days. I'm just glad to get to play for once, though I can already tell reality is going to come crashing down hard come Monday.

No, the competition isn't what's got me zoned out. If anything, I've still got some nervous energy to burn, though I turned down Evie's offer to go out and party it up with some of the other competitors tonight.

Drew's avoiding me, just like I've been avoiding him all week. And it's bullshit. If anybody's got some explaining to do, it's him. Alan showing up unannounced was just icing on the clusterfuck cake yesterday.

And then there's Cooper. Cooper, who took me out, who kissed my brains out in the back of a bar, who got me off harder than I've ever managed to do on my own. Cooper who kissed Drew.

That's the hold up right there. Cooper kissed Drew. My brain's had that memory playing on loop nonstop since yesterday morning, like I don't even know where to start processing it.

I know why he did it, of course. Coop was just helping me out, and maybe by extension, Drew. Coop knew my ex would freak out if it came out that Drew and I were dating. Even though we're not.

It's confusing. I'm confused. That's all it is.

I am not massively turned inside out by the thought of them kissing. And touching. And doing other things. That would be inappropriate. And wrong, probably. If anything, I should probably be pissed at Cooper. Right?

Enough. It's been a week since Drew kissed me, and if you don't count that little interlude where Alan called me over, we haven't spoken since that night either. Time to put on my big girl pants and fix this.

Obviously, Drew and I have been through too much together to let this come between us. He's not my only friend, but he's sure as hell the one I rely on most. I can't lose him. Who else is going to put up with my abominable taste in men? Not to mention my haircuts. I've had people unfriend me on Facebook for less.

He's the most stable part of my universe. He's too important to let some little physical attraction mess things up. I made it go away the first time he rejected me. By God, I'll manage it again. Somehow.

Resolved, I pull together the first outfit I get my hands on. A quick stop at the liquor store for a bottle of Drew's favorite whiskey and I'm standing on his doorstep less than thirty minutes later.

The wind is brisk. In fact, it's fucking freezing out here. And I don't even know if he's home. Hell, Saturday night, he could be out with his other friends for all I know. Or on a date. Surely—

The door flies open.

"Are you insane? It's fucking freezing out here, Bailey." Drew pulls me inside. "Your hair's wet, for God's sake. What's the matter with you?"

I try to answer, but my teeth are chattering too hard. Drew shuts the door behind me, pulling the bag out of my hand and setting it on the tiny table beside the door.

"Forgot my hat," I manage to say through chattering teeth.

"Too late in the season for that, dummy," he says, not much conviction behind it. "You want something to drink?"

I point at the brown bag on the table. Drew pulls out the bottle and his eyebrows go up.

"You knock over a bank or something?"

"Sh-Shut up and get me a g-glass already," I say, pulling off my scarf as I head for his couch.

Drew comes back a moment later with a blanket tucked under his arm and two squat, heavy-bottomed crystal glasses. He pours me a drink and waits until I tuck the blanket around my legs before getting his own.

"Better?" he asks. I nod.

We sit in silence for a long minute, long enough for me to wonder what the hell I thought I was doing barging over here like this. Now that I'm here and in his face, the last thing I want to do is talk about things. Drew seems to be having the same idea, considering he hasn't looked at me since we sat down.

"So how'd the competition go for you today?"

"Fine," I answer. Feeling is starting to come back in my toes. "I wasn't automatically eliminated, so I can't complain. It's been a fun ride."

"I'm glad to hear it," says Drew. "I know the network gets their next big show out of it, but I really wanted it to be enjoyable for the contestants too."

"You definitely managed that," I say, clinking my glass to his in toast. "Here's to a job well done." Drew toasts me back, finally looking at me as he takes his drinks. He knows something's up, but I still can't bring myself to talk about what I really want to talk about, so instead I change the subject.

"Speaking of jobs well done," I say, studying the amber liquid in my glass. "I thought Cooper was outstanding."

Drew stands up abruptly, drink in hand, and walks over to the bookshelf across the room. He fiddles with some picture frames, avoiding my gaze.

"He did pretty well, all things considered," he says after a pause.

"What things?"

"Hmm?" Drew glances my way.

"What things considered?" I ask. "I wasn't privy to whatever went on behind the scenes. What happened?"

Drew turns to face me.

"What exactly are you asking, Bailey?" he says, his voice hard.

"I was just asking about Cooper and how well he did with the competition. Why do I get the feeling you're talking about something else entirely?"

Drew doesn't answer me.

"This is about him kissing you," I say, light dawning.

"Leave it—"

"No," I say. "Bad enough we're not talking about the fact that *we* kissed—"

"Why do we have to talk about any of it?" he asks, exasperated.

"Because that's what friends do, goddamn it."

"Really," says Drew. "Apparently friends also spend whole weeks avoiding each other. Is that how it works?"

My face feels hot. "You were avoiding me, too."

Drew sighs. "You're right. I'm sorry."

"Sorry for what?"

He takes his time answering me, draining his glass first. "I'm sorry I've been avoiding you instead of just talking to you about... things."

"What things?" Like I don't know what things. But my heart is in my throat and I have no idea what he's about to say next, only that if he tells me we can't be friends anymore that it's going to tear my heart open in a way nothing else ever has.

I should probably work out why that is, but it'll have to wait.

"You know what things." Drew's tone is quiet, serious.

I have to swallow hard before I can get the words out.

"You mean because I'm attracted to you," I say. The words come out clear, even if my voice is shaking. "We've talked about this before. It's not an issue. It doesn't have to be an issue. I can—"

"Bailey."

I'm mortified to feel my eyes welling up with tears, but I can't let him speak, because if he's thinking of ending ten years of friendship, I'm going to delay it as long as I can.

"If you need space, I'll give you space. It doesn't have—"

"Bailey, stop."

"To mean we can't be friends." By the time I finish the sentence, the tears have spilled over. I swipe at them, trying to make the evidence disappear before he can see, but Drew's already crossing the room. He's in my space and there's not even the smallest hope he doesn't see.

"Bailey," he says gently.

"I know it's messed up, but I swear—"

This time he doesn't speak, just stops my lips with his.

The kiss is brutally sweet, for all he barely touches me. It's enough to stop me babbling. Who am I kidding? It's enough to stop me breathing.

"There are no circumstances under which we will not be friends," says Drew firmly. "Do you understand? There is nothing you could do that would make me leave you."

"But—"

"Nothing." Drew cups my face in his hard, callused hand, his thumb resting on my bottom lip. "Do you understand? Nod if yes."

I nod, but I can't keep my lips from twitching.

He sighs. "What?"

"What if I become a serial killer?"

"Do you have plans to start killing people?" Drew asks with obvious patience. His thumb is still on my mouth, making thinking difficult.

"Not at the moment," I say faintly.

"You let me know if that changes," says Drew. He drops his hands to my hips, guiding me backward until the wall stops us.

"We should probably talk about this," he murmurs, leaning close, rubbing his nose gently across my cheek. I'm about to agree with him —because obviously this is crazy and we'll ruin our friendship and if he doesn't kiss me again soon I'm going to scream—when Drew drops his mouth to my neck and nips. My entire body lights up like a billboard at night and I gasp.

"You like that?" I can feel his grin against my shoulder.

"Yes."

"Good," he says. "I've wanted to do that forever."

"What—" My voice cracks. I clear my throat and try again. "What else have you wanted to do?"

Drew hums. The vibrations send shivers down my back, making me tremble.

"Should I tell you?" Drew asks, pulling aside the wide neckline of my sweater to nibble at the flesh there. "Or show you?"

"Whatever you do, you better not stop." I feel his smile again before his hands tighten on my hips. He boosts me up, propping me against the wall, and my legs wrap around his waist. I grab his shoulders quickly, the out-of-control feeling making me panic.

"Easy, Bailey girl," murmurs Drew. "I've got you."

"You're going to hurt yourself," I say, though it's a lie and both of us know it. Drew chuckles.

"You weigh practically nothing," he says. The conversation screeches to a halt when Drew steps forward, pressing us into the wall and pressing him firmly into me. His erection is thick and firm and sits exactly where I need it, and I'm grinding my hips against him before my next breath.

Drew swears and pulls back slightly, making me whimper.

"You're going to kill me," he says.

"Not yet," I say, not quite sure how I'm still forming words when all I can think about is getting rid of the clothes between us. Luckily, Drew seems to be on the same page. He presses my legs down and slides his hands down the back of my leggings, squeezing my flesh and groaning again.

He's too tall for me to reach his mouth on my own, so I thread my fingers into his hair, the blond strands catching the dim light from the lamp across the room. Drew doesn't protest when I pull him down for a kiss.

The heat is overwhelming, so much more than the sum of our parts, like we might set the air on fire between us if we keep touching. I can't unbutton his shirt fast enough, getting so frustrated that I give up on the tiny buttons and yank the two halves apart. Buttons plink all over the floor. I dare a glance up at Drew, wondering if he's going to be mad about the damage.

Nope. Definitely not mad. A little shocked, maybe.

"Sorry," I whisper. He shakes his head, apparently speechless. I take advantage of his momentary immobility to get my mouth on his chest.

Seriously, the man is a work of art. I don't know how I've made it ten years without touching him like this.

My lips close over a small, tight nipple and Drew groans, startled back into action. He pulls his hands off my ass and yanks my pants down, taking my underwear with them halfway down my thighs. The rest of the world stops around me when he sinks to his knees.

"Need you," he murmurs, his mouth raining kisses over my abdomen as he shoves my sweater up out of his way. "Need to taste you, Bailey."

I want to say something clever and funny and encouraging, but then Drew's mouth is on me, right where I need it, and there aren't any words in any language for the way it feels.

"Drew."

He doesn't stop, tonguing and touching and pressing one thick finger deep until I'm bucking against him, riding that touch for all I'm worth until I come. Drew rides it out with me, pulling back only enough to watch me come down off the high, holding me gently until I can open my eyes again. When I look down, the expression on his face takes my breath away all over again.

14

DREW

Bailey's eyes are unfocused when she finally opens them, gazing down at me like she's never seen me before. The way I feel right now, I can understand why. Kneeling before her petite, perfect body, I don't know how I made it so many years without touching her like this.

Whatever Bailey sees on my face makes her gasp, before bending down to kiss me again. It's hot as hell, knowing she must taste herself on my lips like this. She pulls me up, kicking free of her clothes, wrapping her gorgeous legs around me as I rise to my feet. I manage to unbutton and unzip my jeans in the process, and by the time her back hits the wall again, there's nothing between me and the heat of her body.

Bailey moans, her hips jerking.

"Drew," she pants. "For the love of God, hurry up already."

I manage to laugh, the sound strained and rough.

"Bailey girl, this is already going to be over too fast if you keep that up." Another thought occurs to me. "And I don't have any protection out here."

That slows her down, though she still doesn't stop her grinding.

"I'm on the pill. And I got tested after Peter the Dick left," she whispers. "There hasn't been anyone since."

"No?" The words fall out of my mouth before I can stop them. "Not even Cooper Hicks?" Bailey's mouth drops open. Even I'm shocked to hear that name coming out of my mouth, especially right now. "You don't have to answer that."

"We didn't have sex," she says, blushing.

"You don't have to explain," I say.

"Uh, considering what we're about to do—what I hope we're about to do—it's kind of relevant." Bailey shifts her hips, and her eyes go wide. "Why does that make you hard?"

"You've been in the room for at least fifteen minutes," I say, feeling my own blush start. "I've been hard. Maybe you just didn't notice."

Bailey shakes her head, a sharp look in her eye.

"Not like this," she says slowly. "It turns you on. But which part? Me being with Cooper? Or just talking about him at all?" One corner of her mouth turns up and she moves her hips more deliberately this time.

"Bailey, wait."

"Not unless you tell me we need to stop for a condom," she says, a challenge in her eyes. I shake my head, any protest locked up tight in my throat. Bailey practically purrs her satisfaction. "Then fuck me, Drew."

The next shift of her hips lines our bodies up just right and the tip of my cock glides in that first scorching inch, causing us both to gasp.

"More," Bailey whispers, her lithe body shaking as she strains against me, trying to take more inside her.

"Like this?" Close as I am to the edge, I shouldn't be taunting her, but I can't help it. Bailey catches on fast, her head coming up to look me straight in the eye as she turns it right back on me.

"Should I tell you about my night with Cooper?" she asks. This time I can't hide my reaction. My dick twitches hard at that name, and the thought of them touching each other makes me shudder.

"Bailey."

"I think I should," she says, squeezing her muscles around my cock, tighter than I can stand and so goddamn hot I'm about to lose my mind. I slide in another couple of inches and Bailey's breath hitches. But she doesn't stop talking.

"He took me to a booth in the back of the bar and put his hand right up my skirt."

At that, my hips buck hard, sliding my dick inside Bailey to the hilt. She cries out, her thighs beginning to shake.

"He slid his hand between my legs." She gasps.

"Did you come?" I ask, my lips right next to hers, sharing air with every breath. I'm pulsing against her now, so goddamn close to the edge I'm about to scream, but I'll be damned if she doesn't go over it with me.

"He fucked me with his fingers. I had to—" Bailey chokes on the last word, crying out as the orgasm hits her hard. Her body clenches tight around me as I pound into her, out of control, out of my mind.

"He got you off in front of all those people," I say, my vision going gray.

"Yes," Bailey sobs. "Yes."

"You and Cooper—" That's all it takes to send me flying, saying his name, picturing the scene Bailey's painted for me. I'm coming so hard, I nearly take us both down. My knees are shaking in the aftermath, but I manage to hold Bailey up a moment longer as we try to catch our breaths.

"Drew," murmurs Bailey. I pull back just enough to meet her eyes, and God help me, she's the most beautiful woman I've ever seen. I can't do anything but kiss her again as I muster enough strength to carry her back to my bed.

The alarm is familiar, but for some reason sounds far away, so smacking my nightstand has no effect on making it stop. I groan as I reach over, feeling around for my phone. When my search turns up nothing, I manage to pry my eyes open.

No phone. I turn to check the other side of the bed. Not there either.

Memory comes back full force, and I realize Bailey's nowhere to be found either. I groan again, scrubbing a hand over my face.

Right. First things first. Pants ended up somewhere in the hallway. Phone is probably with the pants. I track them both down and shut off the alarm. The apartment is empty of all other noise, telling me Bailey's not hiding in another room. She's long gone.

I'm not happy about it, but I'm also not surprised. Any talking we managed to do last night ended abruptly, either by my choice or hers.

Three times? No, four. Christ, no wonder I'm sore. I can't stop a grin imagining she must be feeling it too this morning.

My best buddy Bailey is absolutely dynamite in bed. Who knew?

The grin sticks around as I shower. Even knowing I must look like a dope doesn't make it go away. The good mood carries me all the way back to the competition grounds, where we're gearing up for the final judging and award ceremony. The competition has gone smoothly for the most part, with any hiccups occurring strictly behind the scenes. I'd set up Google alerts, and as far as I could tell, no tabloids were reporting any scandals, real or imagined. There have been a few speculative pieces on the drama between Cooper and me, but apparently most places decided to go with covering the event itself.

As wins go, this is a big one.

There's still some work to do today, but by and large my job here is done. So long as Cooper doesn't burn the place down, we should be home free.

Cooper.

Shit.

That might be the only part of last night I'd forgotten about—that crazy story Bailey told me the first time we—

"What's up, Drew? You feeling okay?" asks one of the techies.

"I'm okay, thanks...Grayson." I fish his name out of my memory, having seen him in the office a few times with my friend James. Grayson gives me a thumbs-up, his dimples flashing for a moment before he turns his attention back to his phone.

I'll have to sort out that mess later. For now, we've got a competition to close.

My earpiece comes to life. "Hicks," says a woman's voice. "Drew Hicks, are you here yet?"

"Right here, Kenna," I say in response.

"You're needed backstage in five minutes," says Kenna.

"Be right there."

I thank my lucky stars there's too much activity backstage today for me to be left alone with Cooper Lawson. Every nerve I have feels raw and exposed today. Given our history of communicating—that weird moment in the stage inventory closet aside—it's best if we don't have to talk to each other right now. I think he'd agree with me, though I catch some side-eye from him as I run down the checklist for the final ceremony.

I peek around the curtain, spotting Bailey in the third row next to her new friend Evie. The crowd beyond the finalists is thick, better than we could have hoped for, considering all the vendors will be shutting down within the hour.

"Right," says Kenna Burch in person this time, standing somewhere behind me. "First, Cooper does his thing, then we'll present the judges. Let the judges do a rundown of the scoring process, then Mr. Greeley will announce the final five."

"Piece of cake," says Grayson, taking the box of equipment from Kenna. "Quit stressing, Burch."

"It is literally my job to stress over this, March," snaps Kenna. I do a double-take, because Kenna rarely snaps at anyone. "What's your role here again?"

Grayson just grins at her, his dimples popping. "Whatever you want it to be, Miz Burch."

"And on that note," I say, stepping between them to draw Kenna's attention away from killing the guy. Grayson clearly has no sense of self-preservation. "I think it's time to start the countdown clock."

Kenna takes a deep breath and checks her own clipboard. "You're right, Drew. Let's get this show on the road." She taps her earpiece to speak and a few seconds later we hear the crowd start cheering, counting down along with the clock on the big screens.

"Ready?" I ask Kenna.

"Showtime," she says. She checks her watch, even as the curtain rises and Cooper Lawson takes the stage.

BAILEY MADE THE FINAL FIVE. I can't believe it.

She's a great home cook and all, and I never doubted her ability to compete. But through some trick of scoring, and that business she managed in the first round with the soup, somehow she pulled it off.

I'm so damn proud of her I could burst.

It'll have to keep, though. We've still got interviews, photo shoots, and tear-down this afternoon before gearing up to film on location. I'll be there as part of the crew, but responsibility for the next phase all belongs to a team somewhere above my pay grade.

"Congratulations, Drew," says Kenna. I return her hug.

"Same to you," I tell her, pulling back. Her beaming smile matches mine. "I can't believe we pulled it off."

"I can," she says, waving me off. "You worked your ass off for this week. And frankly, so did I."

"I couldn't have done it without you."

"Of that, I am well aware," says Kenna, still smiling.

"Where's your assistant?" I ask, my grin turning teasing. Kenna's expression goes a little sour.

"You mean March?" she asks. I nod, smirking when she rolls her eyes. "He's not my assistant any more than you are. I don't know what's got into that kid this week, but if he doesn't watch himself, I'll—"

"I would pay actual money to hear the rest of that sentence," says Grayson March, coming up behind Kenna. She closes her eyes briefly before turning to face him.

"Me too," says Cooper, trailing along behind March. "What are we talking about?"

"Miz Burch here was about to tell us just how she'll punish me if I don't watch myself."

At that, Kenna throws up her hands and stalks off. Grayson March clearly gets under her skin—it doesn't appear to faze him, though.

"If that's what you're into," says Cooper, making Grayson laugh.

"We'll talk about that another time," says Grayson, still chuckling. "Anything else you need from me, boss?" This question he directs to me; I shake my head.

"Cleanup crew has the rest," I say. "Unless you're working the photo shoot or something, we're done here."

"Nice. I'm out of here." Grayson takes off with a wave, leaving me alone with Cooper.

"So," says Cooper, shoving his hands in his pockets.

"So," I say. "Bailey made the final five."

"I heard," says Cooper, trying not to smile. Of course, he heard. He's the one who announced the names.

"Pretty exciting."

"So all three of us will be on location next week," says Cooper. My mind trips over that and stays there.

All three of us. Holed up in the mountains for five days.

"You okay there?" Cooper asks. "Hello?"

"I'm fine," I say. "I hadn't thought of that."

"What, you hadn't thought of all three of us?" Cooper raises a brow, the hint of a smirk on his face. "Shame. I sure have."

15

COOPER

Drew goes beet red.

What is it about Drew Hicks that dismantles the filter between my brain and my mouth?

"It's a joke, dude," I say.

"Of course," he says. I'm surprised he lets me off the hook that easy because he clearly doesn't believe me.

"Are you flying down with the crew on Tuesday?" I ask, just to change the subject. Why the hell am I still here? I should be partying it up in the winners' circle.

"I think I'm going to drive myself down," says Drew. "It's only four hours away."

The final five will compete at some upscale resort in the mountains a couple hundred miles east of the city.

"No rest for the wicked then," I say.

"You ought to know," says Drew, the corner of his lips twitching with the hint of a smile. It makes me want to lick him there.

The random impulse startles me, but Drew mercifully doesn't have time to comment since the cleanup crew picks that moment to dismantle the stage curtain, letting shafts of light fill the backstage area.

It's absurd, really. I left this stupid crush behind in college, maybe even before then. I still shouldn't have such a strong reaction to this guy, not after all these years. Not after the way he's treated me.

And how has he treated you? Except the times you deliberately provoked him and that one lightning-strike episode in the closet backstage, Drew's gone out of his way to make sure you didn't screw up your chances with Sizzle this week.

"I guess I would," I say, conceding the point. "And with that in mind... what would you say to a truce?"

"A truce?"

"We have five days in the godforsaken wilderness—"

"It's a five-star resort."

"—and almost round-the-clock filming to look forward to next week."

Reciting our grueling production schedule next week has somehow amused Drew, bringing his grin back full force and goddamn it, I want to kiss him again.

"And Bailey will be there," I add. Drew watches me carefully, his grin fading slightly, only to be replaced by a look of such heat my heart starts pounding.

"Yes, she will." He looks me over slowly. I feel the weight of his gaze on my body like a touch. God, I hate him. "All right, Lawson. You've got yourself a deal."

Drew stretches out a hand and I take it reluctantly. The rough skin of his palm chafes against mine, making me shiver.

"You're right," he says, holding on just a little bit too long. "It's going to be quite a week."

Before I can ask him what exactly he means by that, the cleanup crew descends on the backstage alcove and we're surrounded by people laughing and chatting as they start packing up equipment. Drew drops my hand like it's on fire and gives me a look, weighty and significant, before exiting the stage area.

It takes me a couple of minutes to get my breathing under control and by the time I do, the crew is looking at me funny, so I clear out as fast as the crowds and traffic will let me.

Several hours and a few beers later, I still haven't deciphered that last look and it's thoroughly pissing me off. Though I've finally deduced that pissed off is my go-to reaction to Drew Hicks, whether it's rational or not.

Mostly, it's not rational. And I'm pretty sure I figured out why.

I want him. I want him every bit as much as I want Bailey. And considering I have ten years of unresolved feelings for her, that fact scares the ever-loving shit out of me.

Music and noise from the pub downstairs drifts up the stairwell as I lock the apartment door behind me. Too many thoughts, not enough space. I need to get out of my own head for a bit, and that means getting out of my little apartment. It's a nice enough space, if tiny. It suits me. More or less. But I'm buzzing with the high of a job well done—if the comments on Sizzle's website are anything to go by —and that last tête-à-tête with Drew and making out in that booth with Bailey. I need to get out of my head for a bit, and Rusty's Pub downstairs is the fastest way to make it happen.

The dining room is still crowded, a good sign for the Sunday night dinner rush. My favorite spot at the end of the bar is open, so I slide into the high seat and scan the room for Rusty, the mountainous bear of a man who owns the building. He'd rented me the second-floor apartment three years ago, right after my parents fulfilled their lifelong dream of moving to the Florida coast.

I'm studying the crowd and don't notice right away when somebody comes to stand in front of me behind the bar.

"Get you something to drink?"

Whoever's asking isn't Rusty. I turn to see a vaguely familiar-looking brown-eyed guy, wiping his hands on the towel tucked into his waistband.

"I know you," he says, tapping a finger on the bar top. "Wait, don't tell me... bourbon on the rocks?"

"That's me," I say, reaching out a hand. "I'm Cooper. You worked the bar at the Sizzle TV gala, right?" We shake hands and the guy gives me a saucy wink.

"Name's Beck," he says. "You were with that gorgeous couple and that bitchy brunette."

"Christ, I'd forgotten about her." I laugh. "What are you doing behind the bar? You must be new here."

"Something like that," says Beck, grinning.

"Cooper!" The booming voice startles us both. "Long time no see, kid. I see you've met my boy, here." Rusty comes up alongside Beck, pulling him into a one-armed hug that even from here looks like it hurts.

"This is your son?" I ask.

"Home from deployment," says Rusty, looking so proud he could burst.

"Knock it off, Dad," says Beck, not without affection.

"Thank you for your service," I say, not sure how else to respond. I haven't met many members of the military. There's no base around here, and if anybody I grew up with signed up, it would be news to me.

Beck nods in reply, excusing himself to wait on a handful of middle-aged women at the other end of the bar. Rusty watches him go.

"They look like they might eat him alive," I say. He laughs, a broad, wide-open sound that makes half the people in the bar turn our way.

"Good for business, he is," says Rusty.

"You must be glad to have him home." Rusty colors up, and I avert my gaze when I see the start of tears in his eyes.

"More than I can say," he says gruffly. "Been home three weeks now, and every couple hours I catch myself checking the news like he's still over there." Rusty pours me my usual, and we chat about pub business for a bit before he heads back to check on the kitchen.

My own parents hit the road as soon as I was done with school and haven't been back since. I can't imagine them worrying about me the way Rusty's clearly been doing for Beck. Then again, what the hell have I been doing with my life? Nothing nearly as dangerous or important as fighting for my country.

The thought is depressing and reminds me why I needed to get out of the apartment in the first place.

My phone chimes in my pocket and I muffle a groan. Not that I don't enjoy my work, I do, but it'd be nice to switch off now and then.

Not a helpful attitude, considering how I make my living.

My followers have been pretty supportive, still checking in and engaging with the photos and posts I scheduled a few weeks ago so I could focus all my attention on the competition this week, but it's nothing like the kind of traffic I usually get. New and novel is the nature of the business, I get that; I expected the lower numbers. But earlier one of my superfans tipped me off that a competitor's blog was actively poaching traffic from the comments on my posts. On an average day, that kind of behavior gets frowned on, but since I haven't been around much online, they've been getting away with it, siphoning traffic to their own sites.

Whatever. I built up my audience from the ground up; I can do it again. Right now, I've got bigger things to worry about.

Like how I'm going to keep my shit together, locked away on some mountain for the next week with Drew and Bailey in close proximity. My contract with Sizzle has a very clear morality clause. If the wrong person caught wind of the things we got up to this week, or worse, if they caught us at it, that contract would be terminated immediately. Definitely no hope of signing on with them again for another show. So it would be in my best interest to steer clear of any trouble, keep things squeaky-clean and above-board between me and... anybody else this week.

Only, I get sidetracked thinking about "squeaky-clean" and between us—all three of us—and the unbidden fantasy those words bring to mind takes my breath away.

This is nuts. I'm too goddamn old to be confusing life with porn, even in my fantasy life. Then again, that's the whole point of fantasy.

"Something on your mind?" Beck's leaning against the bar a few feet away, polishing glassware and grinning like he can see inside my head. I clear my throat.

"Work stuff," I say, tossing back the rest of my drink and nodding when he points to ask if I want a refill.

"You work for Sizzle?" he asks. I know it's just bartender talk. Rusty's a natural at it; wouldn't surprise me one bit if his son is the same way. But it gets my mind out of the porno gutter I keep falling into the last few days, so I accept my drink and answer him.

"Sort of. I'm a contractor," I tell him.

"What kind of work?" he asks. It's the kind of small talk that makes it easy to pay attention to other things, like the repetitive way Beck wipes the glass in his hands, then duplicates the action for every mug he picks up. I think he's counting the number of times he wipes them, and I wonder if that's military training or a compulsion of some kind.

"Hosting for a live, televised event," I answer. "Plus some online media stuff."

Beck nods, interested but not invasive about it.

"Did I hear Dad say you have the second floor here?"

I nod and remember I'd recently heard noise on the third floor for the first time since I'd lived there. "Are you the one who moved in upstairs?"

Beck nods.

"Then we're neighbors," I say. "You need any help getting things moved in or anything, just let me know."

"I appreciate that," says Beck. He excuses himself to tend to some more customers and once again I'm left alone with my thoughts.

Which is not where I need to be, because as soon as Beck walks away I'm picturing myself sandwiched between Drew and Bailey, and if I get kicked out of Rusty's for public indecency, he'll never let me live it down. I lay down some bills to cover my tab and the tip and nod at Beck as I head for the back stairwell. I've got to get this shit locked down, and now. Out of my system, out of my head, and just be done with it already.

It's hours later, in the dark, slanting light sliding through the blinds of my bedroom window that I give in to the urge, rocking my hips into the mattress, imagining her lips, his hands, and everything in between until I come, gasping into my pillow, groaning quietly until I'm spent.

This is going to be a disaster.

16

BAILEY

My short return to normalcy Monday morning does not begin smoothly.

"What do you mean, you're leaving tonight?" says Mr. Heckman, my boss. "You just got back!"

"I made it into the final round," I explain for the second time in ten minutes. "I fly out tonight to film for the rest of the week. But I'll be back on—"

"I don't think so," says Mr. Heckman. "What does this look like, McDonald's? How am I supposed to cover you for another six days? With no notice!"

"I've already talked to Althea and—"

"No," he says, dropping back down into his desk chair. "No. It simply can't be done. I can't believe after all these years, you really care about your position at this bank so little as to treat us this way."

"Mr. Heckman," I try again, but he's not hearing me. Gary Heckman has been general manager of this bank since I was in diapers. Needless to say, change is not something he finds comfortable. I tamp down my frustration and wait him out, knowing from experience he'll only bluster a few more minutes. It'll be easier to talk him down after that.

"Ms. Ross, do you realize your name was submitted for a promotion a couple of weeks ago?"

That catches me off guard. This isn't exactly a large company—I knew there were some openings for assistant managers since the bank opened a new branch a couple of towns over.

"Imagine how embarrassed I was to have to tell the bank president that you couldn't be relied on in a position of authority like that," says Mr. Heckman with an audible sigh.

Are you fucking kidding me?

"Are you joking?"

"Not in the slightest," he says, frowning and leaning forward to rest his elbows on the desk. It's his "Now Listen Here" pose. "You taking off almost a week for some silly baking show was bad enough, but this has just confirmed I made the right call."

Unbelievable. Absolutely unbelievable.

"I've hardly taken a day off since I started this job," I say, so frustrated I'm near tears. But I'll be goddamned if I cry in front of this pompous blowhard.

"And that's the kind of commitment we need from our employees," says Mr. Heckman, his eyes on the massive monitor on his desk now. He's all but dismissed me from the room already. "Not this back-and-forth, time-off-with-no-notice nonsense. You're free to return to your desk."

I slip out of the glassed-in office and walk back to my desk.

The first time I got passed over for this promotion was easier to explain—they'd just hired the bank president's niece right out of college, and she was ever so slightly more qualified than me anyway. It was harder to take that personally, since I'd only been working here a year at the point.

This is something else.

I spend most of my day trying to avoid the well-meaning murmurs and pitying glances from my coworkers, keeping my head down and getting as much work done as I can so next week isn't a complete backlog.

By the time I get home, I've got about thirty minutes to pack before I have to leave for the airport if I'm going to make the flight

Sizzle booked for me. I overheard some of the other contestants say they all got earlier flights. I'm the only one who still had to go to work today.

I'm still blown away that I made it this far in the competition, though I know it was purely by chance. Three other contestants scored higher than me and would have made the number five slot, but they got disqualified after the judging for various reasons. It's a fluke, but goddamn it, I made it.

Any residual anger at my boss has faded by the time I get to the ticket counter. He's only doing what he thinks is right, same as anybody else. He's just another person in my world who doesn't respect me. And isn't that just a slap in the face.

You're the one who sat there and took it. You're the one who let them. Don't put this all on other people.

And damn me if that voice in my head doesn't have a point this time. Maybe it's time I start thinking about respecting myself. I made it to the final five, for God's sake. Fluke or not, that's not nothing. And I'm excited about it, my current moping notwithstanding.

The line at the counter isn't moving, so I pull up an old file in my cloud storage app. Coop asked me a few days ago if I was working as a caterer; it's been so many years I'd almost forgotten about it but sure enough, the file is still there. It was a project for one of my business classes in college—I'd worked up a full business plan for a catering business, right down to funding sources and scouted locations. The information is ten years out of date, but the bones are still good.

Reading through those pages, I feel more like myself than I have in years. Like putting on a favorite old sweater you'd misplaced and thought was lost. By the time they call for first class to board, I'm tapping out notes, highlighting things that need to be changed or updated and practically buzzing with energy again.

Screw Mr. Heckman. He doesn't want to give me that promotion, fine. Maybe it's time I start looking to promote myself.

"Aren't you a sight for sore eyes?"

I gasp and almost drop my phone, turning to see Cooper Lawson standing in line right behind me, grinning.

"What are you doing here?" I ask. Because I'm clearly an idiot when it comes to this man. His grin tells me he's perfectly aware of that fact.

"Knitting a sweater," he says, lifting a brow. "What do you think I'm doing here?"

"Is this—Are we on the same flight?" I'm stammering. Why am I stammering? This is Cooper, for God's sake. I might have the hots for him, but that's nothing new. I managed to ace that chem class, despite having him as my distracting, if otherwise helpful, lab partner. What's the damn deal?

There's a chance it might have something to do with fucking Drew all night after the competition on Saturday. Maybe. Possibly also because Cooper's name came up more than once between us, often in the form of a moan. Which is kinky as hell and more than a little wrong.

Cooper watches my face with no small amount of amusement.

"Looks like," he says, waving his boarding pass and pointing me forward when the line moves. Five minutes later, I'm getting my ancient laptop out of my bag and reveling in the super-deluxe experience of business class when he plops down into the seat next to me.

"No way," I say.

Cooper smirks. "I may have sweet-talked the flight attendant into switching seats for me. But if you'd rather spend the next hour chatting with Mr. Fritz up there..." Coop tilts his head in the direction of a sweating, heavyset older man draining his glass of champagne and playing poker on an enormous tablet.

I shake my head and Cooper grins.

"Thought that might be the case," he says. "Though it doesn't say much for me, if you had to think about it that hard."

I nudge him with my elbow.

"Not that hard," I say. Cooper slides a hand around my arm before I can pull back, using it to pull me close enough to whisper.

"Looking good, Ross." His eyelashes brush my cheek, making me shiver despite the wool blanket draped across my lap. "Missed you the last couple of days."

"You just saw me yesterday," I say breathlessly.

"For a minute," he says, shaking his head slowly and letting go of my arm. "It's not enough."

"No?"

"Not nearly enough," he says, keeping his voice low. I'm forcibly reminded of our little indiscretion at the bar a couple of nights ago and feel my face heating up.

"Lucky for you," I say, clearing my throat and trying for cool as hard as I can fake. "We've got five days of filming ahead of us."

Cooper looks at me, taking in my flushed face and the absolute lack of chill in my expression. His smirk turns to a grin.

"Lucky for me," he says.

The flight attendant stops to offer us champagne.

"Why not?" says Cooper, accepting two glasses with a grin. He hands me one and raises his own in a toast. "Cheers. Here's to you, Bailey Ross."

"I'll drink to that," I say, tapping his plastic cup with mine. "Here's to me."

A beat of silence passes as the flight attendant moves on to the passengers across the row.

"How long is this flight, anyway?" Cooper asks.

"Forty minutes, give or take." I catch him watching me as I turn back from the window to face him. "Why?"

"Just wondering how long I get you for," he says. "You realize I haven't had you alone this much since we were in college?"

"We're hardly alone," I say, glancing around the cabin as the plane starts to taxi down the runway.

A slow grin lifts the side of Cooper's mouth.

"We weren't exactly alone the other night, either," he murmurs. "But that didn't seem to bother you."

He means the night at the bar. Good Lord. What have I gotten myself into?

"Nope." I drain the rest of my glass and stare at the cup in my hand. They're tiny servings, really. Of course, I haven't eaten yet today —too anxious at work and too busy this afternoon—so maybe I should take it easy on the drinks. Thank God it's a short flight.

"Nope, you're not playing," asks Cooper. "Or 'nope,' it didn't bother you?"

I'm pretty sure that smirk means he's got me pegged, but I take a shot at denial anyway.

"I mean, nope, not playing," I say. My breathless delivery gives me away and Cooper's grin widens.

"Now that's a damn shame," he says thoughtfully, sipping his own drink. "I thought five days in the wilderness might be just the thing to help you unwind."

"What wilderness?" I ask, laughing. "It's an exclusive resort, not some cabin shack in the woods."

"All the same," says Cooper, unfazed. The emphasis he'd put on the word "unwind" pulls at me, like he knows exactly what it would take to spin me out.

And he does. If memory serves, the man knows exactly what he's doing.

"What about Drew?" I ask before I can think it through.

His smirk disappears and Cooper scowls. "What about him?"

"Aren't... Didn't you? You guys—" I have absolutely no idea how to ask him what I want to know.

"Oh," he says. Light dawns, chasing the scowl off his face. "You mean Drew and me."

"Well, yeah," I say. "What else?"

Cooper looks up at me through his lashes. "You tell me, Ross."

A vivid memory of Drew pounding into me, pressing me up against the wall, Cooper's name in the air between us flashes before my eyes and I feel my cheeks go red.

"Well, now. What have we here?" Cooper brings a hand up to touch my cheek. "That's quite a blush, Bailey. Something you want to tell me?"

I shake my head, fast enough to make me dizzy. Or maybe it's the altitude. Or maybe it's just because he's sitting so close. I can see just the barest hint of a tattoo peeking through the collar of his shirt. He didn't have that tattoo back in college. The urge to trace its lines with my tongue comes out of nowhere, making me blush even harder.

"You and Drew," I blurt. "You kissed him backstage."

Cooper takes a deep breath.

"I did."

"Why?" I ask, trying to get a handle on my own breathing before I hyperventilate from overexcitement. I've never been so turned on in my life. "Alan would have taken your word for it. You didn't have to kiss Drew to prove anything. So why?"

Cooper takes his sweet time answering, his eyes searching my face for something before he speaks again.

"Why did you kiss him at the gala?"

I've done a lot more than kiss Drew since then, but I see what Cooper's getting at. He doesn't look mad. If anything, he looks curious, and if he's anywhere near as turned on as I am right now, maybe he won't be mad if I tell him the truth.

So I do.

"I wanted to," I say, so quietly I'm not sure he hears me at first. Then Cooper ducks his head to meet my eyes.

"So did I."

The connection between us goes electric, raising the hair on the back of my neck, making me shiver. Cooper holds my gaze, the heat there burning me from the inside out.

"You want him," I say.

"I want you," he counters, but he doesn't deny it otherwise. Silence reigns for a long moment, and Cooper takes my hand, our fingers intertwining.

Maybe it's the champagne. Maybe it's the shitty workday, preceded by several shitty years of shitty relationships. Or maybe it's the universe trying to nudge me into action. Whatever the reason, the next words that come to mind spill out of my mouth before I can let fear get ahold of them.

"What if you could have us both?" I ask Cooper.

17

DREW

The blandly named Blue Ridge Resort and Lodge is gorgeous, even swamped with camera crews as it is now. The ceilings peak over several levels of balcony railings, and the glassed-in wall gives the lobby a nearly three-hundred-degree mountaintop view of the Blue Ridge Mountains. What started as a flurry a couple of hours ago has ramped up to a full-on snowstorm, enough so that I'm worried about the last of our crew getting here tonight. Including Bailey. She was one of the last scheduled to fly in.

So was Cooper, but I'm not thinking about him right now. I bite my lip to remind myself of that for the third time in twenty minutes, but I'm not sure it helps.

Ty arranged for us to share a suite. It's not a big deal, obviously. The resort was running out of rooms, and Greeley had us doing the stick-together song and dance this week, so my boss figured it'd be an easy fix—win-win for everybody. At least it's a suite and not a single room.

Not that that's crossed my mind at all. And guess who probably gets to tell Cooper about the arrangements? If he ever gets here.

Room arrangements notwithstanding, the lodge was a good choice for the finals. Idyllic and picture-perfect everywhere you look, plus the conference rooms are perfectly sized for the number of mini-kitchens we set up today. And it's just exactly far enough from the city to make it inconvenient for fans of the network to turn up for selfies. Filming this week should be a breeze, assuming we don't all get stranded in this snowstorm. But I guess there are worse ways to spend a week.

Snowed in. In a deluxe mountain resort. With Bailey. And Cooper. Who's sleeping next door.

Not to mention all my coworkers and the other contestants. And my boss. And my boss's boss.

But who's counting?

The person in line ahead of me finally gets her room key and the concierge nods my way.

"Hi, I'm with Sizzle TV. I need to check whether one of my... one of our contestants has checked in yet."

"ID please," says the attendant, eyeing me skeptically. I hand over my pass and after a long moment that has me seriously considering whether I'm about to be hauled out by security, the attendant gives a tight nod. "Of course, Mr. Hicks. The name?"

"Bailey Ross."

A moment of tapping later, the attendant nods again.

"She checked in about thirty minutes ago," he says. I thank him and step aside, pulling out my phone. Still no answer to my texts. Considering the way she left a couple of nights ago, maybe I shouldn't be surprised Bailey's avoiding me again.

The desk is curved, like the lobby itself, so I hear the commotion before I see anything. An exasperated woman, swearing, and a smacking sound.

"What kind of place is this? I'll have you know I'm one of the finalists!"

Stepping around the guests still in line, I move around to see one of our competitors, Tracy, slapping the desk with her palm and all but stomping her feet in a temper. Bailey stands a couple of feet away, looking wary.

"I'm very sorry, Ms. Elffers," says another attendant behind the desk. There are three of them crowded around one computer monitor. A security guard has moved from the lobby door to the edge of the counter where other stragglers have gathered to watch the episode. "There's really nothing I can do. The suite—"

"I told you, I don't care if it's a suite, damn it! I will not be shoe-horned in with some... some..." Tracy Elffers stammers, jabbing a finger in Bailey's direction.

"Watch it, lady," snaps Bailey, her own temper starting to show, which means they've been at this a while now. "I'm a finalist too."

"Whatever," says the other woman, rolling her eyes and turning back to the desk. "I want another room."

"Ms. Elffers, again, I'm very sorry—"

Before Tracy can wind herself back up, I step around the group of onlookers and up to the desk myself, handing over my staff badge to the attendants.

"I'm Drew Hicks, Sizzle production staff," I say. Tracy comes up short, surprised enough by the interruption to take a breath. "What's the problem here?"

"These people," Tracy sneers at the attendants, "refuse to give me a room of my own. They insist I'm to shack up with her." She points at Bailey without so much as turning her head.

"The staff members have been moved into suites as well, Ms. Elffers," I say. The attendants bob their heads in agreement.

"That's right, sir," one of them says. "We had a last-minute reservation for a conference this week. Because of the storm, they didn't have anywhere else to get rooms. I'm afraid the entire resort is booked for the next four days."

"Well, now," I say. Tracy puffs up like she's about to start boiling over again. "Seems to me we can all make some concessions, given the circumstances. Right, Ms. Elffers?" I say. She turns that sneer on me. Can't say I'm surprised, considering she has no idea who I am, and even if she did, I suspect it wouldn't matter.

Her condescension is distasteful, but my job is to make sure the show goes on, so I take a deep breath and remain calm. Catching Bailey's eye, I wave her closer.

"I refuse to share living space with this person," says Tracy, getting louder. People all over the lobby are watching us. "Or anyone else for that matter."

"If you would please keep your voice down," I say quietly. Before she can turn that temper back on me, I hold up a hand and address Bailey. "I believe I have a solution. If I can find you another suite, would you be all right with changing rooms?"

"Yes," Bailey says emphatically, only barely audible over Tracy's much louder "Finally!"

"Ms. Elffers," I say, my voice so quiet she's forced to step closer to the desk to hear me. "Let me remind you that you signed a contract, and finalist or not, it can be terminated at any time, for any reason the network deems worthy. Do I make myself clear?"

Tracy hears the thinly veiled threat this time, and nods tightly, closing her mouth. Bailey grips my arm.

"You heard the people at the desk," she mutters. "Where are you going to find an extra room?"

"I happen to have a suite also," I murmur. I thank the attendants, and disappointed by the anticlimactic end to the drama, the crowd in the lobby begins to disperse.

"What about your roommate?" Bailey asks. I pick up the suitcase next to her feet.

"Come on," I say. "I'll explain upstairs."

THE DOOR of the suite clicks shut behind me as Bailey turns, laying her coat over the back of the sofa in the common area between the two bedrooms.

"Jeez," she says, whistling low. "You definitely won the room lottery. This is beautiful."

She had a point, but the producers had picked this place on purpose.

"Not a bad camera angle to be had," I say, setting her suitcase down flush with the wall.

"So what's the story?" Bailey asks. "Somebody call in sick or something?"

"First things first," I say, grabbing her hand. I pull her closer, the scent of her body wash making me ache in a way I no longer had to shove to the back of my mind. Instead I lean in, savoring the way it came a little stronger off the delicate skin right below her jaw. Before she can ask me anything else, I do what I've been thinking about for the last three days straight and kiss her.

Bailey's lips part on a gasp. When she melts into me, her body lining up with mine in all the best ways, my arms go around her waist and I deepen the kiss. It's liberating, being able to touch her like this. Being able to enjoy it after all these years of constantly trying to keep her into the friend zone.

My fingers twist in her hair just a little too hard and Bailey breaks the kiss, huffing out a laugh.

"You're so beautiful," I say, instead of apologizing like I meant to. "I mean—"

Bailey catches my hand and presses a soft kiss there, her mouth lingering, her eyes bright with tears, or laughter, or secrets. Or maybe something else.

"Well, this is cozy," comes a drawling voice from across the room. Bailey chokes on a gasp, whirling around to see who's caught us.

Cooper stands, arms akimbo, propped up on the door to his room, hair still wet from his shower.

That is, I assume he took a shower. Given that all he's wearing is the thick hotel towel wrapped around his waist, it seems reasonable.

That Cooper Lawson can make me babble inside my own head is infuriating.

"Guess you got here all right," I say, stupidly.

"Looks like," he says, the hint of a smirk on his lips. "All right there, Ross?"

Bailey clears her throat. Twice.

"Long time no see," she says. Cooper grins.

His body is ridiculous. Lean and long, but tightly muscled, one of those smaller guys who can outperform half the meatheads at the gym without breaking a sweat. A drop of water drips from his ear, over the tattoos on his chest before disappearing into the valley of his abs, and the silence between the three of us stretches.

And stretches. And stretches some more.

"Um, Coop?"

"Yeah, Ross?"

Bailey clears her throat again, her hand gripping mine harder by the second.

"Where are your clothes?"

Cooper's smirk dials up to eleven at that, and damn me if that look doesn't turn me on. Hard.

So hard. Embarrassingly hard. If Bailey moves to the side, there'll be no hiding it. Then again, I think that's what this is... no more hiding. Not for any of us.

Hence Cooper in that goddamn towel.

"What do you think, Hicks?" he asks, just standing there, letting us gape at him.

"About what?" My voice is so rough, it's a wonder the words come out at all.

"About my clothes," he says.

"You're not wearing any clothes," I say automatically. I'll admit, I haven't exactly been following the conversation all that well. My eyes drop to his towel, my breath stuck in my throat, waiting for something to happen to it. Like I could magically make it fall with my gaze alone.

This is not like me. Passive is not how I'm wired. At all. That stupid, ridiculous towel has broken my brain.

"Thank you, Captain Obvious," says Cooper, rolling his eyes and finally moving into the room. He doesn't bother to hold the towel's knot, just strides across the common area like he doesn't care if it falls. "Tell me something. Did you arrange for us to be roommates?"

"Ty."

"Ah," he says. "Then you're still babysitting me this week."

"Not so much," I say. "Ty figured since we'd already been stuck together for so much of the filming that maybe we wouldn't care about being assigned to the same suite. Not everybody is as gracious about sharing as I am."

My mind was on Bailey's room predicament and the bitchy Ms. Tracy Elffers when I said it. Then my brain catches up with my mouth, and my face heats.

"Interesting choice of words," says Cooper, looking between Bailey and me.

"No shit," she agrees. "I think Drew was referring to my room assignment." At Cooper's frown, Bailey sighs and falls back onto the oversized sofa, tugging me down to sit next to her. "My roommate kicked me out. Said she refused to share. Drew took pity on me and brought me up here."

"The couch is a pullout," I say, pointedly not watching Cooper fiddle with the knot in his towel. "I'll sleep here. You can have my room."

"Or mine," says Cooper, the suggestion clear in his voice. I chance a look at his face.

The smirk is gone, as are all signs of that high-handed amusement he wears like a damned second skin. He studies Bailey for a long moment before meeting my eyes, and I have the most insane idea that he can see every X-rated thought in my head right now.

Hell, maybe he can. God knows I'm tired of hiding it from him, from both of them. So I let him look, let him see every bit of it—all the looks I cut short, the things I didn't say, the late-night fantasies. I let him read my face like an open book as I remember every second of being inside Bailey, of pounding into her as we cried out his name.

A heartbeat later, Cooper's kneeling on the floor in front of us.

"Coop—"

He cuts Bailey off with a hard, fast kiss, bracing his weight on our thighs where they're pressed together on the couch.

"You're right, Hicks," he says, pulling back slightly and glancing my way. I can't breathe at all. "Sharing is better."

Then he's kissing me, going full-tilt, stealing the air from my lungs. Bailey's whimper disappears into Cooper's growl, her hand clutching at my thigh as Cooper makes quick work of my shirt.

This is madness. This is absolute insanity. There will be no awkward-but-short morning-after with this. For one heart-stopping second, in my mind all I can see is that there aren't any mornings-after at all, just the three of us, locked together over and over. I can't see an end to it because it doesn't end, and it scares the holy hell out of me. It's enough to make me pull away from him, sucking down air and resting my head on the back of the couch as Cooper works his way down, kissing and licking my chest until I'm about to tear the upholstery off this couch.

He tugs at the button on my jeans and I lift my hips to help, helpless to do anything but what he wants. Bailey kneels up beside me, her mouth at my ear. I can hear her panting already and we've barely started. When Cooper finally gets my dick free, Bailey groans, and that sound coupled with Cooper's mouth on my cock takes me right to the edge.

18

COOPER

So much for "needledick."

Christ, Drew's body doesn't quit; muscles for days, flexing and curving and planing out in all the right spots, nothing feminine about him whatsoever.

The thick head of his cock almost triggers my gag reflex, but only almost. And only because I'm so out of practice. He's so worked up his hips hitch against the air, trying to get to the back of my throat. I close my eyes to concentrate on taking him and when I manage to swallow around him, his and Bailey's twin moans have me looking back up to see.

Bailey's got a hand at her throat, her sweet full lips parted and panting, her eyes glued to me. Sucking off Drew Hicks was already on my top ten hottest encounters ever, but Bailey watching me puts this right at the top of the list. She looks like she might come just from watching us. I make a mental note to exploit that particular detail later and turn my gaze to Drew.

With his head thrown back like that I can't see his face, but the tension in his body tells me he's hanging on by a thread. I pull off him slowly, winding my tongue around the head of his cock to test my theory. He sucks in a breath, his abdomen clenching hard. Yep. I shouldn't feel smug that I got him there so fast. But I do. Probably not very sporting to tease him about it either, but I've never claimed to be a good person.

"Looks like somebody could use a breather," I say, working his spit-slick cock with one hand. That brings his head down, just so he can glare at me properly. My face feels like it might split, I'm grinning so hard.

"Smug is not a good look on you," he says.

"Liar." I let him go to wrap both hands around Bailey's hips and lift her off the couch, setting her on the floor beside me. The glazed look on her face is hot as hell. I have to kiss her, and because she's Bailey, I get lost in her, forgetting why I pulled her down here to begin with. When she works her fingers over my chest and down to the towel now tented in my lap, I break the kiss.

"Jesus, Ross," I say, catching her hand before she succeeds in stripping me. "You're a menace. Hold that thought."

I climb to my feet, adoring the pout on her face and the confusion in her eyes so much I bend down to kiss her again.

"Supply run," I whisper, my eyes darting over to see Drew watching us hungrily. "Maybe you can help keep him occupied for a minute."

Bailey grins, rising up on her knees.

"I can handle that," she says. "Hurry back."

The lights in our suite are dim so I leave them on; through the open curtains, the light pollution from the city an hour away is bright enough to light the heavy gray clouds even at night. I expect it's a romantic look, what with the mountains and snow and trees, if you're into that kind of thing. Me, I'd rather be looking at the view back on the couch.

Breathing deeply to force myself to calm down, I retrieve the shopping bag from the drugstore Bailey and I found after our flight landed. On my way back I again pause in the doorway, no less blown away by the sight of Drew and Bailey together than I was the first time—than every time I see them together. My chest tightens, heavy with how right they look, how unbelievably gorgeous they are together, and now, tonight, with how goddamned lucky I am to be walking back toward them.

I consider dropping the towel before I join them, but something tells me it might come in handy, so instead I head back to the couch, taking the seat right next to Drew.

"You want to sit that close, might as well be in my lap next time," he mutters. Drew glances at my towel but doesn't make eye contact. He's got one hand in Bailey's hair, his fingers flexing as she blows him.

"Maybe next time," I say, watching her technique. I'm pretty confident in my cock-sucking skills, but you never know when you might learn something. And I'm looking forward to learning all I can from these two.

Bailey catches me watching and grins as she runs her tongue over his sac, making Drew shiver. His hand lands on my towel-covered thigh.

"You're overdressed," he says.

"You looking to get me naked?" I ask, delighted when they both promptly answer "Yes." Bailey takes that as her cue.

"Drew's got a point," she says, releasing Drew with a long stroke of her hand that has his cock slapping against his stomach. She scoots in front of me, sliding her palms over my knees and presses up under the fabric slowly, forcibly reminding me of the night I got my hand up her skirt. Can't say I ever thought about wearing a skirt myself— not my kink—but if it feels this goddamned hot, maybe I should start.

And that's a bit *too* kinky, even for me. Too much for our first time together.

Not that I'm counting on a next time.

Right, because this isn't a thing. This is just... I don't know. Jungle fever? Except we're in the mountains. Mountain fever? Whatever it is, it's temporary, and I need to remember that.

Bailey watches me carefully, taking her time unwinding the thick roll of fabric at my waist, drawing it over my skin deliberately as she opens me up. Even the air around us feels like a stroke to my cock at this point.

Except for the sound of our breathing, it's awfully quiet on this couch.

"Don't tell me you've never seen a dick before, Hicks," I say. I'm just inventing reasons for him to fight with me now, but when I finally get up the nerve to look over, the stark want on his face has me gripping my balls, trying to stave off that point of no return. It must have the same effect on Bailey, because she's got one hand on my leg and one hand digging in the pharmacy bag.

"Get down here and fuck me, Drew," she says, tossing the box of condoms at him. And Christ, it's hot, watching him hop-to when she tells him to. Definitely something to explore next time.

There I go again, "next time."

That voice of reason shuts down real quick when Bailey lowers her head to take me in her mouth. She did this once before, that night back in college.

Apparently she's learned a thing or two in the last ten years.

"Jesus, Bailey." I use both hands to pull her head back gently before I erupt in her mouth. "What do you want?"

"Like this," she says, turning to capture my thumb between her lips. "Let me suck you while he fucks me."

It's all I can do to force the words out. "If you're sure."

Bailey laughs, releasing my thumb with an obscene pop. "Always wanted to try this. Never had the chance before."

The sound of foil tearing has us both glancing back to watch Drew stroke the condom over his length. My mouth goes dry as he pulls Bailey's ass up, spreading her knees and lining himself up. Bailey keeps her hand on my cock, kissing me everywhere she can reach except where I need her mouth the most.

"God," she whispers. "Oh, my God."

"Good?" I ask. When he bottoms out, Bailey presses her face to my hip, panting.

"Just wait," she says. "You'll see."

Drew's eyes snap up to mine, going wide when she says it and his hips start moving before any of us are ready. Bailey finds her balance, rocking back just enough to take the head of my cock in her mouth. It's not the most artful blow job I've ever had, but I imagine balance is a tricky thing when you're getting railed as hard as she is. And the view... Sweet Jesus, the view.

Drew goes from zero to sixty between one thrust and the next, and the buildup of the last couple of weeks—hell, the last couple of months of us working together—hits me all at once and I thrust up a little too far, gagging Bailey and drawing moans from all of us. Drew drops down over her back, his fists on the ground, his face buried in Bailey's neck. I sweep her hair out of his way as she works me over with her mouth, watching them both work up a sweat.

"Too close." I realize Drew is murmuring against Bailey's neck. "Too close. Don't want to come yet, but fuck."

Bailey pulls back a little, turning her head as though she's going to answer him, but Drew's already thrusting again, rocking both their bodies into me when his mouth grazes the tip of my cock.

"Fuck." My hand fists in Bailey's hair and she gasps. Drew catches my eye for half a heartbeat, then swallows me down and it's over. Bailey's crying out her orgasm, and I've got one hand wrapped around both their heads and Drew doesn't let up for even a second, sucking me hard as I shoot down his throat, groaning hard.

It's several minutes and lots of heavy breathing later before somebody grabs that towel and drops it back in my lap.

"Guess you planned ahead," says Drew, still a little breathless.

"Guess maybe I did," I say, tracing the lines of Bailey's cheek where she's resting on my thigh, a blissed-out look on her face.

Drew scoots over to lean back against the sofa, mirroring Bailey's position on the floor. Without thinking about it my hand goes to his hair, drawing my fingers through it and rubbing his scalp. He sighs once, then goes very still. It takes me a beat too long to take my hand away.

"We should head to bed," he says, glancing at Bailey first, then me. I nod and wait for them both to stand before rising off the couch, wrapping that towel around my waist again. Bailey smothers a grin.

"What?"

"Nothing," she says. She grabs her suitcase and follows Drew into the bedroom opposite mine. I move to follow and stop.

Drew said "head to bed" like he was talking about sleep, not more of... whatever that craziness on the couch was. I'll be sleeping in my own bed, obviously.

And yet, I stand there for a moment, indecision riding me far longer than it should.

"Lawson." Drew's voice snaps me out of it.

"What?"

"Get in here."

Guess that answers that.

Bailey shuts herself in the en suite bath. I hear the shower switch on and wonder just what the hell I'm supposed to do now.

When in doubt, brazen it out. As mottos go, it's a little perfunctory, but it's served me well so far. Especially when it comes to Drew Hicks.

I don't wait for an invitation this time; I crawl into the middle of the king-sized bed and fluff the pillows up behind me. When I catch Drew watching me, I fold my hands behind my head, flexing my abs as hard as I can.

He notices.

"Make yourself comfortable," he says dryly, tossing the boxers he held back into the open dresser drawer beside him. His body really is ridiculous. Thick and strong, enough meat to hang on to. If one were so inclined.

The towel around my waist twitches visibly. Drew notices that too.

"I think I will," I say. My mouth goes dry as he walks slowly to the side of the bed, climbing up to kneel next to me.

"You're awfully agreeable all of a sudden," he says, the hint of a smile at his mouth.

I absolutely will not laugh, not when he's making fun of me.

"I like you like this," he continues. Drew sets his hand on my shoulder, shoving me back into the pillows when I try to sit up.

"You would," I say. My brain clearly isn't back online yet because I can't stop staring at his mouth and I know he's teasing me, but I can't bring myself to get mad about it. Not with his cock right there, getting thicker by the second.

"I—" Drew stops before he finishes the thought as the bathroom door opens. It takes me an extra second to see why he's staring. When I tear my greedy eyes off his body and look over at Bailey, I realize why.

She's taken the fastest shower in history apparently, and is now wearing only an old band T-shirt and as far as I can tell, nothing else.

Hang on. That shirt—

"Ross," I say, sitting up straight. Drew lets me this time. Maybe because my voice has gone scratchy. "Ross, is that...?"

Bailey glances over at me, suddenly shy. Considering everything that just happened between us I find it adorable, but it barely registers because she nods.

"What?" asks Drew. "What is it?"

"My old band T-shirt," I say. "You kept it?" Bailey nods again, biting her lip and giving me a smile, taking my breath away. It's too much.

"Coop let me borrow this shirt back in school," Bailey tells Drew, though her eyes never leave mine. "I meant to give it back before the end of the semester, but..."

"No you didn't," says Drew. He sounds very serious, and I should probably be worried about that. This is his girl, after all. I'm just here for... I dunno, fun or whatever. They have a much longer history together, one that doesn't include the likes of me. Even if I met Bailey first.

I can't believe she kept that shirt. Seeing her wear it ten years ago blew my mind. Seeing her wear it now?

I don't think my heart will survive it.

"Get over here," I manage. When she gets close enough on the bed, I pull her into my lap. Drew starts to shift away, but I stop him, wrapping a hand around his wrist. He looks down at our hands, then back to my face. Then to Bailey.

"Stay." It's Bailey who says it out loud, since my voice has disappeared again. He looks between us again and nods, pulling up the bedsheet and turning to switch off the light.

I SLEEP like the dead somehow, waking up to the same gray dimness filtering through the hotel suite curtains. The alarm clock next to the bed says I've got thirty minutes before the first alarm goes off, and as tempting as it is to close my eyes and snuggle back under the blankets, I know Bailey's somewhere in this bed wearing my damn shirt.

I somehow ended up between them, Bailey turned on her side facing the bathroom door and Drew flung out like a starfish, his leg thrown over one of mine. When I shift up the pillow a little, his thigh brushes up against my balls, making my already stiff dick jerk at the unexpected contact.

Keeping my lower half as still as I can, I turn to Bailey, curving a hand around her hips. She shifts and sighs in her sleep but doesn't wake up.

Which gives me an idea.

19

BAILEY

It was the heat that woke me. The covers were suddenly far too warm long before I was actually awake, I fumbled with them, trying to make my legs work enough to kick the heavy fabric away. Only there was a heavy weight holding my hips down, wedged between my thighs.

A soft growl clued me in.

Cooper.

And Drew.

Holy shit.

I'd slept with Cooper *and* Drew. At the same time. And then we *slept* together, actual sleep. I'd never slept with a lover before in my life, at least one who I wasn't engaged to.

Before I manage to work myself into a panic, Cooper shushes me, pressing close to whisper in my ear.

"He's still asleep, sweetheart. I want you to myself a little bit longer."

"Yeah?"

"That's what you get for wearing my shirt all night," he says, not quite as quiet this time as I think he was aiming for.

It thrills me, making me shiver. Or maybe it's his hand, stroking me gently.

"No panties," growls Coop.

I shake my head, afraid to open my eyes. It's too much, all of it. The two of them, and this place, and... *Oh my God, what am I doing?*

All I know is I don't want it to stop. I've never seen anything so hot in my life as the two of them touching each other, touching me, inside me. That prospect has my eyes opening fast.

"Get up here," mutters Cooper, slapping my thigh softly. I shake my head, not sure what he means. Coop points down at his lap. At first I think he's indicating his erection, flushed and hard against his stomach, but then I realize Drew's got him pinned at the hip.

"What should I do?" I whisper, turning into Cooper. For some reason fooling around with Drew asleep next to us feels a little like getting away with something. Maybe it's because we want to get caught.

Cooper's next words tell me he's on the same page.

"Sit on my face," he murmurs, stealing the breath from my lungs. Like those are words you just say to somebody. Jesus. But that's Coop in a nutshell. Outrageous to a fault.

"How—?"

"Turn around and back that sweet ass up here, Ross. If I don't get my mouth on you in the next ten seconds, you're not going to like what happens next."

The threat's enough to jumpstart my adrenaline and I do as he tells me, arranging my knees on either side of him like he said. The second his mouth touches my flesh, we groan so loudly I think we might wake the entire hotel. I don't have a lot of experience with this position, but the vibrations from Cooper's mouth and the sheer enthusiasm with which he goes to work on my body is enough to melt my brain. All I can hear are my gasps. Cooper's moans are little more than extra sensation between my legs.

I guess we're loud enough, though, because the next time I manage to open my eyes, it's just in time to see Drew leaning up to pull the shirt over my head.

"Jesus. Drew." Startled, I lift up away from Cooper's magic mouth, accidentally leaning hard into Drew at the same time.

Cooper tightens his grip on my hips and yanks me back down, but not before I hear him mutter, "About time."

Guess he had a plan all along. I don't have time to argue though, as Drew throws the blankets off the bed and kneels up, straddling Cooper's hips. Coop goes still.

"Don't mind me," says Drew, leaning over to grab the bottle of lube from the bedside table. He pours it into his hand to warm for a moment before slicking himself up. "I'm just along for the ride."

He takes Cooper's cock in a firm grip, smearing the lube between them.

Cooper groans beneath me and I realize he can't see a thing, what with my ass in the way. It must be like being blindfolded, just letting somebody else handle him this way. The thought turns me on more than I thought possible, causing me to rock into Cooper's mouth. He takes the hint, redoubling his efforts on my clit, sliding two fingers right where I need them.

"God, Cooper."

"Feels good, doesn't it, sweetheart?" says Drew, his own hips grinding as he works their cocks together with both hands. His grip is harder than I'd ever dare, squeezing and pressing, massaging firmly then lightening up enough to stroke with his fingertips. I can never guess what he's going to do next; it's mesmerizing to watch. "What do you think? You gonna let Cooper make you come this way?"

I moan again, no longer able to form words as Cooper works me over with his fingers and tongue. This weird position, with every part of me on display, suddenly seems like the hottest idea ever invented, with Drew's eyes on me and his hands on their cocks and Cooper's mouth on my clit. In the end it's the sight of them together that sends me over the edge, crying out in the dark.

I hear Cooper gasping and then he's coming too, thrusting his hips hard enough to make Drew bounce. It works for Drew, too, because that sets him off like he was barely holding on in the first place.

A long moment later, after I've slid off to one side and Coop's wiped his face on the sheet and Drew's planted his fists on the mattress to catch his breath, somebody's alarm starts blaring loudly from the other room.

GETTING ready for the day is an experience. Despite two deluxe bathrooms and plenty of mirrors to work with, there's somehow never enough space for me to get ready for the day without getting felt up by one man or the other. Yet we manage to make it to the second-floor ballroom—Sizzle's temporary HQ—without incident. Once the elevator doors open, Cooper takes off into the crowd, milling around without a word. Drew squeezes my hand swiftly before heading in the opposite direction. Having compared schedules on the ride down, it was likely we'd all be on our own most of the day.

Filming doesn't start until tomorrow for the Final Five episode. Drew said today is all promotional stuff—interviews, photo shoots, last-minute setup and the like. I spend two hours waiting for hair and makeup to get around to making me presentable, then another couple of hours waiting for my turn to talk to Archer Burke, who's acting as host this time around.

All this hurry up and wait suits me down to the ground today. If I were at home, I'd be doing Bailey's Trademarked Freak-Out Routine —often involving hair dye of some hue, and possibly also property damage, if my last episode is anything to go by. Here in front of all these people though, I'm left to deal with my feelings.

Like an actual adult. What the fuck.

There are a lot of them—the feelings. Feelings for Cooper, obviously. The kind that started years ago and never got resolved. That they never got resolved is my own fault, of course; I can admit it. But dealing with them here and now... that's new for me.

And Drew. All the feelings for Drew I've had, also for years. Some are old, some are new. A lot of them are overwhelming.

Hell, *all* of this is overwhelming. Or it should be. I should be freaking out. It's kind of what I do, and that's one of the many ways this whole situation is different. I'm different when I'm with them. With Drew and Cooper, I don't have to be anybody but me. There's no pressure, no sense of disappointment or unmet expectations. They take me as I am. Hell, they want me as I am, both of them.

And yeah, both. That's the kicker. It's a lot to deal with.

I don't have to defend myself to them. I only ever have to ask for what I want, and it's done—no explanations or rationalizations or arguments or "maybe some other time." They respect me.

The thought sets off a small explosion in the vicinity of my chest.

"You all right, sweetie?" The makeup tech working on another contestant the next chair over gives me a worried look. I nod, taking a deep breath.

"Just a bit crowded," I manage. The makeshift dressing room is overrun with people. The tech nods knowingly and launches into a story about the worst job she ever worked, featuring a tiny trailer and sixteen people in the dead heat of summer. The story distracts the others around us, thank God, since everybody who could hear her was looking at me sideways, waiting for me to freak out or something.

Which still isn't out of the question. It never occurred to me, not until right this minute, how gratifying, how unexpected it is to be honored like that, the way my guys are with me. And Drew and Cooper do it automatically.

Why is that so rare? Do I really expect to be treated otherwise? Is that how people see me?

Worse... is that how I see myself?

Thinking back, I remember plenty of compromises, concessions made or requests delayed or denied. I cannot for the life of me remember any one time where I stood my ground and refused to give in.

Except these last couple of weeks with the competition.

With Cooper. With Drew.

Entering this competition was just another way of acting out, I think. My subconscious mind just got fed up with Peter, with my boss, with my mom. With me, not taking action and never taking myself seriously.

I think about that for a long time, through the makeup room and the on-again, off-again schedule of interviews for sound bites. The thought stays with me as I smile for promotional photos with the other contestants and the pep talk we get from somebody named Greeley later in the afternoon.

If Drew and Cooper can treat me with that kind of recognition and respect, why can't I treat myself the same way? What does that say about me? Besides the fact that I've clearly never done it before, I'm not sure.

It's time to change that. No more settling. No more bowing in the face of something I want. No more Trademarked Crazy Bailey. From now on, I'm in charge around here. Even if it's only over my own life.

Before I can chicken out, I tap out an email to my boss informing him that I'll need to change my hours at work when I return next week. I'll need more time to get that catering business off the ground, and if he doesn't like it, well... so be it.

It's time to get to work.

I'm the first one back to the suite after the contestants get dismissed for the day, and I take the opportunity to shower as long as possible. Which is about how long it takes to scrub off the many layers of makeup I've been wearing for the last ten hours or so. I could go back down and party it up with the rest of the contestants and the staff members down in one of the resort lounges, but the risk of running into Tracy Elffers again is more than I care to deal with. Besides, Drew and Cooper will be back soon.

Instead, I crack open the champagne somebody thoughtfully left in our full-size refrigerator and pour a glass, settling down to wait.

20

DREW

"Back when I worked with WPNG, they managed a better spread than this." Tracy Elffers sneers at the coffee in her hand, then redirects her disgust to the caterers' table at large. "Boutique service, you know. Such a wonderful station."

"I'm sure they'd be glad to have you back," I say innocently. Tracy's glare is so furious, I fight the urge to check my face for singe marks. She knows damn well WPGN went under years ago, but she's not sure if I know that, so the snark goes unmentioned.

I don't know what's gotten into me today. It's been one for the record books. Busy as hell, with me acting as Ty's gopher more than I have in years. Since I'm really just here as support, not a major part of the crew, I'm helping wherever I can. Turns out today "wherever I can" is all over this damned hotel.

I wouldn't mind, except my brain has been somewhere else for most of the day. Thank God other people are in charge today, because otherwise this show would be falling apart. Last night was...

I swallow hard, refocusing on the room, casting about for something, anything, to distract me from my thoughts. Last time I got caught up thinking about last night, I managed to spill coffee in exactly the wrong place, shorting out a power strip that led to something important in one of the interview rooms. That was over an hour ago and though I apologized to the crew profusely, I'm still expecting to hear about it from Ty.

Tracy continues her litany of complaints for her audience, currently consisting of a group of interns and one of the younger competitors who apparently mistook "drama" for "celebrity" last night and became a Tracy fan. I leave them to it, scanning the room for my boss, immediately bumping into somebody. Not the first time today that's happened, either. At least there are no drinks involved this time.

"Sorry, sorry—" I start apologizing long before I figure out who I've hit this time.

"Not a problem," says Cooper, straightening his shirt and smirking at my dumbfounded expression. "You can plow into me anytime."

My face goes lava hot. "Cooper."

He laughs, not bothering to keep his voice down.

"Relax, Hicks," he says, patting my cheek. I don't think it's my imagination that he lingers far longer than he should in a room full of our colleagues. "Nobody's paying a bit of attention to us."

"Hicks!"

The call comes from a corner off to my right. Cooper grins and shrugs when I shake my head at him.

"Duty calls," he says, his eyes twinkling.

"Right." Punk ass sonova—

"Hicks! Get your ass over here." It's Ty, and that tone means I don't have time to fuck around.

"I'll deal with you later," I say, keeping my voice low. Cooper's laugh disappears into the crowd as he wanders off.

You can plow *into me anytime you want.*

He can't possibly mean what I think he meant. I mean, you don't just say that to a guy if you don't mean it. Right? Especially not one you've slept with—and I don't mean sleep in the literal sense. Sure, we've fooled around a couple of times. That's not the same as... what I think he meant.

It takes all of fifteen seconds for me to get across the crowded hall to the door Ty's holding open for me, but fifteen seconds is all it takes for my face to return to boiling hot.

"You okay?" Ty asks. "You look a little overheated."

"The crowd," I say vaguely, ignoring the fact that the whole floor is kept at a perfectly controlled seventy degrees, snowstorm notwithstanding.

"Yeah," says Ty. "Come on in. We need to talk."

Turning into the smaller conference room, I see Kenna already sitting down with Archer Burke. At the far end of the table sits Bob Greeley.

"What's going on?"

"Come on," says Ty, ushering me in so he can close the door behind me. The sound from the crowd outside dulls considerably.

"Sit down, Mr. Hicks," says Greeley.

"What's going on?" I ask again, my stomach pitching. "Did something happen? My parents—"

"Nothing like that, Mr. Hicks," says Greeley, shaking his head. "As far as I know, your family is fine. I apologize for alarming you. However, we have something very serious we need to discuss."

Not my parents. Okay. The fear recedes a bit and my stomach slows its roller-coaster ride, but the gravity on the faces around me doesn't make me any less worried.

"We've received reports that the delayed start of the final ceremony last week might have been due to deliberate sabotage," says Greeley.

"Are you joking?"

"Not in the slightest," he says tersely. "That delay cost the company a minimum of six figures in advertising revenue. Let me assure you, the network takes this accusation very seriously."

"Of course," I say, not quite understanding where he's going with this. "Anything I can do to help, just let me know."

"That's why we're here," says Burke. I haven't had much reason to deal with Archer Burke. He's Ty's biggest competitor at the network —their fan base is almost identical, and they've been competing for the same time slots for at least a year, maybe longer. I know Burke's had a major hand in getting this competition to pass with the higher-ups, but beyond that his presence right now is a mystery to me. Maybe he's Greeley's man.

Kenna raises a finger and Burke nods, letting her go ahead.

"Your name has come up as one of the possible suspects, Drew," says Kenna gently.

The silence that follows her soft-spoken words is deafening.

"Excuse me?"

Ty shakes his head. Greeley stares me down like some shitty TV cop questioning a suspect. Burke doesn't look up from his tablet.

Kenna tries again. "I told them this was a waste of time—"

"You're goddamned right it is," I say, shoving back from the table. I walk to the only window in the room, forcing myself to breathe before I start screaming.

"We have evidence you were nowhere to be found during the time in question," says Greeley.

"So your evidence is my absence?" I say, not ready to turn and face him yet. I've worked for this company for three years. I've worked my ass off for these people.

"You're not being formally charged," says Ty. I snort. "Mr. Greeley just needs to ask you some questions."

That has me spinning to face them.

"You actually buy this?" I ask him. I've supported my boss every step of the way these last couple of years. If anybody in this room knew me, it was him, though Kenna clearly had her own ideas about what was going on.

"No." Ty and Kenna say it at the same time. Burke still doesn't look up, tapping away on his tablet. Taking notes for Greeley, I assume.

Unbelievable.

"Do you have an explanation for your whereabouts just before the final ceremony last week?" asks Greeley. His voice is stern, more of that TV cop bullshit. If it weren't my career, my character at stake here, I'd have laughed.

But the question forces me to stop and think.

"I'd have been backstage," I say slowly.

"That's what the staff assignment board says," agrees Kenna.

"If that's what the board says, why are you asking me?"

"No one remembers seeing you during the time of the delay," says Greeley.

"We paid a security firm to keep people away from the stage," I say, rubbing my eyes. "Of course, there was nobody else back there."

"Other staff members were allowed backstage," says Burke. "As were the contestants."

"A security oversight, certainly," says Greeley, smug and justified.

"All the contestants would have been called down to the competition floor by then," Ty points out. "We have them on camera."

Greeley nods. "Which brings us back to Mr. Hicks."

"I don't know what to tell you," I say, shoving my hands in my pockets. "If the staff assignment says I was backstage, then that's where I was."

Except that was the day we were delayed at the start of the ceremony. Which means... Cooper.

That was the day I shoved Cooper into that storage closet.

Shit. Shit fucking hell.

Which means I have an alibi. Except I can't tell my colleagues anything without outing Cooper, or without outing our relationship.

Not a relationship. Involvement. Whatever.

I turn back to the window to buy myself time to regain my composure. There's nothing else I can say at this point that will convince them; I certainly can't tell them the truth.

"Mr. Greeley, I know you said this is urgent, but the show is on a deadline here," warns Burke in a low voice.

"Right, right," says Greeley. "Mr. Hicks, I strongly urge you to reconsider your position on this. We'd like to see this investigation resolved as soon as possible. Any information you can provide would be useful."

Christ. The guy really does think he's playing in some police drama. I nod, unable to force any niceties. He might sign my paychecks, but politeness has its limits, even for me.

I hear Greeley and Burke chatting as they exit the conference room until the door snaps shut behind them.

"What the hell, Drew?" Ty yanks on my elbow until I turn to face him. Kenna's standing at the table watching us, gripping the back of her chair so hard her knuckles are white.

"You know it wasn't me," I say. Ty's mouth flattens to a thin line. "You know it."

He pauses long enough to make my stomach clutch.

"I know," he says finally with a sigh. "What I don't know is why you wouldn't tell Greeley where you were."

"I was backstage." The protest sounds weak, even to me.

"I believe you," says Kenna. "But backstage where? Can anybody vouch for you?"

"Since when do I need somebody to vouch for me?" I ask, ducking the question. I run a hand through my hair, frustrated as all hell. "Since when is this about me and not about figuring out who the hell would want to sabotage a cooking competition?"

"There are obvious answers to that," says Ty. "DQ'd contestant."

"Or current contestants wanting early access to the list of winners," says Kenna.

"Rival network," says Ty.

"Corporate espionage," says Kenna, nodding.

"Okay, okay, I get it," I say, waving a hand in surrender. Jesus. "But you made my point for me. Where on that list of possible suspects do I come in?"

Kenna flexes her hands on the chair and bites her lip.

"Spit it out, Kenna," I say, checking my watch. We're almost done for the day and I have a sudden pressing need to get back to my suite as soon as I possibly can.

"You didn't answer my question," she says quietly.

"What question?"

"She's right," says Ty, looking at me with the first hint of suspicion I've seen from him. "Can somebody vouch for you, Drew? Anybody."

I hesitate long enough this time that Kenna sighs and Ty swears.

"Give me a couple of hours," I say, stopping Ty just as he's about to stalk past me for the door. "Just... I need some time. Give me until the morning."

Ty looks at the floor for a moment, then nods. This time, when he heads for the door, I don't stop him. Kenna avoids my eyes as she gathers up the last of her things.

"We've worked together a long time," she says, finally meeting my eyes. "If you need something... if you need help, I hope you'll come to me."

I swallow hard, nodding my thanks.

I make my way to the elevator in a daze. Greeley's little interrogation act took long enough, almost everybody's cleared out of the conference level, so I ride up to the twenty-second floor alone with my thoughts.

I've never given anybody reason to doubt what I say, yet in the last twenty minutes, four of my colleagues—two of whom I consider friends—have all but called me a liar. Like I'd sabotage my own event. Of course, after this, I'm more keenly aware than ever that this event —any of the events I've managed for Sizzle, or the classes I've taught, or anything at all—none of it is really mine. I put my best work into that place. I pulled out every trick I knew to make sure the competition went as smoothly as possible, and I'd done a damned fine job.

Except for this.

Sabotage. Who the hell would want to mess up the final ceremony? Ty and Kenna had made their point; the list of possibilities isn't short. But really, who would go to the trouble? It doesn't make any sense to me.

Sure as hell doesn't make any sense that I'd do it. But then, I have the distinct advantage of knowing exactly where I was during the time frame the damage was done. The rest will be up to the cops, or whoever's investigating, to figure out.

Maybe I should have just told them the truth, that I was making out with somebody backstage. Unprofessional as hell, maybe, but not unbelievable, as excuses go. Only they'd ask who I was with. They'd want to question the other person. To him.

To Cooper.

Yeah, telling the truth back there was out of the question. Failing that, the best I could do was to not lie, even though the disappointment on Ty's face and the concern on Kenna's were almost enough to make me reconsider.

It wouldn't just be outing Cooper, either. I didn't think of it sooner, but there's a damn good chance getting caught with me would mean the end of his contract with Sizzle. I know how much he wants this contract. Even though the job's almost finished—once we're done filming this week, Cooper's contract is fulfilled—I know there's been talk about hiring him as a temporary show host to fill in for some of our regulars.

Losing that opportunity for me... there's no way it's worth it to Cooper.

So I'm glad I kept my mouth shut, even if it means waiting until Sizzle's investigators find out who actually caused the damage. Cooper's job is safe, and maybe that means Bailey and Cooper and I might have a shot.

21

COOPER

Tuesday lasts for-fucking-ever. Ever have one of those days that isn't bad, but you'd just really, really rather be somewhere else? That was today.

Not that I had anywhere else to be, since both the people I wanted to be with were on the same floor, working every bit as long as I was today. You'd think, considering the resort isn't all that big, that maybe we'd have been able to spend some time together, maybe sneak away for a minute.

Not even once. Balls to the wall all day today, that was my schedule. The closest I got to tracking down one of my busy lovers was literally running into Drew on my way to yet another interview. I barely had time to flirt, let alone suggest we make use of the stairwell.

Not that I'd gone out of my way to find a secluded stairwell. Ahem.

Flirting was worth it, though, judging by how red he got. Christ, I'd been half-hard just from seeing him. It happened when I saw Bailey too, the brief couple of times I'd glimpsed her across the room.

I make up yet another flimsy excuse for why I can't go to dinner with some of the friendlier crew members and finally make my way back up to the suite, breathing a sigh of relief the instant the door shuts behind me. The only sound in the suite comes from the shower in Drew's room, bringing a wide smile to my face.

Finally.

Drew got dragged off into a conference room by his boss a little while ago, so I'm pretty sure it's Bailey I'm about to pounce on. My breath comes faster as I imagine the scene I'm about to walk into—only to hear the water shut off and the heavy glass door slide open.

Damn. Shower sex will have to wait. I veer back to the kitchen and open a bottle of wine I find sitting on the counter. Pouring three glasses, I've only just taken a sip when Bailey peeks her head around the corner.

"You're back!" she says, coming up to hug me from behind. I set the glass down and turn, scooping her up into my arms properly. Bailey whoops and squeezes her arms around my neck like she's afraid I'll drop her. As if.

"Missed you," I murmur, breathing in the clean scent of her. Her hair is still wet, pulled back into a knot. I can't resist tonguing an errant drop of water off her shoulder, and Bailey sighs.

"Missed you, too," she whispers. "Now put me down before you hurt yourself."

I laugh, setting her back on her feet. "Not likely, short stuff. How was your day?"

"Busy," she says. "How about you?"

"Same," I say, handing her a glass of wine and watching her take a drink. "I thought about you all day."

"Yeah?" That makes her smile for some reason.

"Yeah," I say. It didn't occur to me while I was planning to seduce Bailey in the shower, but I realize I don't know what the rules are for having two lovers at once. Is it copacetic to make a move on one of them if the other one's not there?

Before I can come to any conclusion—besides the obvious priority to get Bailey naked ASAP—the lock beeps and Drew opens the door. Bailey's smile gets wider. So does mine.

Only Drew's not smiling at all.

"What's wrong?" asks Bailey.

Drew tries a smile and fails spectacularly. I've never seen him look so down.

Defeated. That's the word for it. I've never, not for a second, seen him look defeated before.

That's the look on his face now—the sad, blank stare, the sluggish march across the room.

"What happened?" I ask. We'd bumped into each other not even an hour ago and he'd been fine. Whatever Ty had called him in for must have been one hell of a shock.

Drew plops down on the couch, elbows on his knees, his head in his hands.

"I need to talk to you," he says.

"We're right here," says Bailey. She picks up two of the wine-glasses, pressing one into Drew's hand before sitting down next to him.

"I mean Cooper," says Drew dully. He stares at the glass in his hand like he's never seen one before. "Actually, it's good you're both here. You need to hear this too, Bailey. Maybe you can help me think of something."

"You're scaring me, Drew," she says, waving me over. I take the seat on Drew's other side; it seems like the sporting thing to do.

Feels strange sitting next to him like this. We've spent most of our time arguing or tearing off our clothes. The G-rated contact is… nice.

The memory of what we all did on the couch last night is having a not-G-rated effect on me, though, so I nudge Drew gently to get things moving along.

"What's going on, D?"

Drew sets his wineglass on the coffee table, sitting back to stare at the ceiling.

"Remember the beginning of the finals ceremony Sunday?"

Bailey nods. "The opening got delayed by several minutes. I never did hear what happened," she says. She eyes me curiously, no doubt wondering why my cheeks are suddenly flushed. I never heard what happened either, but I sure as hell remember what I was doing at the time.

Namely Drew in a closet backstage.

I clear my throat.

"It was sabotage," says Drew. "Somebody tampered with the sound booth on purpose. Cost the studio several hundred thousand dollars in advertising as a result."

"What?"

"That's crazy," I say. "But what's that got to do with you?"

Drew finally meets my eyes. The misery in his gaze has me bracing myself before he speaks again.

"They think I had something to do with it," he says.

Our shocked silence doesn't last long.

"Horseshit," spits Bailey.

"That's the dumbest thing I've ever heard," I say at the same time.

Drew looks between us and laughs, the pain on his face evaporating. It'd be a relief to see, except his eyes get suspiciously damp.

"I should have known," he says, scrubbing his hands over his face.

"Known what? You're making me crazy, dude," I say, elbowing him for real this time. "Out with it already."

He starts at the beginning, with Ty calling him into the conference room earlier tonight. When he's finished, Bailey's full-on furious.

"This is absurd," she says. "I can't believe they'd accuse you of sabotaging your own project. What possible motive could you have?"

"Good question," says Drew. He's glanced at me a couple of times the last few minutes, and I'm pretty sure I know what he's not saying. So I say it for him.

"He was with me," I tell Bailey. She cocks her head, frowning, so I go on. "During the blackout, or technical difficulty, or whatever they're calling it. Drew was with me. I'm his alibi."

"Oh," says Bailey, looking relieved. "That solves everything, doesn't it? You just go with Drew tomorrow and tell Mr. Greeley... What? I'm missing something."

Drew rubs his eyes, focusing on the ceiling again.

"About that," he says. "We weren't exactly talking shop at the time."

"What do you—" Bailey's eyes go wide. "Oh. *Oh.*"

"Yeah," I say, tongue in cheek.

"Okay," she says, a little breathlessly this time. "Maybe you can tell me more about that part later. But I still don't see what the problem is."

"What do you mean?" says Drew. "I can't out Cooper like that."

"I mean, he was with you, but what does it matter what you were doing at the time? Even if you had your cock down his throat, nobody has to know it. Just tell them you were talking."

Everybody shifts, the tension in the room getting thick.

"If I tell them where we were," says Drew, tugging at the collar of his shirt. "They'll know which security cameras to pull footage from. And even though there aren't cameras in that particular closet—"

"Fucking cameras," I mutter. "That's why you pushed me in there." I start popping the buttons of my cuffed sleeves.

"They'll see what happened leading up to, um, that," finishes Drew.

"The morality clause in my contract includes fraternization," I explain, since Bailey still looks lost. "If I'm caught fraternizing with any employees, the network would have clear cause to terminate my employment."

Two sets of eyes follow my hands as I go to work on the buttons at my collar. For the moment, I ignore them.

"They're going to find out anyway," I say to Drew as I work. "You realize that, right? If there's security footage backstage, it's only a matter of time. We'll go to Greeley first thing tomorrow to make sure you're seen as cooperating. But it's going to come out either way."

"How can you be okay with that?" Drew asks. His voice is thick, distracted. I take my time with the last of the buttons, slowly tugging the shirt off and dropping it on the floor next to me.

"It's done," I say, rubbing a hand over the tattoo on my chest. If I'm going down, you can be damn sure I'm going to make it worth my while.

"There has to be another way," says Drew. His voice is thick and I can tell he's about ten seconds away from being thoroughly distracted. I intend to make sure of it.

I knew what I was getting myself into. It's not like I planned to go sneaking around the competition and trying to get caught, but I knew the risks, with him and Bailey both. If the network found out she and I were involved too, I'd be done for sure.

If they found out it was all three of us, together? Bailey'd get cut from the show, certainly, and there was no small chance Drew and I would both be out of work.

But I don't think about that now. I don't think about how long I've waited for this kind of career break, not when it's my fault Drew's in such a mess, and that Bailey's shot at stardom is at risk. She acts like it doesn't matter to her if she wins, but why else would she sign up? Of course it matters.

I can't fix it. All I can do is scrape together whatever I've got left, whatever they'll let me take from this. I'm not foolish enough to think this thing between us can last beyond a few nights in a hotel suite.

So I'll take what I can get. Tomorrow can take care of itself.

I fist a hand in Bailey's shirt and pull her over Drew's lap to kiss me. Her startled whimper hits my heart like a drug, and I need more. Now.

"Get these clothes off," I mutter. Bailey whimpers again, gripping my shoulders so hard her nails bite into the skin. The pain spurs me on. Drew takes up the challenge, his hands working between our bodies as he tugs Bailey's shirt up over her head, separating us for a moment until I can get my mouth back where it needs to be.

Desperation colors the air around us, and though I'm keenly aware it's coming from me, I can't help it. If this is the last time I get to be with them, I'm going to take it all.

"Bed," I say, pulling Bailey's legs around my waist so I can carry her. Drew follows, but stops in the doorway. I lean down, chasing Bailey's mouth as I lay her out on the bedspread.

"Problem?" I ask him over my shoulder.

"Cooper," says Drew. Something in his voice has me standing up to look. "I don't think—"

"I do," I say, cutting him off. "Get over here."

Bailey nods, watching between us.

"Please, Drew," she says softly. It's her words, not mine, that have him moving toward us. That's going to piss me off later, but for now I have other things to worry about.

I pull Bailey's tiny excuse for underwear down her legs, throwing them somewhere behind me and kneeling at the foot of the bed.

"Coop, I—"

"Later," I say, shoving her knees wide and setting my mouth to her body. Bailey cries out, her fingers tangling in my hair, holding me in place.

I'm not going anywhere, sweetheart. Not yet.

She's already damp, the scent of her arousal causing my heart to pound. We didn't have time for this last time and I'm not going another day without it. Digging around in my jeans I retrieve the condom I'd—admittedly optimistically—pocketed earlier, making quick work of my zipper and rolling it over my painfully stiff erection.

"Need you," I murmur, moving up over her body and kissing her hard. Bailey slides her tongue across my lips, tasting herself and making me crazy.

"You have me," she whispers. A heartbeat later, I'm sliding home, Bailey's back arching hard as I drive into her.

"Christ," I say, dropping my head to her shoulder. "Christ, Bailey."

"Yes."

The intoxicating wet heat of Bailey's body means I've lost track of Drew for the last few minutes, so the hand on my hip startles me out of my rhythm. Bailey's breath stutters as I slow us down, forcibly yanking myself back from the point of no return.

Drew's hand slides across my stomach and up over my ribs to grip my shoulder, pulling me upright without pulling me away from Bailey. His arm wraps tight around me as he brings our bodies together, his thick erection already slick and sliding up across my ass.

"Cooper." My name is nothing but a gasp when he says it like that, but I hear the question in it. He's already covered and slick with lube —he knows what I want. Maybe better than I do.

"Do it," I tell him, hooking an arm around his neck to pull him down with me so the three of us are breathing the same air. Bailey's eyes are wide, hot with want as she watches our faces.

"You're sure?" he asks. She looks at me. I can feel them both waiting. I think they must want it as much as I do.

"I'm sure. Hurry up, Drew. Fuck us."

22

BAILEY

Drew looks as overwhelmed as I feel in the wake of Cooper's proclamation. In all the years we've been friends, I've only seen that look on his face a couple of times.

'Course, if anybody could bring it on, it's Cooper.

Never in my wildest dreams did I actually think we'd end up here. Fantasies maybe, but nobody ever expects a fantasy to happen in real life. Cooper's gone totally still, but I can feel him pulsing inside me. Part of me wants to scream at them for stopping, but a bigger part is hooked on what I think is going to happen next. Except what I think is about to happen is the kind of thing that only happens in porn.

So I hear.

If this all turns out to be some crazy fever dream and I wake up in my own bed at home alone, I won't be surprised one bit.

Drew shakes off his hesitation, or maybe he just can't wait anymore, because he produces a condom and bottle of lube out of thin air, making quick work of them both. Bracing one hand on the bed beside our bodies, he keeps his eyes on Cooper's back as he goes to work opening him up.

Above me, Cooper's eyes slam shut and he moans.

"Okay?" asks Drew.

"I'm fine," snarls Cooper. "I'm good. Keep going." Drew's lips twitch. For all he gripes about Cooper, he sure seems to enjoy the snark. Under the circumstances, I guess I can't blame him.

My knuckles bump Coop's stomach, spoiling my attempt at covertly getting a hand between my legs. His eyes open, narrowing on me.

"Are you touching yourself?" he asks. He doesn't wait for an answer, shifting up on his hands to give me room.

"I'm not," I lie, mostly to distract him. He smirks. Drew watches us, the hint of a smile turning to a grin.

"Liar," says Cooper. "Do it again."

"I don't—"

"Now, I know you were not about to tell me you don't do that kind of thing," says Cooper. Drew does something good with his hands and Coop's voice catches on the last word. He takes a deep breath to compose himself. "I happen to know you better than that, Ross."

"You think so, huh?"

Cooper's grin turns wicked.

"Do you not remember the night we—"

I slap a hand over his mouth, cutting off his words. He sucks at my fingertips in retaliation, making all my muscles clench, including the ones clamped around his body. It sets off a chain reaction: my moaning, Cooper's groan as he thrusts into me.

"Uh-oh. Keeping secrets?" asks Drew, meeting my eyes over Cooper's shoulder. Coop's eyes are still closed. Whatever Drew's up to must feel awfully good, if the look on Coop's face is any indication. My face is hot with arousal and just a hint of embarrassment.

"Not exactly," I say. "Do you remember me telling you about a drunken striptease?" They both freeze, staring at me.

"That was Cooper?"

"You told him about that?" This from Coop.

"I might have been under the influence of tequila," I admit, staring at the ceiling. "On both occasions."

"So you're the one who got her started on pole dancing," says Drew, resuming his work with a smile on his face.

"Is that right?" Cooper asks me, his voice unsteady as he tries to keep up with the conversation. "Shame I missed that phase. Maybe you can show me sometime."

"Anytime," I say, wrapping a hand around his neck to bring him down to kiss me.

"If anybody's showing anything, it'll be you, Lawson," says Drew, his eyes hot and intense as he watches us. "I didn't know you could dance like that."

"It's... been a long... time," says Cooper, gasping a little now.

"I noticed," says Drew, his focus narrowing on Cooper's ass.

"Oh, shut up," says Cooper. "You're taking forever. Stage fright? Or have you forgotten how it works?" Even laid out for the taking, Coop can't turn off the snark.

Cooper glances back in time to see Drew's grin turn sinful, the grin I didn't know he had until the night he pinned me against the wall in his hallway and made me come my brains out. That Cooper's the one to bring it out of him this time warms some dark spot inside me, and the glow spreads. Before Cooper can talk any more shit, Drew takes himself in hand, lining up and leaning in. I'd give my left arm for a mirror right now so I could see it myself. His hands drop to Cooper's hips and Cooper stops breathing altogether.

"You okay?" Drew's panting the words out, his abs flexing hard. I thank every deity I can think of, karma, and the universe itself for putting me exactly here to see this, lack of mirror aside. There's no hotter sight on the planet than their faces right at this moment.

When Drew stops, Cooper starts to move, his hips thumping mine rhythmically in a grind, and mother of God does it feel good.

"Cooper," says Drew, still panting but sounding worried now. He pulls back, giving Cooper time to answer.

"For fuck's sake, don't stop." Cooper slides his hands under my shoulders, his elbows on the bed, his whole body shuddering. Drew takes him at his word, mimicking Cooper's actions and grabbing his shoulders for leverage.

At the long, slow drive, Cooper makes the most arousing sound, a soft groan that's higher than usual.

"Shit, Cooper," says Drew, visibly struggling to hold himself still. Cooper sucks in air, still grinding his pelvis against my clit. I'm not going to be able to wait much longer, but Cooper looks like he's about to die with pleasure.

"Too much?" I ask, brushing hair out of his unfocused eyes.

He shakes his head no, followed by an immediate "Yes."

Drew pulls back slowly and Cooper's mouth drops open. I kiss him, helpless with need, trying my damnedest to hold back and make this last as long as humanly possible. In the end, it's Drew who loses control first.

"Can't wait anymore," says Drew. "Hope you're ready for this." He hitches a knee up on the bed and cants his hips, bucking into Cooper —into us both—and it all goes haywire.

Cooper and I are the first to go, his orgasm kicked off almost instantly by mine. The pleasure is intense, protracted every time I open my eyes and see them above me.

Drew's release hits a long moment later. "Oh fuck, oh fuck, oh fuck."

The sweat on my skin cools all too soon as Cooper pushes his and Drew's combined weight up off of me. The guys sprawl out on the bed beside me.

The silence in the room is deafening. My heart eventually returns to normal.

"So... how 'bout them Yankees?" I ask, staring at the ceiling.

Somebody's laughter shakes the bed. I turn to see Drew smiling at me, propping himself up on an elbow and looking down at us. When he sees Cooper's eyes are still closed, lying still between us, Drew frowns but doesn't comment.

"Since when do you like baseball?" asks Drew.

"Also, it's the middle of winter," says Cooper, sounding winded. "This is what you might call the off-season." He's not moving, and his eyes are still closed. Drew and I share a concerned look and scoot closer.

"Hey," I say to Coop.

"Horses," says Cooper. Still not moving, still not looking at us. Drew takes a shot, tracing Cooper's cheek with his nose. "What do you want?" The snark is back, but Cooper's shiver is visible from here.

"You okay?" Drew asks quietly. Coop's snark isn't enough to lift the concern from his gaze. Cooper sighs and opens his eyes, blinking as he focuses first on me, then on Drew.

"I'm fine," he says at last.

"Just fine?" I ask.

Cooper's lips twitch, his eyes dropping down briefly to my breasts. "Maybe better than fine," he admits.

"Look at me," demands Drew. Cooper obeys, and the effect on Drew is immediate, his cock stirring to attention. I noticed that yesterday, how compliant Cooper gets after a good orgasm. Clearly Drew's noticed too and intends to use that knowledge every chance he gets.

He studies Cooper's face for a long moment until Coop starts to look uncomfortable under his scrutiny. Drew nods, letting up and smiling at me.

"Yeah, he's all right," says Drew. "Just fucked out."

Cooper groans and rolls his eyes, covering his face with both hands. "Oh, shut up."

"There'll be no living with him after this," I say to Coop, prying a hand off his face so I can kiss him.

"I know it," says Coop mournfully. "Goddamned Marvel comics."

"What's that now?" Drew asks, thoroughly lost.

I nod at Cooper in sympathy. "I know," I say. "The movies didn't help."

"What the hell are you two talking about?"

"America's ass," I say. "Not enough he's one of the good guys. Had to go and make him Chris Evans too." Cooper sighs, nodding.

"Wait, are you talking about me?" Drew asks, looking horrified.

"Sorry, dude," says Cooper, crossing his arms behind his head and looking completely at ease for the first time all evening. "It's a fact. If you don't want to get called Captain, maybe you should skip the gym every once in a while."

"Unbelievable," mutters Drew. His face has turned a dark sunburnt pink.

I climb over Cooper to tackle Drew back to the bed before he can leave. Not that he couldn't throw me off without breaking a sweat, of course.

Which is really freaking hot, if I think about it too long. I think about it anyway because he's here, naked, and we've fucked. All three of us. And the world didn't end. Drew and I are still friends, and he's still here with Cooper and me.

Hoo boy. Speaking of hot.

"Penny for your thoughts," says Drew, the smile back in his eyes as his embarrassment starts to fade. Cooper takes a break from trying to pierce the ceiling with his gaze and looks at me, his breathing finally back to normal. I figure what the hell and tell them the truth.

"That was hot. *So* hot."

Drew laughs. Cooper snorts.

"Like, really, *really* hot," I say. "We should do that again."

This time they both laugh.

"Maybe some of us need to recover," says Cooper.

"Speak for yourself," says Drew, reaching between us to palm his rising erection. Cooper's eyes go wide and I feel mine doing the same.

"Holy cow," he mutters. Drew grins, and I know that look. I brace myself just in time as he grips my hips and flips us, throwing me back onto the pile of pillows at the head of the bed. Drew grabs a towel and the lube and sets them on the nightstand next to me, eyeing Cooper at the foot of the bed.

It's going to be a long night.

WAKING up the next morning feels like the one and only time I ever got a mud bath—my limbs aren't quite cooperating and everything feels way heavier than normal.

"Morning, Bailey girl."

It's Drew, and unless I miss my guess, there's fresh coffee somewhere in this room, too. The possibility is enough to get my eyes open.

"What time is it?" I ask, rolling toward him to stretch. He watches with pointed interest, and I remember too late that I'm not wearing pajamas. When I try to pull the covers back up, he yanks them away.

Cooper appears at the door, whistling when he sees me.

"That's a sight I could get used to," he says, his voice rich with appreciation.

"You and me both," says Drew. "To answer your question, it's early. Not even seven yet."

"Then why the hell are you both already dressed?"

"We're going downstairs to catch Mr. Greeley before he makes any more stupid accusations," says Cooper, his face going carefully blank.

That's right. Drew's job is on the line. Cooper's, too, though he's been quick to gloss that over any time it's come up in conversation the last twelve hours.

"We probably won't be back up before call at eight," says Drew. "Think you can manage to get to the conference level on your own?" The worry on his face isn't for me, that much I know.

"I think I can handle it," I say, sitting up and wrapping my arms around him before he can get up off the bed. Drew tolerates the hug for a second, breathing deep before he wraps his arms around me tight, squeezing me hard.

"It's going to be all right," I whisper.

"I'm not so sure," he whispers back. "Cooper's contract—"

"Enough about my contract," says Cooper in normal tones. Drew fixes his eyes on the wall behind me.

"If I get you fired—"

"Pretty sure you weren't the only one backstage that day," says Cooper. I don't like the blank look he's holding onto like a mask, but I think I get it. Coop has a hard time letting other people in, and I suspect if his emotions are involved it's that much harder for him to let go. It makes me wonder just what it is he's holding back. And from whom.

If my heart thrills a little at the possibilities, at the implications... well, I stomp that bitch right back to her corner and tell her to shut it.

"Gotta run," says Drew, squeezing me and kissing me softly. Coop comes over beside the bed to do the same.

"See you downstairs, Ross," Coop says, making it a leer and wagging his eyebrows to make me smile.

"Not if I see you first, Lawson."

Drew rolls his eyes, and the door clicks shut behind them as they go.

The shower is my third in twenty-four hours, but I revel in it anyway, taking note of every slight bruise and red fingertip-shaped mark on my body. They'll fade before the day is out, but for now I wallow in the memories they bring. I'm finally forced to pull my clothes on as the clock ticks closer to eight. Halfway through drying my hair, my phone rings. I frown at the display.

"Mr. Heckman, good morning," I say. The bank doesn't open for another hour. I can't imagine what would have him calling me now.

Then I remember the email I sent him so impulsively, changing my availability.

"Ms. Ross," he says. "Do you have anything to say for yourself?"

"Pardon?"

"I have an email here claiming that you need to change your availability," he says sternly. "Ring any bells?"

"I sent you an email about changing my schedule, yes," I say slowly.

"Are flexible hours listed in the terms of your employment contract?"

I don't exactly have a contract, unless he's talking about the generic employee paperwork I signed when I started at the bank, so I don't say anything.

"I can assure you, that is not a condition of your employment," he continues. "I'm calling to inform you that your request for reduced hours has been denied. Now. Do you have anything to say for yourself?"

I can think of only one thing to say.

"You'll have my resignation by the end of the week."

Mr. Heckman splutters and I end the call. There's nothing he can say to change my mind, and anyway, it's almost time for me to report downstairs.

I'm going to finish filming this cooking competition. I'm going to lose—no illusions there. But then in a couple of days I'm going to go home and start my own goddamn life. No more waiting for permission. No more waiting for somebody else to recognize me for it.

It's my turn.

23

DREW

Bailey didn't win.

I'm surprised and pretty disappointed. I really thought she had a shot; hell, it's why I encouraged her to sign up in the first place. She's a kickass cook and a grade-A human being. I saw some of the early footage, and though I know it's still going through a heavy editing process, Bailey looks amazing on camera.

Of course, she does. Bailey's never looked anything other than amazing to me, even all those years we stayed in our clearly-marked friend zone corners.

She takes the news better than I do. After the on-camera announcement, she congratulates the winner with way more warmth than I could have managed in her shoes. A couple of the other contestants don't even try to act gracious, including Tracy Elffers, who doesn't bother to conceal her shock and disgust.

The contestants will go through one last round of exit interviews this week, and there's already a tentative reunion date scheduled, depending on how the ratings turn out when this thing airs, but otherwise, we're done. It's finally over.

I take a deep breath, searching the crowd for Cooper. Bailey will be tied up for another hour yet, but maybe he and I can get out of here.

Something's happened to me this week. I can't explain it, but sometime between falling onto that couch with Bailey and Cooper and today something's different.

I'm stunned to realize it's hope.

Despite the threat still hanging somewhere over my head, despite my family's expectations, despite the insane unlikelihood of our situation... Cooper and Bailey have given me hope. No matter what else happens after this, I think we've got a shot, a real honest-to-God shot at making this thing between us work.

Sure, it's complicated, but what isn't?

"You might want to dial it back a little," says Kenna, appearing next to me with no warning. "Smiling like that after your girl just lost might maybe send the wrong kind of message."

I tone it down to a grin. "What can I say? It's been a good week."

"Yeah?" Kenna looks up from her phone and narrows her eyes, studying me. "Not what I'd expect from somebody under investigation for corporate sabotage."

"Oh, please," I say. "You know that's bullshit as much as I do."

Kenna nods, going back to her phone, tapping away.

"I know," she says. "It makes me wonder, though."

"What?"

"Just what it is that makes you smile like that anyway," she says. I get the impression she's doing her best to keep a lid on it, but she's curious as hell.

"Hey," I say, bumping her with my elbow to get her to look at me. "We've been working together for a long time. I think of you as a friend."

She smiles. "Same goes, Drew. You know that."

"So ask me sometime," I say. Kenna cocks her head in question. "I can't talk about it right now. Maybe not even anytime soon. But we're friends. I trust you. So ask me sometime, and I'll tell you why I'm smiling."

Kenna looks at me for a long moment. There's never been even a hint of attraction between us, despite how lovely she is, or I'd never have said anything so unprofessional. But she stuck up for me after Greeley's nasty accusation, and if there's anybody at work I can count on to back me up, she's the one who'd do it. Ty too, probably, but since he's my boss, I don't plan to go outing my suddenly-atypical love life to him if I don't have to.

Kenna finally nods again, accepting my words after thinking about it, then neatly changing the subject.

"You heading out in the morning?" she asks.

We make regular office small talk as I continue to scan the room for Cooper. After several minutes, the crowd finally begins to thin, and I figure he must have already gone upstairs. Bailey's been whisked away to the room for her interview, so she'll be busy for at least a little while longer. I've long since been dismissed, and the thought of catching Cooper upstairs alone is more pull than I can resist.

"Think I'm clearing out," I say to Kenna. "You need anything done before I head up to pack?" She shakes her head, waving me off.

"I'll see you at the office on Monday," she says.

"Right. I'll see you on Monday." And I leave her to it, taking the elevator with a handful of gossiping production assistants who've apparently got big plans to take over the hotel lounge in the next twenty minutes.

When I get to the room, I find out I was right. Cooper's shower is running and I don't want to waste this opportunity. Who knows when we'll all be able to share a bed again, let alone a hotel suite like this?

The fantasy is brief, and silly, but vivid enough to make my heart pound in my chest. The three of us, locked in a suite just like this one, no schedules, no work or obligations, no other people around. Just us. You'd think we'd be sick of each other by now, considering how much Cooper and I have clashed, and how firmly drawn that friend zone line was between Bailey and me all those years. But it's been smooth sailing. The only hitch has been Greeley and the ridiculous accusation of sabotage.

Guess that's life, though. It'd be smooth sailing all the way if it weren't for other people, or places, or things.

I have to laugh at my own thoughts—lovestruck idealism isn't my usual reaction to having my job threatened.

Not that I'm in love.

But I might be, and Christ, isn't that a scary thought. My heart pounds harder as I pull my shirt over my head, planning to give Cooper the shock of his life.

I could love them. This thing between the three of us could work. We've put it together in this little bubble away from the rest of our universe, but it could work out there. Why not?

My family is one reason. Cooper's career is another. Not to mention how other people will react. Three people in one relationship isn't exactly something you see every day.

But it does happen. So why not us?

I toe off my shoes, making quick work of the buttons on my shirt. Tomorrow we go back to our normal lives, though "normal" is going to change if I have anything to say about it. We haven't talked about it yet, the three of us, but I see no reason this has to end between us.

Unless... they don't want to pursue it, of course. The thought stops me short. I know Bailey well enough to be confident she's on the same page as me.

Well, maybe not quite the same page. Not the "L" word page. She's been unusually levelheaded about this whole thing, which I'm taking as a sign we're headed in the right direction. It was all the wrong guys who got her acting out like a rebellious teenager, dyeing her hair and setting shit on fire.

Granted, I guess taking on Cooper and me at the same time isn't exactly what you'd call sane. Or mature. Or rational.

I shove the whirling thoughts away, dropping my jeans on the floor outside Cooper's bedroom. When Bailey gets here, she'll have no trouble finding us.

She's my best friend. That part hasn't changed, and it won't change if I have anything to say about it. But I want more from her. Cooper, too. We don't have the greatest track record of like-minded thinking, but I can handle it. I can man up and ask what he's thinking. Ask him to be mine—to be ours. And I know Bailey's on that page; she'll back me up.

He left the bathroom door open a crack. Steam swirls in the air as I push the door open enough to slip inside, still wearing my boxer briefs for the moment.

Cooper stands under the rainfall showerhead, the big one hanging from the ceiling right in the middle, his arms braced on the tile, head hanging to let the hot water pound away at his shoulders. Swanky place like this, there's two other showerheads to choose from. The lights play over the muscles of his arms and back, shifting into shadows every so often as he breathes. He doesn't move from that spot as I watch, obviously unaware he's not alone anymore.

Even as I tell myself to stop being a creep, my dick thickens as I watch him, imagining all sorts of ways I could touch him like this, catching him off guard. No time to pull that armor on, or that damn chip he carries on his shoulder. Helpless against anything I wanted to take.

My cock turns to granite at the thought, the shame coursing through me having no effect on my arousal whatsoever. If anything, it makes me harder.

"You getting in, or what?" Cooper asks, tossing the question over his shoulder.

Guess he wasn't quite as unaware as I thought.

He doesn't turn, just glances back over his shoulder to take me in. My hand drops to squeeze my junk, the gesture as automatic as Cooper's eye roll. And fuck him for making me want him more when he does it.

Why his rough edges turn me on so hard, I'll never understand. I love to see how Bailey softens him up, but those edges never completely go away.

And Bailey's not here right now.

"You asking?" I say.

Cooper turns his gaze back to the wall.

"Bite me," he says.

My blood heats, my breath comes faster. I don't even bother kicking off my shorts, instead stepping into the wide shower and pulling the glass door closed behind me. By the time Cooper turns to look at me, I'm crowding him up against the wall with my body flush against his back, my stiff cock grazing his ass through the now-soaked fabric of my shorts.

"What the—"

"Shut up," I growl, one hand going around his throat. The other slides over his hips, squeezing hard to keep him from turning around. "You want me to bite you? That can be arranged." I set my teeth to his shoulder, waiting for him to throw me off, cuss me out. Hell, maybe he'll laugh me off. Ever since this thing between us all started, I can't predict which Cooper I'm going to get.

He's motionless under my hands for a long time. Just when I'm certain I've fucked it up, read him completely wrong, just when I'm about to apologize and get the hell out from under the scalding hot water, he arches back into me. I bite down to keep him from moving before I can think it through, too soft to break the skin but harder than usual. Cooper sucks in a breath, his hips rocking back against mine.

"Tell me to stop." The words are barely audible over the water flowing around us and the beating of my heart, but my lips are at his ear and I know he hears me. Cooper shakes his head.

"Fuck off."

"That's not 'stop,'" I say, grinding my hips into him, gripping his hands when he tries to shove me away. The shower is definitely not the best place for this, if it's really going down the way I think it is.

"Fuck off, Hicks," he growls. I manage to pin his hands to the wall over his head, trapping his wrists in one hand, reaching around with the other to grip his cock.

He's every bit as hard as I am.

"If you want me to stop," I say, licking into his ear as I pump him fast, the water keeping him slick. "You know what to say."

Cooper growls again, the tension in his body coiling like a spring. He arches back hard, trying to buck me off, but he never, not once, tells me to stop. When I can tell he's close to coming I let go, his thick length slapping up against his stomach as I pull off him. The sound it makes drive me insane with want as I watch him shudder and swear at me.

"You fucking prick. I swear to God," he mutters. I ignore the swearing, still holding his wrists as I wrest my aching cock free of my soaked underwear, dragging the head over the crack of his ass as I stroke myself.

"This what you want?" I ask.

"Fuck *off*."

"You're repeating yourself, Coop," I say, biting his shoulder and humping hard against him. I could come like this, no question, but I want more. Using the grip I still have on his wrists, I manage to push us both out of the shower, shutting off the water and getting us both to dry land before we end up maiming each other on accident.

Whether we maim each other on purpose, well, that remains to be seen.

The clearer it becomes that he's letting me get away with this, the hotter it gets me. He's cursing every step of the way, but Cooper lets me manhandle him out of the bathroom until I can shove him face-down on the bed.

"Christ, your ass," I murmur, distracted for the briefest moment by the sight of him bent over. Never one to waste an advantage, Cooper shoves his weight up, trying to escape. I wrestle him back down immediately, this time pinning both his wrists behind his back. He manages to get his hips back away from the edge of the bed, but I can work with it. I kick his feet wider, forcing him to his knees, his legs spread wide, his forehead buried in the sheet.

"You must want this bad," I say, taunting him as hard as I can as I shove my wet shorts down my thighs, working them off and kicking them away before I drop to my knees behind him. I'm trying to figure out how to get him to my room—we tucked the lube and condoms away in Bailey's suitcase in there—when Cooper shocks the hell out of me with a groan.

"Yes."

24

COOPER

It's humiliating, how much I want him like this, but even the shame I feel fans the flames in my blood. Drew's gone still behind me, but I can feel the length of him, rock-solid and dripping onto my skin. He buries his face into my shoulder, kissing the back of my neck, whispering my name and making me long for things best left unsaid.

Much as I want to provoke him further, to force him to fuck me until my brain shuts off, I want this more.

"I want—" I can't stop the words from leaking out of my mouth.

"Tell me," says Drew, panting. "Anything."

A soft sound at the door has us both going unnaturally quiet.

"Don't mind me," says Bailey softly. She walks to the edge of the bed, dropping a bottle of lube and a handful of condoms in front of me. "I'm just here to watch this time."

"You like to watch?" Drew sounds surprised.

"You ought to know that by now," says Bailey with a small smile. Bailey's never been a liar, but the heat in her expression rids me of any fear that she might have been upset we'd started without her. Much as I want Drew, I'm not about to blow my shot with Bailey over a minor miscommunication.

She puts that fear further to rest when she takes the chair near the window a few feet away, sliding her legs wide and hiking up her skirt until I see the flash of lacy fabric beneath and a hint of her flesh beyond it. My heart skips a beat.

"Like I said," she says, reaching into her shirt to stroke her breast. "Don't mind me." She waves at us, an obvious command for us to carry on now that she's settled.

Drew wastes no time, seizing the bottle of lube and smearing it all over my crease until I can feel it dripping over the back of my balls.

It's too much—Bailey's obvious enjoyment and Drew's suddenly soft touch. It's too soft, too easy, and it makes me want so much from them both that I'm about to scream.

Instead, I buck hard, throwing Drew off balance enough to sneak out from under him. He recovers quickly, snagging me by the ankle before I can get all the way over the bed. His grip turns painful, my panic subsiding as arousal takes the lead once more.

"You know what to say if you want me to stop."

Drew uses his hold to pin me to the bed even as I try to scramble away while he climbs over me. He uses his forearm to pin my shoulders, compensating for every move I try to make. He's strong, but I didn't know he was this strong, for fuck's sake. It's infuriating, like everything else about him, so I stop half-assing it, using every bit of energy I've got to fight him off. I can hear Bailey gasping from her chair and it makes me fight him all the harder, knowing she's watching.

"Drew, maybe—"

"No," I cut her off. The worry in her voice is clear but I don't want to stop. I don't want to slow down and explain, and I sure as hell don't want Drew to back down.

"Should I tell her, Coop?" taunts Drew. He somehow manages to flip me on my back one-handed—jacked-up sonofabitch, how did he do that?—and gets right up in my face as he pushes me into the bed, driving our cocks together. The friction is unbearable and not enough and if he doesn't do something soon, I'm going to die.

Since when does he call me Coop?

"Should I tell her you were begging for it, just a minute ago? Legs spread, ass in the air. Absolutely begging." He drags the words out, licking at the corner of my mouth until I can't breathe for wanting him to kiss me and hating him for every minute of it.

I fight him, bucking with everything I've got left and swearing a blue streak. But I can't catch my breath, and when he pulls his hips back just as I drive up, the head of his slick, covered cock catches on my hole and the tip of his fat dick slides inside of me, stilling us both.

"Tell me to stop," says Drew, moaning it this time. I shake my head, out of words, out of air, out of my mind. Instead, I drive my body down on his, taking him faster than he'd do it himself. Bailey's whimpers echo in the sudden quiet of the room, barely audible over the blood rushing in my ears. I'd wanted the fight, wanted him to fuck me like he still hated me, but now I can see his face and for all the emotions written there, hate isn't one of them. Not anymore.

Between the two of them, I'm lost. Bailey's cries as she pleasures herself and Drew's face above me, spilling truths I don't think he wants me to see. Both of them, letting me in, letting this happen between us.

Too much.

My release hits hard, untouched except Drew thrusting into me—another first for me. Bailey's vocal climax in the corner and the lingering grip of my body around Drew's prove too much for him and a moment later he groans, going still inside me before slumping over on his elbows. My hands trace grooves of the muscles on his back before my brain switches back on and I jerk my hands away, pushing him off to the side so I can make a beeline for the bathroom.

Bailey gets there first.

"Oh, no you don't," she says, sliding between me and my escape hatch.

"I'm just getting—"

"Don't lie to me, Cooper Lawson," she says, her eyes narrowed. "You get back in here and talk to us."

"Let me get—"

"I'll get it," she says, shoving me back away from the bathroom door with more force than her tiny self ought to be packing. I step back, watching her shut the door behind her and hear running water a minute later.

It's cowardly, but I don't want to turn around. Drew's silence makes me sure of that. Bailey comes out of the bathroom, washcloths in hand, and rolls her eyes when she sees me standing right where she left me. She tosses a towel to Drew and grabs my hand, dragging me back to the bed, pushing me down to sit beside him.

The warmth of his thigh against mine wars with Bailey's hands for my attention as she wipes me down. Despite the mind-melting orgasm I barely survived not five minutes ago, my cock stirs with interest at her touch. My response seems to mollify her a little, and she's got a hint of a smile on her lips as she sits back on her heels to look at me.

"Want to tell me what that was all about?" She splits the question between us, her gaze going back and forth. I don't dare look at Drew, shaking my head.

"I'd be interested to hear the answer to that, too," says Drew.

"You don't know?" asks Bailey.

"He was like that when I got here."

"Hardly," I say, unable to keep from rolling my eyes at that. "I was minding my own business when you got here. You're the one who barged into the shower."

"The shower, huh?" says Bailey, a flush rising to her cheeks. "Lord, that's hot." Bailey feathers a touch over my cheek, tipping my chin up when I try to avoid her eyes. "What's going on, Coop?"

Drew's fingers thread themselves between mine. I have to squeeze my eyes shut against all the goddamned feelings. Fucking feelings. Such bullshit.

"Sizzle decided to terminate my contract," I say. Drew sucks in a breath, his fingers tightening on mine.

"What happened?" asks Bailey, incredulous. "There's no way they were dissatisfied with your work."

"No," I admit. In fact, Greeley had gone out of his way to praise my work before he fired me. "It was the investigation. They saw us on the security feed backstage and decided I wouldn't be a good fit with the company going forward."

"This is my fault," says Drew, sitting up and tunneling his hands through his hair before meeting my eyes. "All of it. I'm so sorry, Cooper." He retrieves his jeans from the floor and hikes them up. Bailey and I pull our clothes back on too, following him into the kitchen area of the suite. Drew pulls three bottles of beer out of the fridge, sucking down half of his right away.

"Last time I checked, there were two of us backstage that day," I say mildly. His sudden agitation soothes me somehow, making it easier to stay calm. Pretty sure that's more perverse than all the fighting-hate-sex we just indulged in, but it's always been that way with Drew. Winding him up calms me down, though I don't like seeing him upset for real. And this is very much for real—in all my self-pitying the last couple of hours, I'd kind of forgotten his job might be at risk, too.

"Will they fire you?" I ask, afraid to hear the answer but ready to help him and Bailey kick some ass if necessary.

Drew shakes his head. "Not unless they find evidence of me tampering with the equipment," he says.

"Which they won't," says Bailey, certainty in her voice.

"Which they won't," Drew echoes. "I expect my boss will have something to say about the security tapes, but I'm not going to lose my job over it." He flushes, looking guilty as hell. I shake my head, heading off yet another apology.

"I'm an adult," I tell him, glaring at him. "It was hardly professional of me, but I knew what I was doing."

"Still," says Drew.

"If they got you on camera doing anything like what I just watched, I can see why it might cause some problems," Bailey chimes in. She's trying to lighten us both up, and I set my beer down on the counter so I can slide my arms around her, kissing her soundly for the first time since this morning. Holding her like this goes a long way to bringing me back to normal.

"Nothing quite so dramatic," I say, moving my mouth to tease along the curve of her neck. "How on earth did I miss this voyeuristic streak of yours? You were a meek little thing back in college."

Bailey laughs, even as she shivers in my arms. "Hardly meek," she says, gripping my shoulders.

"He's got a point," says Drew. He's propped a hip against the counter, watching us over the top of his beer. "But then again, I can see the appeal." He studies the pair of us, making no move to involve himself but tracking every move we make. When Bailey moans softly into my mouth, I see goose bumps break out over his body, his nipples going hard.

"What time is checkout?" I ask.

"Noon," murmurs Bailey.

That gives us about fourteen hours to ourselves. Hitching Bailey up so she can wrap her legs around my waist, I set her on the counter beside Drew.

"Not much time then," I say, going to work on her blouse.

THE NEXT TWO weeks are a whirl of texts and phone calls and late nights where nobody gets enough sleep. I spend an inordinate amount of time at the computer, doing my level best to recover my audience's attention, using every trick I can think of to bring my numbers back up. The most successful turns out to be a video compilation of my worst kitchen fails, all recorded at various points over the last couple of years. There are a lot. Cooking is definitely not my thing, despite my foodie persona. And it turns out my audience digs that—the comedic element fits with the rest of the material I've built and plenty of my fans have chimed in with their own kitchen-fail stories, giving me a whole new direction to work with.

My nights are spent chasing Bailey or Drew, or both when I get really lucky. He's been working overtime for Ty on their next project, trying to keep from drawing any extra attention while the network continues their investigation into whoever tampered with the competition finals that day. Bailey's been busy working on something secret while she's finishing up her final days at the bank; she swears she'll tell us about it soon.

Every minute we spend together makes for another day I don't want to be away from them. Nobody dares to bring it up, though I'd swear Drew was about to a couple of times—I think he wants to talk. About us.

I'll put that off as long as possible, thanks. I'm well aware there's every chance that this is his shot with Bailey too, and that they might decide their years of friendship mean they're meant to be together, all by themselves. At which point I'll be shit out of luck, so we can have that conversation maybe never.

Before I know it, it's a cold, sunny Sunday afternoon and I'm standing at Bailey's door. She shuffles out, locking the door behind her and taking my elbow as I escort her down to my car out of the cold.

"You ready for this?" she asks as I slide into the driver's seat.

"Ready as I'll ever be," I say. Twenty minutes later, we roll up to Drew's parents' anniversary party.

25

BAILEY

A banner announcing the thirty-fifth anniversary of Roy and Sandra Hicks clues us in on which entrance to use as Cooper pulls his car around to park. The event center is gorgeous, tasteful and subtle. Driving past, you'd think it was some upscale home, not party-rental facilities.

I haven't seen Drew's parents in ages. I've met plenty of his extended family over the years, between dating Alan and being friends with Drew; I assume that's the reason for my invitation today. Any awkwardness I felt over seeing my ex-fiancé has mostly fallen away over the years, though I suspect he's gone out of his way to avoid talking to me at get-togethers like this one. Today, however, we couldn't avoid each other if we tried.

I sneak another glance at Cooper. He's holding up well so far, if looking a little gray. I'd be less worried if we'd managed to get out of the car by now, but he's holding onto the steering wheel like the car might start driving itself any second.

"Okay there, Coop?"

My question startles him enough to jerk his hands off the wheel, wiping his palms on his dress slacks. He's as dressed up as I've ever seen him, except that night at the gala, and damned if adulting doesn't suit him just as much as his usual guitarist-meets-hipster style.

"I'm good," he says, licking his lips nervously.

"Most days I'd be the first to agree with you on that," I say, nodding. "But you look a little nervous."

"This is fucking nuts, Ross," he mutters, scrubbing a hand over his face. "You've met these people before."

"I have," I say, reaching over to squeeze his hand. "I promise, they're not going to burn you at the stake. At least, not on sight."

"Funny girl," he says, glaring at me.

"I try."

"I know Drew said they're all chill with him being bi," he says, "But still..."

"But it's still meeting the parents."

"And I'm still not crazy about leaving you out of it," says Cooper.

"I'm not either, but you know it's for the best," I say. I'd made my peace with that sometime over the last couple of weeks. I know Sandra and Roy, not to mention the aunts and uncles and a bunch of the cousins. I know they love Drew and want what's best for him, even if they have conflicting ideas about just what that might be at times. He didn't like us coming here like this, Cooper and him as boyfriends and me by myself. Neither did Cooper. But we all agreed it was for the best; it'd hardly be respectful to Sandra and Roy if we came out at their big celebration.

All that aside, Cooper's walking into it all a little blind. Which only makes me admire him that much more. The boy's got balls of brass. Both my boys do.

"What are you smiling at?" he asks, his eyes narrowing in suspicion.

"Just thinking about what we get to do when the party's over," I say, aiming to distract him. It almost works.

"Get drunk as hell?" he asks, making me laugh.

"Maybe that too," I say. "We haven't done that together since college."

Cooper's amusement slides into a leer.

"Know what else we haven't done since college?" he asks. I know exactly what he's talking about and my face goes beet red.

"Nope," I say. "Not going to happen."

"Really?" The crestfallen look on his face makes me laugh all over again, though I'm still blushing hard enough to light an airport runway.

"I mean, we're not going to talk about it now," I say.

"So that's not a hard no to—"

"Save it," I say, smacking his arm. He chuckles again, then takes a deep breath. "You ready for this?"

"Ready as I'll ever be," he says again. He's out the door and circling the car before I can get my seatbelt all the way off, opening the door and extending a hand to help me out.

"What lovely manners," a beaming older woman comments as she walks by, heading toward the Roy and Sandra party banner. Cooper looks at me, making a face.

"Hey, you're already scoring points," I say, taking his arm as we walk up the steps to the wide wraparound porch. "That was Drew's great-aunt—"

"Please," says Cooper, holding up a hand to stop me. "I beg you. I'm already going to forget the name of every person I meet today. Don't give me extra homework already."

I grin and bite my tongue. As we make our way through the crowd looking for Drew, I spot his parents holding court at a well-appointed table near the buffet line.

"There he is," murmurs Cooper. He leads me across the wide porch, shifting around seats and the freestanding heaters churning out enough warmth to allow guests to remove their coats despite the outdoor seating.

"I was beginning to wonder if you changed your minds," says Drew. He kisses Cooper on the cheek and pulls me in for a hug. "You look amazing," he whispers.

"Thanks," I say, smiling at him.

"Careful," says Cooper. "You're going to make me jealous." I can't tell if he's joking, but I guess that's the point, since Drew's cousins are standing right there.

"Hey, Eric, Daniel. Good to see you again," I say, waving at the twins.

"This must be the new boyfriend," says Eric. Tall and every bit as broad as Drew, Eric offers his hand to shake.

"Guilty as charged," says Cooper.

"Careful there," says Drew, looking every inch the proud boyfriend showing off his lover. "My cousins are cops."

"So I probably shouldn't bring up my rap sheet over dinner," says Cooper glibly, making Drew's cousins laugh.

"Hang on, you have a rap sheet?" Drew asks, making them laugh harder.

"Bailey," says Alan, coming up behind me and taking my elbow. "I didn't know you'd be here today."

"Yes, you did," I remind him. "You asked me about it at the cooking competition, remember?"

"Hmm," says Alan, pursing his lips as he takes in Drew's arm wrapped around Cooper's waist as they chat with the twins. "Look, Bailey... can we talk for a minute?"

I have no idea what he wants, but it's a party and talking is the thing to do, since the buffet's still being set out. I wave at Cooper to let him know I'm going and allow Alan to guide me around the corner where no one's been seated yet. It's hardly hiding, but we have this section of the porch to ourselves for the moment.

"What's up?" I ask, wishing I hadn't taken off my coat. The heaters work well out here, but we're standing too far away from them now.

"Nothing, I just wanted to talk to you," says Alan, offering his suit coat. I accept it gratefully. "It's been a long time."

"It has," I agree, wishing he'd get to the point.

I want to watch Drew and Cooper being a couple. They're fucking adorable like this. I think they could be that sweet together if Cooper ever really lets his guard down, or if Drew ever stops provoking him. Seeing them together like that makes something inside me go warm and bubbly. Not the same kind of warm as when I watch them... do other things together. But the feeling is warm all the same. It's the silliest thing, but when I see them together like that, it makes my heart smile. I can't explain it any other way.

"I thought maybe we could catch up sometime," says Alan. He's noticed my distracted state and is getting visibly annoyed, but I know what it looks like when a Hicks boy is keeping a lid on his temper. Guess you could say I've been here before. "Why is that funny?"

"It's not," I say, patting his arm and tamping down on my amusement. Alan doesn't take too well to being laughed at. "Maybe we can catch up after the meal."

"That's not what I meant," he says, running a hand through his hair anxiously. "Bailey, are you listening to me?"

"Of course," I say. Most of my mental processes are wrapped up thinking about Cooper's nonexistent rap sheet and wondering if either of the boys have access to a pair of handcuffs.

"Is that a yes?" Alan asks, taking my hand.

"Sorry, wait," I say, shaking my head. "What did you say?"

"I want us to try again, Bailey," says Alan slowly, looking me in the eye. "I've been thinking about us lately, and the truth is—"

"You want us to, what? To date?" My voice breaks on the last word, going a bit shrill.

"Keep your voice down, please," Alan mutters. "I just thought... Look, it's been such a long time. We've both grown since college. I've changed. You certainly have."

More than you know, buddy.

"Alan, this is really not a good time to be talking about this," I say, stalling for time. It's a party for fuck's sake; somebody should be wandering around the corner by now. There are people all over the porch and dining hall. Just not here, interrupting this painfully awkward conversation.

"If you need time to think about it, sure," he says, clearly disappointed. "But I really hope you'll consider it." He looks earnest, and... something else. I can't put my finger on it, but that hint of something is enough to cut short my rising panic.

"Why ask me now?" I say, more suspicion in my voice than anything.

"Huh?"

"Why now? Why ask me here?" I say, gesturing around. "Your parents are having this gorgeous party to celebrate them. I know they

195

don't get to see all your relatives as often as they'd like." A light dawns. "Is that what this is about? You want to be able to tell them we're getting back together."

Alan shifts on his feet, twin pink spots appearing on his cheeks. "It's not that—"

"Then what is it?" I interrupt. "Is it Drew? He brought Cooper... it's because he has a date this time." The spots in Alan's cheeks go bright red. "And I'm guessing you don't."

"Come on, B," he says, using his old nickname for me. "You know what my grandfather is like. He's been on me for ages now about settling down. And now he's got Mom and Dad starting in on it."

"Right," I say, somewhat less than charmed.

"B, come on," says Alan. He takes both my hands in his, pushing up the cuffs of his jacket to get to them. At this point I'd rather freeze than wear his coat, but we're standing right in front of beveled glass double doors in full view of the rest of the guests and the last thing I want to do is cause a scene. It'll only bring more trouble for Drew, not to mention mess up his parents' celebration. I bite my tongue and let Alan talk.

"We were good together once," he says.

"We were," I say. "Ten years ago. Then you dumped me for a sorority sister." She'd been on her way to med school, but I didn't exactly give a fuck about being fair right now. "What the hell makes you think it would work this time?"

"So I guess maybe there are still some hard feelings," Alan says, trying to joke. "That's okay. That's good, actually. It means there must still be something between us."

The only thing between us right now are my hands, fisted tight to keep from punching my idiot ex. Alan takes my silence for assent, apparently, because he brings his hands up to cup my face.

"What the fuck is going on here?" It's Drew, and he sure doesn't seem to care if he draws attention. Which is lucky because everybody in the ballroom on the other side of the glass doors turns to see who's shouting on the porch.

"Mind your own business, Drew," says Alan.

196

"Get your hands off her," growls Drew. I step back, happy to help Alan comply.

"What the hell is—" Cooper halts next to Drew, a hand on his elbow as he takes in the scene. "Bailey?"

"I'm okay," I say, stripping off Alan's coat and tossing it back to him.

"We should head inside," says Alan, once he registers all the eyes on us through the glass.

"Why were you touching her?" Drew is normally not remotely aggressive. He can be assertive when the situation calls for it, but I've never known him to fly off the handle about anything, not the whole time I've known him. Yet his hands are fisted, his shoulders tight with restraint, and if he were anybody else on the planet, I'd swear he was about to punch his brother.

"That's between Bailey and me," says Alan, trying to wrap an arm around me. I take another step to the side, dodging him and putting myself next to Cooper, who wraps me in his arms.

"There is no 'Bailey and you,'" says Cooper.

"Like you'd know," sneers Alan. "You barely know her."

That makes Cooper smile. "Better than you might think."

"Back off, Alan," I say. "And in case you were wondering, my answer is no."

"Bailey," he says, starting toward me. Drew stops him with a hand on his shoulder.

"She's taken, asshole."

"No, she's not," says Alan.

"Yes," says Cooper, his arms tightening around me, "she is."

Alan stops and stares at the three of us.

"You're here with my brother," says Alan to Cooper.

"Yep."

"So who...?"

"She's with us," says Drew tightly.

"Us," echoes Alan, still not getting it.

"Both of us," says Drew, wrapping an arm around my shoulders, sandwiching Cooper in between us.

"Mother of God," breathes Alan. "I always knew you were an

idiot." He starts laughing. "Jesus Christ, Andrew. Grow up." Alan keeps laughing as he walks away. Our audience inside is nearly silent, the only sound coming through the other set of open doors the clattering of trays and plates as the caterers continue their setup. Every eye is on our little drama on the porch.

I see Drew's father pushing his way through the crowd, rounding the same corner Alan had directed me past.

"Andrew," he says.

"Dad," says Drew, taking a deep breath and withdrawing his arm. "This is Cooper Lawson, my boyfriend."

"Mr. Hicks," says Cooper. It's the closest I've ever heard him come to sounding meek. Drew's father gives Cooper a short nod.

"And you know Bailey," finishes Drew.

"Your girlfriend," says Mr. Hicks, drawing a matching wince from all of us.

"I didn't plan for you to find out like this," says Drew, regret thick in his voice.

"No, I expect you didn't," says Mr. Hicks. "But that's out of your hands now. Your voice carries."

Cooper laughs abruptly, slapping a hand over his mouth to cut it off.

"Sorry," he says quietly. "It's that teacher's voice." I want to say Mr. Hick's lips twitch with humor, but it must be my imagination. He looks absolutely mortified.

Sound picks up from the ballroom inside, a mass of whispers and quiet conversations drifting through the open doors somewhere on the porch. If we can hear that much, it's no wonder everybody heard Drew.

"What is the meaning of this?" A stern, angry male voice precedes its owner by several beats. Mr. JD Hicks stalks around the corner, his walking stick thumping hard every few feet. He's a burly bear of a man with the energy of somebody half his age. I've only met him once before, at a cousin's wedding many years ago. He hasn't changed —he intimidated me then, too.

Cooper's expression is unfazed, but I can tell he's having trouble processing. We never got around to talking about exactly what's going on between the three of us, let alone whether to tell anybody. Or what to tell anybody.

Looks like we're going all out, though.

"Grandfather," says Drew, the anger in his voice tempered with respect. If JD Hicks is intimidating to me, I can't imagine what it must have been like growing up as part of his family. If anything, Drew's spine stiffens, bringing him to his full height. "This is Cooper Lawson. And I believe you've already met Bailey."

"Andrew." The elder Mr. Hicks sets both hands on his walking stick and keeps his gaze on Drew, not bothering to look in our direction. "Your parents have put up with your dithering for years. Bad enough to have left a perfectly sound career to flounder away at some television studio. Now this?"

Drew's jaw tightens. "Grandfather, I—"

"No," says Mr. Hicks. "We have tolerated your indecisiveness quite enough. Boyfriends, girlfriends, odd jobs. No commitment, no strings, no responsibility." This last one he punctuates by striking the porch with the end of his staff. "You were raised better than that."

Drew looks to his father. "Dad, you can't possibly think—"

"I don't know what to think," says Drew's father quietly. He appears to be the only Hicks on the porch with any concern for being overheard. Surveying the crowd quickly, I can't see Drew's mother in there anywhere. I can't imagine she'd put up with this if she knew what was going on.

Drew's parents always struck me as open-minded, generous people. It never occurred to me that they might have a problem with his bisexuality, and certainly not with his career choices.

"You really ought to have known better," continues Drew's father, looking disappointed and sad. Mr. Hicks harrumphs in agreement.

"Your son is one of the best men I've ever met," says Cooper, stepping forward suddenly.

"You're awfully forward for someone showing up uninvited to a family occasion," says Mr. Hicks, glowering at Cooper.

"Drew invited him," I say, stepping forward and sliding a hand into Cooper's. I can't stand here and listen to this anymore.

"Don't get me started on you, young lady," says Mr. Hicks, turning his glare my way. "It's bad enough, you turning up here when Alan doesn't want you anymore."

"That's enough." Drew steps between us and his family. "You've made it clear we're not welcome here. It's time for us to go." He turns, taking Cooper and me each by the elbow and pushing us gently back the way we came. We're pulling our coats on as his father and grandfather round the corner, whispering heatedly at each other.

"Andrew, we aren't finished with this conversation," says Mr. Hicks.

"You've made your views perfectly clear, Grandfather," says Drew tonelessly. "My life and my choices do not meet your expectations. I doubt they ever have, and I don't expect that to change. You don't need to worry about that going forward."

"What is that supposed to mean?"

"It means we're leaving," says Drew, helping me into my coat. "Congratulations, Dad. Give my best to Mom. For whatever that's worth."

"Andrew, wait," says his father. Drew shakes his head.

"You don't get it," he says. "You only see how I've disappointed you. Can't you see that every step I've taken these last few years, every move I made that disappointed you... every single one brought me closer to being myself?"

Drew's father closes his mouth. Alan comes up behind him, his arms crossed, looking defiant.

"This is who I am," says Drew quietly, taking my hand and Cooper's. "These are the people who accept me for that, who maybe even love me for it. If you can't accept them, we're wasting our time here."

He tugs on our hands and the three of us walk back to the car as one.

26

DREW

"Where to?" Cooper asks. Bailey's shoving me into the back seat, none too carefully, so I'm too distracted to protest when she directs him to my place. Just as well. Cooper takes us out of the parking lot and I have to make an effort not to turn back to see if my family is still watching us from the porch of the house. Bailey's got an answer for that too, jerking my chin down in a grip firmer than I knew she had in her.

"Look at me," she says.

"Do I have a choice?"

"Drew," she says, all business. I comply. It's no hardship—my Bailey girl is beautiful, more so right this minute than she's ever been. My heart skips a beat, thinking of the last half hour and the last several weeks, and it dawns on me that I don't just love her. She'll always be my best friend. Somewhere in the last few weeks, I've gone and fallen in love with her.

Bailey's eyes widen at whatever she sees in my face and she pulls me close for a kiss. The kiss is soft, full of things I don't dare to say out loud, but I think Bailey hears me anyway if the look in her eyes is any indication.

"Starting without me, huh?" says Cooper. I catch his eye in the rearview mirror and grin. He smirks back. "Knew I should have gotten that camera installed."

"Something for the bucket list," says Bailey. She slips out of her seatbelt.

"Safety first," Cooper singsongs.

"We're almost there," says Bailey over her shoulder as she straddles my lap. "Do me a favor and don't wreck the car."

Cooper mutters something too low for me to hear, but I'm distracted again, arms full of Bailey.

"That was hard," she murmurs, working her lips up the side of my neck. I tip my head back to give her room. "But you have to know how proud I am of you."

"Yeah?"

"I couldn't be more proud," she says, her tongue making wicked magic. She shifts her hips over my lap, tugging her skirt out of the way. "I had no idea things had gotten that bad."

"You really want to talk about this now?" I ask, helping her slide her skirt up out of the way. I bounce back and forth between watching her work herself over me and Cooper's hungry gaze in the rearview mirror. Traffic is mercifully light this afternoon, and he's kept to side streets to avoid being seen, I assume. Glad somebody's brain is still functioning well enough. Mine cut off some time ago.

Bailey grinds her pussy down on my cock through my clothes and if I thought I was getting through this day with any dignity intact, she's on the verge of proving me wrong. The friction is exactly perfect and not nearly enough, and a wet spot forms on the front of my dress slacks. Bailey must notice. She lifts her body away, canting her hips back to look down.

"God, that's hot," she says.

"What's hot?" asks Cooper.

"He's wet. Leaking through his clothes," says Bailey, tossing the comment back at him over her shoulder as she keeps her gaze on me. Cooper groans.

"We'll be there in like, ten minutes," he says. "I don't suppose you plan to wait that long."

"Nope," says Bailey. She licks her lips and climbs off my lap, sliding down to kneel on the floorboard.

"Maybe we should wait," I manage to say. My hands go straight to her hair, belying the words and making Bailey grin up at me.

"I will if you really want me to," she says, her fingers tugging my belt apart. "Do you want me to stop?" She lingers there a long moment, feathering her fingertips over my zipper before tracing the length of my erection through my clothes.

"You're killing me."

"It's one kind of death," she says, nodding. "But you didn't answer my question." She moves faster this time, keeping her eyes on mine as she leans in, bracing her hands on my hips and touching her tongue to the growing wet spot.

"Jesus, fuck."

"Tell me what she's doing," demands Cooper. I can tell he's driving as fast as he can without drawing attention. We'll be at my place in no time and I'm afraid of coming in my pants if Bailey keeps it up. I tell Cooper that much, making him moan and Bailey laugh.

"You're right," she says, slapping my thighs. The sting is just another layer of sensation at this point, and it's my turn to moan as she scoots back up into the seat beside me.

"Tease," I say, squeezing my eyes shut and fighting to keep my hands off my cock.

"You're welcome," she coos, patting my knee.

"Funny."

"I'll tell you what's funny, is that I'm buying a car with bench seats in the front," says Cooper. "Or putting in that camera. Maybe another mirror."

"Doesn't seem very safe," says Bailey, teasing him now. Her gorgeous face is flushed, and she keeps pressing her thighs together. Looks like teasing is a double-edged sword for my girl.

"Hurry, Coop."

They laugh at me, but a short while later we're pulling up to my apartment and it's comical the way we all hurry inside. They must be as eager as I am.

Cooper crowds Bailey against the wall as I close the door behind us, kissing the breath out of her. I'm struck by a wave of gratitude so big it nearly drops me to my knees. These two are going to be the death of me.

Or maybe the life of me.

They're beautiful, both of them. Separately, together. So much more together like this. I never thought I had so much inside me for anybody, let alone for two people.

Cooper's notched himself between Bailey's thighs, rocking up against her, pressing her into the wall when she catches me watching them. She tugs on Cooper's hair, jerking her chin until he looks back at me.

"You're beautiful," I say to them both. It comes out mangled and choked. I clear my throat and start to try again because it's not right to feel this much and say nothing. "You didn't have to do that, back there."

"Yes, we did," says Cooper. He looks determined, setting Bailey back on her feet and turning to face me fully. He fists a hand in the front of my shirt and yanks me into a kiss. It's brutal, overwhelming, more than my heart can stand. Just when my knees feel like they might give out, Cooper pulls back to kneel on the rug at my feet and I stop breathing altogether.

Bailey steps close to kiss me, her touch as soft as Cooper's had been hard.

"Yes, we did," she whispers. Then she drops to her knees next to him.

They go to work on my clothes, yanking and tugging. I hear soft laughter and watch them swapping kisses. My shirt gets thrown somewhere and my trousers fall to the floor around my ankles. Bailey starts to pull my shorts down but Cooper grabs her hand, halting the motion.

"Not yet," he says, laughing when Bailey pouts. He leans over to kiss her full bottom lip. "Your own fault, Ross, talking all kinds of dirty in the car like that. I'll carry that image in my head until the day I die."

Cooper leans in, nudging my cock with the tip of his nose. I make an undignified gurgling noise that, thankfully, everyone ignores. I can feel the heat of his breath on the wet fabric over the head of my dick. I hold my breath again, anticipating his touch.

Waiting.

And waiting.

I glance down to see Cooper grinning up at me.

"Fucking teases, both of you." I sound terribly put out, which makes sense considering I am.

"We wouldn't do it if you didn't like it so much," says Cooper. He traces my length with his fingers, much like Bailey had in the car. Only this time the touch doesn't stop.

The wet cotton of my underwear slips against the sensitive skin, giving me chills.

"Take it out," I beg. My hands are pressed to the wall behind me to keep me from doing it myself.

"Oh, I could get used to this," drawls Cooper. "You're awfully pretty when you beg, Andrew."

I've never much liked my full name, but when he uses it like that, especially like that, it makes me shiver.

Bailey strokes my calf lightly, watching Cooper with affection. She's in love with him. I think she has been for a long time, though it's only been in the last few days I've been able to see it.

Not that we've talked about it. Not that we've talked about anything important. We talk about our lives and our work and they ask me about the investigation at Sizzle, which still hasn't been resolved, and sometimes we talk about our families and sometimes about our pasts. But we aren't talking about this thing between us. And we aren't talking about what happened at my parents' party today. We're going to have to talk about it eventually.

Why does that feel like the beginning of the end? Everything is working, working better than I ever thought it would. In my wildest dreams, I couldn't imagine a relationship like this working so well. So why can't we talk about it?

I can't answer for Bailey or Cooper, but I know why I can't. I'm afraid of losing this.

Cooper shoves Bailey back to the floor, peeling her skirt and stockings off, pulling her blouse off over her head. He leaves her bra, something I've noticed he likes. Bailey's clearly caught on too, if the sheer variety of colors of underwear I've seen this week is anything to go by.

Coop spends a long moment tracing the violet lace over her breasts before tugging her back up, this time to sit astride his lap. He pulls her hands to his pants and Bailey takes the hint, undressing him without fuss or comment. I'm about to join them on the floor when Cooper stops me.

"Stay there," he says, one hand on my thigh, the other wrapped around Bailey's waist. He leans up carefully so as not to throw her off and takes the breath out of my lungs as he wraps his lips around the head of my dick, fabric and all. He sucks lightly, humming at something Bailey does with her hands, sending a shock wave all the way up my spine. He backs up, finally yanking my shorts down around my thighs.

"Back pocket," he says to Bailey. I hear the sound of foil tearing, but the sound comes from somewhere far away as Cooper wraps a hand around the root of my cock, now leaking freely from the tip. He swipes a thumb over the head, smearing pre-cum before taking up a lazy, rhythmic stroke.

"Ready?" Bailey says. I nod before it dawns on me that she's not talking to me at all. I look down just in time to see her kneeling astride Cooper's thighs, sinking down on his cock with a heady sigh. Cooper groans, his grip tightening around me. When I can't stop my hips from bucking up into his fist, he grins, opening his eyes to focus on my face.

He holds my gaze as he whispers in Bailey's ear.

"Secrets don't make friends," I gripe.

"You're such a child," he says in a normal tone. I slide my dick through his fist again.

"Hardly."

Cooper snorts. Bailey laughs. As one, they lean in and lay their open mouths on either side of my shaft.

"Jesus. Christ." I can't keep my hands off them now, my fingers tunneling through their hair. Cooper's is too short for much of a grip, but Bailey's blond hair is long enough to wrap around my fist so I do, keeping as tight a hold as I dare as they work me over. First matching their strokes like some kind of filthy performance art, then alternating. When Bailey sucks me into her mouth, Cooper moves to tongue my balls. If I didn't know any better, I'd say they'd planned this, but this is just how it is between us.

Bailey pulls back, swirling her tongue around the head as she backs off. I look down to see her brace herself, one arm wrapped around my leg for balance, the other clinging to Cooper's shoulders as she starts to ride him. Cooper hums again, the vibration making me crazy with want. He picks up where Bailey left off, wrapping his lips around the head of my cock and sucking hard before taking me deep. I groan, releasing Bailey to hold his face as he bobs up and down.

"More," gasps Bailey. Cooper lets me go and it's all I can do not to whimper in protest. I don't feel quite so bad when a few seconds later, Bailey does whimper as he pulls her off his lap.

"Turn around."

She's so quick to do as he says, I'd tease her about it if I had any blood left in my brain. But I'm desperate for him to touch me again, too. Bailey gets on her hands and knees before him and Cooper doesn't hesitate, sliding into her body in one thrust. Bailey shudders, moaning so loudly I can feel it in my bones. Coop shifts, moving them closer, resuming his place around my cock as he begins thrusting into Bailey.

We've tried this position a couple of times; it's more challenging than you'd think. I'm distantly awed by his coordination, even as I'm doing my best not to come in his mouth instantly. But Coop's going for the gold this time, he pauses again, tugging Bailey up by her shoulders until she's braced upright, her hands on my thighs. Coop whispers in her ear again and resumes his thrusting, tighter and faster now as their mouths work me over together. The next time Bailey takes me deep, I can't hold it back any longer, coming hard, arching into their combined touch. It sets Cooper off, and a moment later, I hear Bailey crying out her release as he pumps into her, his hands all over her body like he can't touch her enough.

In the soft, sweet aftermath, it dawns on me that this is supposed to wear off, this high I get with them. The heat that seems to build anytime we're together. It's supposed to be fading.

It's not fading. If anything, it's getting stronger.

27

COOPER

Bailey whimpers as I pull out of her body, and again when I kiss her shoulder before sitting back to deal with the condom. Drew looks like he's blown a fuse, a little vague and still not quite focused. Can't blame him. That was some next-level fucking.

Not just fucking.

Of course, it was just fucking. That's all this is. That's all this can be. Any day now Bailey and Drew are going to figure out they were meant to be together all along and they'll be ready to settle down, get serious, all that white picket fence shit. Just because I've gone and gotten goddamn feelings for them doesn't mean this is forever. Relationships between three people don't work.

I suppose they must, or else "throuple" wouldn't be a thing. But it's not a thing here in this room, so I'm not getting my hopes up.

Liar.

The voice in the back of my mind sounds suspiciously like Bailey's. I shove the thoughts away, heading to the bathroom to clean up. I can hear Bailey and Drew laughing softly in the other room and I cuss my foolish, aching heart even as the rest of me thrills at the memory we just made in Drew's hallway.

I'll be able to keep that, at least. I know better than to think I can keep them, but I'll have these few weeks.

"Where'd you go, Coop?" calls Drew. He started calling me that after the week in the mountains, just like Bailey does. I don't even think he's noticed.

The two of them are chatting in the kitchen by the time I track them down.

"You get lost?" Bailey asks, tugging me into the chair beside her at the table. Drew's got his head stuck in the refrigerator, naked as a newborn, his ass in perfect profile from where we sit. Bailey and I both just watch him in silence. When he finally shuts the door and looks over at us, he blushes bright red.

"Knock it off," he says. I hold up my hands.

"You're the one flaunting," says Bailey. Her voice sounds a little thick. I have a feeling we won't be in the kitchen much longer.

"Nothing in the fridge," says Drew apologetically. "Takeout?"

"Chinese," I say.

"Pizza," says Bailey at the same time. We look to Drew.

"Why do I always have to be the tie-breaker?" he says with mock exasperation. Bailey gives him the cute-puppy eyes. I cross my arms and do my best to look intimidating. Not an easy feat, sitting naked at a kitchen table.

Drew laughs.

For a few glittering hours, everything is perfect.

I CREEP out the next morning before they wake up, leaving a note by the coffee maker because Bailey won't let me hear the end of it if I don't at least say something. I plead work, which isn't a lie. All that time off around Sizzle's cooking competition took a chunk out of my numbers, which require steady content to maintain. I knew I was probably going to lose some traffic with the downtime, but I got so excited by the prospect of finally getting some professional recognition by a network that I let things slide.

Never again. I'm making up for lost time and then some.

"Hard at work today," says Beck, coming out from behind the bar.

Rusty's doesn't do much business mid-morning, especially considering the nasty weather today. Also, it's before noon on a Monday, not exactly peak pub hours, though I expect their die-hard lunch crowd will be trickling in soon enough.

Beck's been behind the bar more often than not when I've been down here these last few weeks. We've established a friendship of sorts, where we both pointedly ignore the fact that his bedroom is right above mine and the walls aren't as thick as they should be.

"Not that hard," I quip.

"Now that's a crying shame," he says with a grin. We also ignore the fact that Beck's a flirt. Man, woman, enby, or otherwise—he's as equal opportunity as anybody I've ever met.

"Don't you have your own work to do?" I ask.

"Nah, Dad's busy in the office and I'm all caught up out here," he says, voice dry. I'm the only other person in the pub right now. "What are you working on?"

"Salvage," I mutter, clicking through the comments section on my Instagram stories.

"Pardon?"

"Just trying to revive my audience," I say.

"That sounds like actual work," he says.

"It is." And lately it feels more like an uphill battle than ever. "Beats the hell out of working for somebody else, though."

I had a feeling Beck would be firmly on my side if I ranted about Sizzle and the investigation and the termination of my contract. Then again, I had no idea where the good bartender role ended and the friendship part began.

The phone rings, taking Beck back to the bar top. A flurry of incoming chatter brings my attention back to the screen.

"Is it true??"

"There's no way. Coop's as straight as I am."

"Nuh-uh. Fucking pervert!"

What the hell?

Somebody posts a link with no other comment and I click through without checking to see if it's clickbait.

It's a tweet from a tabloid, linked by that same sleazebag vlogger who tried to poach my audience while I was working on the show for Sizzle.

On one hand, I should be over the moon. I'd never get tabloid-level exposure normally. It's the kind of publicity you can't buy.

Except it's about Drew and Bailey. There's a photo of the three of us at the gala, standing in the middle of the ballroom.

Sizzling-Hot Threesome Suspected of Network Sabotage!

The article is tiny—barely a paragraph—but it mentions all three of us by name. The comments on my account are coming in faster than I can screen them.

"Is it true??"

"You really swing that way, bro? Gross."

"Bitch is hot, though."

Some are enthusiastic in offering their support. Some are speculative. More than a few are negative, some horribly so.

Christ. What the hell do I do now? I can't exactly tell the truth, but with that photo out, I can hardly deny it.

What am I saying, of course, I can deny it.

"It's a tabloid. Don't you all have better things to read?" is my first response. I don't mention that this is all just a scam cooked up by the other vlogger to steal my audience, because even though it's clearly a play in that direction, it's not wrong. None of that report was wrong. They mentioned the sabotage, the investigation, the fact that Drew and Bailey and I are romantically involved, but there's only insinuation, no accusation. Enough to draw attention, not enough to bring on a lawsuit.

Goddamn it. God. *Damn*. It. I knew it couldn't last forever.

FOUR HOURS of constantly clicking and typing and excuses later, I give up and crack open the whiskey I'd bought off Beck downstairs. I'd gone back to my apartment after my phone started pinging nonstop with notifications, enough to annoy even the most callous of Rusty's regulars. Several hours spent, and with none of the online fires extinguished, I'm giving up.

I close the laptop decisively and decide that three in the afternoon is still five o'clock somewhere, toasting the liquor bottle in the air to nobody in particular.

"Here's to the end of my career," I say. "It was fun while it lasted."

There's no containing the story. I don't know how the tabloid got ahold of it, but it almost certainly must have been somebody at Sizzle, likely somebody we worked with during the competition. Who else would think to call us a threesome? Somebody must have seen us that week, though I haven't the faintest idea who it might have been. I'd spent the better part of today going over every minute of those weeks in my mind but came up with nothing. I really thought we'd been discreet.

I'd have been a whole lot less surprised if it came out that Drew and I were involved, considering the security footage they found of us backstage at the live event. Or if somebody had seen me leave with Bailey that one night she and I... reconnected.

The memory of just how we connected, with my hand up her skirt in that dimly lit dive bar, resurfaces and I let it. It feels nice, unlike every other moment of this day so far.

Some people are pissed at my apparent bisexuality, some at the thought of me being involved with two people. Plenty of them are pissed I'm involved with anybody at all, which kind of surprised me. I didn't realize my single status mattered at all, but apparently it did.

Doesn't matter that I've denied it all over the place. My website actually crashed at the initial amount of traffic, but came back up fast enough that people are still leaving comments. I used every social media account I've got to try to talk my way around the tabloid piece, but it's no use. If this had happened to any other online personality, I'd have been green as hell with jealousy over all the attention. As it is, all I can do is wait for it to be over. There's no coming back from this.

And God help me... what happens when Bailey and Drew find out? If they haven't already.

I haven't heard from them since I left that note this morning. Normally, that wouldn't be cause for concern; Drew's still got a job after all, and Bailey's got a couple of days left at the bank. Is it possible they won't be affected by this?

A boy can dream.

Drew was brave enough to out himself to his family, despite knowing they wouldn't approve. What happens when the entire world finds out?

28

BAILEY

The text messages start over my lunch break, but I'm too busy daydreaming about Cooper and Drew to check them. I've heard from Evie a few times the last couple of weeks, though it's been mostly short "congrats!" types of messages. When we swapped phone numbers, I didn't actually expect her to keep in touch, but it's been nice to hear from her, even if it's largely in GIF form.

Drew and Cooper went out of their way last night to blow my mind, I think. Every time I think the shine must be starting to wear on the three of us being together, they do something to make me fall for them even harder. Whether it's Drew's all-around considerate actions or Coop's newfound ability to cooperate, every moment we spend together seems to bind us closer together. So much so that I'm starting to think maybe a define-the-relationship talk is unnecessary. The three of us, we just are. We're a fact.

After what happened with Drew's family, I'm terrified of taking us for granted, but I can't help how I feel. It feels certain, real. Solid.

So when Evie starts sending me screenshots of Cooper's website, you might say I'm caught a little off guard.

"Ooh, Bailey, you've been holding out on us!" Twenty-year-old

Shana at the next teller window leans over the partition between us, a sly grin on her face. "Those guys are hot."

A handful of my coworkers start migrating in our direction. Given the dead zone that is our lobby after lunch, it's prime gossip hour. And it looks like I'm the topic of choice today.

"Hold that thought," I tell Shana, trying to play it cool. "I'll be right back." I snag my phone and haul ass to the ladies' room, locking myself in a stall before swiping to open the messages from Evie.

It's Cooper's website all right, plus shots of several of his accounts on social media. Apparently, somebody reported a story about Cooper and Drew and me—there's a photo of the three of us from the opening gala. I look fat as hell, but the guys look amazing. I don't remember there being photographers around at that point, but whoever took the picture definitely captured the air of intimacy between us. I do remember how it felt standing there with them that night, long before anything happened between us. It's staring me in the face, out there on the Internet for all to see.

According to the screenshots, Cooper's been posting about this for hours and his strategy is clear: deny, deny, deny.

I don't understand. Obviously, somebody's spreading gossip on purpose; that part I get. I didn't really expect to get through a TV show competition without some kind of drama or exposure of some kind, though it's all been small potatoes so far. But I didn't win, and the finale hasn't even aired yet, and nobody knew my name at the gala. There's no reason to care, for anybody. Why bring up this shit now?

Cooper's phone goes straight to voicemail. I keep it simple, asking him to call me back when he can. I imagine this must be something like damage control for him, trying to keep a lid on his reputation.

Nothing to worry about. That's all it is, damage control. He's not avoiding you.

I text Drew instead of calling, knowing he'll be at the studio today. I wonder if they've already heard. I hope to God this doesn't cause more problems for him. Exonerated or not, he doesn't need any more negative attention at work.

I'm just about to gird my loins for dealing with my coworkers when my phone buzzes with an incoming call. I answer immediately, thinking it must be Cooper.

"Hey," I say, a little breathless with relief.

"Bailey Annette Ross," says my mother. "What is the meaning of this?"

"Oh," I say weakly. "Hi, Mom."

"Is it true? Are you out of your mind?" My mother huffs and continues before I can come up with an answer to any of those questions. "I always knew there was more to you and that other Hicks boy, but I never thought you'd expose yourself like this."

"Mom, I—"

"Don't interrupt me, young lady." I can tell she's been working her way up to this. She barely stops for breath. "Old Mrs. Daniels stopped me in the middle of the supermarket—the supermarket, for God's sake—to ask me about my daughter's whoring. Do you have any idea how humiliating that was?"

"It's not whoring," I manage, cracking open the bathroom stall door a fraction so I can keep an eye on the door. Shana will be barging in here any second now, or one of the other girls from the floor, to see why I've been in here so long. They'll figure it out that I'm avoiding them, but there's nothing I can do about it right now.

"Don't you dare make jokes," says my mother. She sounds genuinely shaken under all her bluster. In all the scenarios I'd imagined, when I pictured telling her about how I'd fallen in love with two men, it never once occurred to me that it would upset her this much.

"I'm not joking," I say.

"Is it true?" she asks again. This time she waits for me to answer.

"Which part?" I have to be careful here. The write-up Evie sent me made it clear that all three of us were involved. That's going to be a problem for a lot of people.

"Any of it," says Mom, seething. I'm not trying to make her angrier, but she won't care about that right now.

"Yes."

Mom takes a deep breath.

"Which part?"

"Pretty much all of it," I admit. "Although, that picture was taken long before—"

"I don't want to hear it," she says, cutting me off. "I don't want to hear any of it. You're embarrassing yourself, Bailey, if you think to continue in this way. It's a good thing they've already filmed that television show. I can't imagine they'd allow you to stay on after all this."

I try to speak again, to defend Drew and Cooper and myself, to explain. But she's not having it.

"Call me when you've come to your senses." With that, my mother hangs up on me.

I'm still staring at my phone a moment later when Shana finally pops her head in the door.

"Everything okay in here, Bailey?"

I swallow hard to get the lump out of my throat before I can answer.

"Yep. Be right there," I say. My voice sounds hoarse. Shana's expression is closed, showing none of the glee I was expecting to see. She hesitates before speaking again.

"Mr. Heckman is looking for you. I'm supposed to tell you to meet him in his office."

I close my eyes, letting my head fall back so the tears don't spill over. My last day is tomorrow. I'm so close to being done here.

Dry it up, girl. Hold it down. You can handle this.

Mr. Heckman has spent most of my final days at the bank pretending I don't exist. Or like I'm already gone. He's not pleased that I handed in my resignation rather than fall in line like he expected. It made me sad after all these years of working well together, but I can't really blame him for it.

I make my way to his office, keeping my head high.

"Ms. Ross," he says, pointing to the chair in front of his desk. The expression on his face is that of someone required to sift through a dumpster; his distaste is plain.

"No, thank you," I say quietly. "Mr. Heckman, I need to leave early today."

He looks up at me sharply.

"I still have unused sick days," I add. "But there's a... personal matter I need to attend to. I really need to get home."

He nods immediately, making me wonder if I've just spared him the trouble of firing me.

"Perhaps that's for the best," he says. "You have enough to cover you through the end of your resignation period. Is that what you're telling me—that you won't be coming back?"

The certainty in his voice tells me my suspicion is correct. Despite already holding my resignation, he'd been about to fire me.

This day can't get any worse.

"Yes, sir," I say quietly. He nods again, rapidly.

"Yes, I think that's for the best." He hits a button on his phone. "I'll have Shana help you pack your things."

Twenty minutes and some confused hugs later, my former coworkers watch me carry the box of personal effects out to my car. No farewell party, no fuss. Just a cardboard box containing mementos of the last three years of my life.

Even knowing I'd been facing this day, that I'd chosen it myself, that it'd be coming soon, I'm not prepared for the sudden sense of loss as I wave goodbye to Shana one last time and start the car.

Evie calls as I'm pulling out of the parking lot.

"Hey, girl," I answer.

"Hey," she says. "You okay?"

I smile. Rather than ask me for all the sordid details, she asks if I'm okay first. Considering we don't know each other all that well, I take it as a sign that maybe we're going to be friends after all.

"I'm still here," I say, putting as much optimism in my voice as I can.

"At the risk of sounding like a reporter," she says, "You've been holding out on me."

I laugh. "What can I say? It's good to be me." At least, I'd thought so up until a couple of hours ago.

"I bet," says Evie, her voice thick with envy. "One of these days I'm going to get you drunk and pry the details out of you."

"You're welcome to try," I say. She laughs.

"Seriously, though," says Evie. "Are you okay? Is there anything I can do?"

I think back over the screenshots she sent and shake my head before realizing Evie can't see me.

"I don't think so," I tell her, pulling up to Cooper's building. We've spent most of our nights together at Drew's apartment and one or two at my place. I've never been here before. It looks like a pub, though the fire escape up the side of the building tells me there must be apartments upstairs. "But I appreciate the thought."

I assure Evie I'm fine and when we hang up a minute later, I'm still no closer to understanding what's happened to my life today than I was before she called. The pub looks mostly empty, so I take a chance and step inside. The bartender waves, setting down his tray before coming over to greet me.

"What can I get you?"

He's tall, thick with muscle, and bristling with energy. Everything about this guy screams "danger" to me, though his face is friendly and open. Good guy to have working a bar, I guess.

"I'm looking for Cooper Lawson," I say. "Do you know where I can find him?" I eyeball the stairs toward the back of the restaurant floor. When I turn back to look at the bartender, he shakes his head.

"Can't help you there," he says. "Coop was in here earlier, but he went upstairs before lunch."

"His car's still parked outside," I say, pointing out the window. The bartender shrugs.

"Wish I could tell you more, beautiful," he says, giving me a half-smile.

"Thanks," I say, heading for the stairs in the back. I can feel the bartender watching me as I make my way up, but he doesn't say anything to stop me. In a bigger city I'd be worried about Cooper's security if he really lives up here, but considering this town's about as American Midwest as it gets, I'm not surprised to arrive at the landing at the top of the stairs unchallenged.

Then again, if the bartender downstairs is any indication, they probably don't need added security.

The first door on the left matches Cooper's apartment number, so

I knock quietly at first. No sound comes from inside, so I knock louder. Another minute goes by. I try pounding with my fist, because a nasty suspicion is bubbling up in my gut and I don't like it, not one bit.

"All right, all right," I hear Cooper mutter from the other side of the door. There's a thump followed by a muffled crash, then the sound of locks turning. Cooper pulls the door open wide, hanging onto the doorframe with one arm.

"Hey, Ross," he says. He doesn't smile.

"You're drunk." Really, really drunk.

"Yep. You?"

I shake my head. "Cooper, we need to talk," I say.

"I don't think that's a real good idea," he drawls. I've never seen him like this, not even back in college.

"Are you going to let me in?" I ask. His head swings around, looking over his shoulder slowly before he looks back at me. It takes him a minute to focus on my face and when he does, he gets sad.

"I don't think so, Bailey girl."

That's what Drew calls me.

"You didn't answer my calls," I say. I don't know what to do with him like this. I wish Drew were here. Maybe I should have waited, brought him with me.

"Turned my phone off," he says. "Too much… you know." He nods at me, waving a hand between us.

"You couldn't have called to let me know? We need to talk about this," I say.

"Nothing left to talk about," he says, frowning. "It's done."

"What do you mean, done?" I say. I'm starting to get mad. "We are not done."

"It's out," he says, not appearing to hear me. The doorframe is the only thing keeping him on his feet right now. "We're out. Nothing we can do about it."

"There's plenty we can do about it," I say, stepping forward. "But we need to talk—"

"I don't think so," he says, shaking his head. His expression drops, looking so sad I want to cry for him. He looks at the floor.

"I'm sorry, Ross. Shouldn't have done it. Didn't want it to end this way."

"Cooper, you're scaring me," I say, stepping into his space, trying to force him to look at me. "What are you talking about?"

"It was fun, right?" he asks, trying to smile and failing miserably. "We had fun. But it's over."

All I can do is stare at him. Cooper's been cagey about this— about his feelings—from the start, but today... today he's denied his involvement with us to all and sundry online. He refused to acknowledge our relationship publicly. He's completely shut me out all afternoon, and now—

Now he's telling me goodbye?

Maybe for once in my life it's time to believe someone when they tell me who they are, what they want.

Cooper can't make it any clearer: he thinks it's over. He said so. So why am I still here, begging for scraps of whatever he might have left to give?

That's not who I am anymore.

"Fine." I meet his eyes one last time. "You know what, Cooper? Fine. You want out, all you had to do was say so." I turn and head back down the way I came.

29

DREW

"**D**rew."

I tilt my head in Kenna's direction across the office but don't turn to look at her, too busy reviewing the production schedules in front of me.

"*Drew*," Kenna insists.

"What? I'm almost done with the—"

"Leave it," she snaps in a loud whisper. "You need to get over here."

That was how I found out about the tabloid article; a couple of whispers over a working lunch, bouncing back and forth between my cubicle and Kenna's desk. I should be thankful she's the one who caught wind of it first, and that everybody else was still out to lunch when the story broke. At least I had a few minutes to get my shit together.

After that, I didn't have a minute to catch my breath. Between trying to get my usual work finished and the emergency meetings to "clean up this mess"—Ty's words—I'd run all over the building this afternoon.

At least I still have a job. At the moment. Greeley wanted to fire me on the spot, but Archer Burke of all people pointed out that despite the salacious nature of the tabloid write-up, it's free publicity and the network could use it to springboard the launch of the competition finale.

"Ride the wave as long as we can," advised Archer. Legal was still trying to get the post taken down, but Ty and Archer suggested playing it up, even going so far as mention cutting together a special ad for the competition finale featuring Bailey and Cooper and me.

"That's despicable," said Kenna when I told her about the idea. I agreed, but the network had to spin it somehow and I had zero control over how that happened.

After the second hour of nonstop notifications, I'd set my phone to silent mode, picking it up only every now and then to see if Bailey or Cooper had checked in.

I check it again now, just in case. Still nothing.

I do have a new missed call from my mother, whom I haven't heard from since before her anniversary party. My stomach drops just thinking about it.

I didn't expect an unconventional relationship like ours to be all smooth sailing, but I really thought we had more time to sort things out. We never even talked about this, about what to tell people. I sprang it on Cooper and Bailey at my parents' party, coming out and claiming them both like I did. After that, I thought we'd be solid. We were on the same page.

So I thought. After today, I'm not so sure.

Cooper denied everything after that picture of the three of us was posted, and he hasn't been seen online since. He's not answering my texts. I don't know what to make of that.

Bailey's supposed to be at the bank this afternoon, and I don't want to bother her at work. If her day's been anything like mine, she's had enough to deal with. I'm worried, but no news is good news, right? I figure to check in with her in a couple of hours, after I've had a minute to decompress.

Only when I pull up to my apartment, Bailey's already beat me there. She's sitting in her car with the engine running. When she sees me park, she shuts the car off, meeting me at the door.

"Come on in," I say, guiding her inside. "It's freezing out here."

I shut the door behind us. Bailey's quiet. It's a far cry from the last time we stood in my hallway alone together.

"I guess you've seen it," I say.

Bailey laughs without humor. "Yeah," she says. "Evie sent me screenshots at lunch."

I nod. "Kenna showed me at lunch, too." I shove my hands in my pockets to keep from reaching for her. Tense as she is, Bailey might as well be wearing a flashing neon sign that says Do Not Touch.

"Have you heard from your family?" she asks.

"I've got some voicemails. I haven't listened to them yet," I admit.

"You should," she says. Her reaction is dulled, like she's closed in on herself. Considering Bailey's had no trouble speaking her mind the last couple of weeks, her behavior surprises me. But what she says is probably right, so I pull out my phone and play the message from my mom.

"Andrew... I saw the article. Your grandfather is absolutely furious with you. Perhaps it would be best if you stay away for the time being. At least until this... situation dies down. Of course, that man in the photo with you says there is no relationship. He claims the article is all wrong. If that's true, please call me back. We'd like to believe this whole thing is just some ham-handed PR stunt for your job, but your father tells me you confirmed the relationship yourself. If that is the case," Mom takes a deep breath, "well, I can only tell you that I sincerely hope you've had time to reconsider your position. I know you think we expect too much from you, but I hardly think it's too much to ask that you keep your private life private. Consider what you're putting your family through, Andrew. I'll be in touch."

I set the phone down on the coffee table, not looking at Bailey.

"What are you going to do?" Bailey asks, her voice soft in the quiet of my apartment.

I don't know what to tell her.

"What can I do?" I ask, voicing the very question that's been on my mind all day. "It's out. There's no hiding it. Even if the Internet wasn't forever, Sizzle is going to spin the story to help launch the show."

Surprise registers on her face.

"Spin it how?"

"Any way they want," I say bitterly. "It's out of my hands."

"Our hands," she corrects me.

"Right."

She keeps looking at me like she's waiting for me to do something. My frustration at the tabloid, at the day, at the entire situation spills over.

"What do you want me to do, Bailey? It's out of my hands, all of it."

This whole situation—hell, this relationship—has been out of my control since the start. I don't know why I ever thought otherwise.

"Do you realize since we started this thing I've lost my reputation, my relationship with my family, and now I've damn near lost my job," I say, running my hands through my hair in frustration. "Twice. I don't know what else you want from me."

"I want you to fight for us," she says, visibly upset.

"That's the thing, Bailey." I turn my back to her, because I don't know if I can say it while I look at her. "It seems like all I've done is fight for us. I'm tired of fighting."

Worse, I'm tired of feeling like I'm the only one who's had to fight. What has Cooper given up for us? Or Bailey? Neither of them have put half as much on the line as I have.

"What are you saying?" she asks. I don't turn around at the question, but her tone makes it obvious: Bailey's furious.

"I'm just saying I'm tired," I say, equivocating.

"Then I guess you'll be relieved to hear Cooper's already ended things," she says without inflection. I spin around to see her standing by the door.

"What are you talking about?"

"I went to his apartment," she says, her chin rising. "He wouldn't answer my calls. When I got there, he was drunk, but he made it very clear this… this thing between us is over."

"That's what he told all those people online, but I thought—"

"You thought wrong." Bailey looks me dead in the eye. "We both did. I'm going home. Maybe it's best if we don't see each other for a while."

"Bailey, no."

She shakes her head when I head for the door to try to stop her.

"You're not the only one who's had to fight, Drew," she says. I hear the tears in her voice, though her eyes stay dry. "Only difference is, I thought you two were worth it."

Bailey steps out into the cold, pulling the door closed with a click.

I'VE HAD BREAKUPS BEFORE. Obviously. Even bad breakups, the kind where I mope around my place and don't shower and get depressed and skip the gym and forget to eat.

That's not what this is.

My entire life has been upended, and all I can think about is them.

It's been eighteen days. Eighteen days of silence, eighteen mornings of waking up and wishing I hadn't. Eighteen hangovers. Maybe nineteen. Drinking isn't usually a vice for me, but I can't think of anything better to do.

I can't go out with my coworkers, not without constant jokes about the tabloid article or the newly spread rumor about Cooper and me making out backstage. My parents have called a few times. Tired as I was of fighting their expectations, I'm not too keen on the idea of letting them know that they were right to expect my latest relationship to fail. Maybe I just don't want to tell them the truth. It didn't just fail on its own. I set it on fire and scattered the ashes.

Every now and then a wave of energy surfaces enough to remind me that I didn't burn it down on my own. Cooper had a heavy hand in it, too. And Bailey, she's the one who walked away.

I'm not sure which part hurts the most.

"Here," says Kenna one morning at work. She pushes a bottle of water into my hands.

"Thanks." I've been subsisting on mostly coffee during daylight hours. Kenna's the only one who bothers me about that. Considering the look she's giving me right now, I think she's about to bother me about something else.

"When's the last time you ate?" she asks. Yep. Right on cue.

"Dunno," I say, turning back to my desk. "What day is it?"

Kenna snorts, though neither of us find it funny. She's quiet long enough, and after a couple of minutes I forget she's there.

"You know you're being an idiot, right?" she says, startling me enough that I to turn to look at her. "Maybe I need to be more specific."

"By all means," I say, waving a hand.

"Those two would do anything for you," she says, stopping me when I shake my head. "I'm serious. I saw the three of you, remember? More than once."

The short weeks I had with Cooper and Bailey have been on replay in my head nonstop. I know what she means.

"Have you tried talking to them?" she asks.

"They don't want to talk to me," I mutter.

"That's a big fat 'no.' How do you know they don't want to talk to you if you haven't tried?"

I know the way Bailey looked at me before she left. I know Cooper's gone radio silent. If he wasn't uploading videos he put together weeks ago, I'd be worried something might have happened to him, but he still posts his stuff right on schedule.

"I know," I say, trying to get her off my back. Kenna snorts.

"I didn't take you for such a flake," she says, sounding disgusted.

"What are you talking about?" She's pissing me off. After weeks of this gray, foggy indifference, it's kind of a relief to feel angry again. "I gave up—"

"Yeah, yeah," she says, talking over me until I shut my mouth. "I've heard all about how much you had to give up. Yet here we are, me wiping your snotty nose again." She ignores my protest and continues. "You need to get them back."

"It's not that simple," I say, shocked into momentary silence.

"Duh," says Kenna. "I doubt anything is simple between the three of you. But you didn't sign on for simple, did you? Or easy? Or uncomplicated? That's not why you get involved with two people at once. Especially not people like Bailey. Or Cooper, for that matter."

"They could have called," I say defensively. "They could have said something the last few weeks. Why is it on me to make the first move?"

"Because you're the only one living in your head, dummy." Kenna leans forward, jabbing her finger into my chest like she means it. "You're the one pining for them. The only person you can control is you. So what the hell are you waiting for? Go get them back."

30

COOPER

"Beck. Beck!" Where is that damn fool bartender when you need him?

"For crying out loud, Cooper, I'm standing right here." And so, indeed he is. Beck appears before me like magic, summoned by the power of my hangover. At least, that's the way it seems to me.

I pull my stool up closer to the bar and Beck eyes me warily. It's been weeks of this—drinking myself stupid, staggering upstairs to sleep it off, then coming back for more when I can't take another hour of humiliation at the hands of the Internet.

Nearly three weeks of this. Nineteen days, but who's counting?

Beck's just standing there, tapping his fingers on the bar.

"You've single-handedly doubled my order for Jim Beam this week," he says.

"You're welcome, asshole," I say, about to order my usual, but Beck's expression is pinched. Like he's bracing himself.

I don't even blame him. He's had to help me upstairs more than once the last few weeks. So has Rusty. I'm not proud of it.

I know I did the right thing. I knew from the outset there was no way it could work between... us.

Bailey and Drew. *It's been three weeks; you can use their names.*

Except I can't. And it's only been nineteen days.

I know I was right. I know it. But I kind of thought being right would suck less.

Because this fucking sucks.

Guess I said that part out loud, because Beck nods and says, "I know, buddy. That's the only reason Dad hasn't banned your drunk ass from the bar."

"Seriously?"

"Look around, Cooper," says Beck. "You see anybody else in here crying into their beers night after night?"

I've had tunnel vision the last few weeks, I can admit it. I've been focused on salvaging any kind of following I can—that and deliberately not thinking about the two people I haven't seen in almost three weeks.

Turns out it takes a lot of whiskey to focus on not thinking about them. That's where living over a pub has come in handy. Because drinking upstairs alone would be sad.

"Rusty's ain't that kind of place, man," says Beck, all matter-of-fact. "You're lucky Dad likes you. I'd have kicked your ass to the curb ages ago."

"Aw, come on, man," I say, but Beck shakes his head. "You're not kidding."

"Not even a little," he says.

"Well, excuse the fuck out of me," I say, annoyed and hurt. The hurt just blends into the vat of aching in my chest, though, so I stick to being annoyed, standing up and shoving my stool back into place. It's all just part of the fucked-up scenery these days.

"Sit down," orders Beck. It's his military voice, all command, no room for argument. Don't ask me how it works, but it does. Before I know it, I'm sliding back into my chair.

"I'm really not into power play," I mumble. Beck snorts.

"Could have fooled me," he says. Another customer calls to him from down the bar. Beck taps the bar in front of me. "Stay here," he says, setting down a glass of ice water.

Any other time in my life, I'd be all about Beck's unique brand of flirting. He's certainly hot enough. Too bad my sex drive appears to have been broken sometime in the last couple of weeks.

Nineteen days. That's how long it's been since Bailey turned up at my door, when somebody told the whole world what we'd been doing. It's been nineteen days since I slipped out of Drew's bed and watched them hold each other in their sleep. Nineteen days since I left a note saying I'd be back to see them that night after work.

Nineteen days since I last woke up and was glad to see another day.

It's so stupid. I'm so stupid. Everything is stupid.

"So here's the thing," says Beck, coming back to my end of the bar. This time he sets a cup of coffee in front of me. I glare at him, but decide fighting is what he's after and I'm all about thwarting authority. I wrap my hands around the mug, just to warm them up. Maybe a sip won't hurt.

"You're in love with them, yeah?"

I choke on my drink, spraying coffee on the bar top. Beck arches a brow and hands me a towel.

"What are you talking about?" I manage wiping up the mess.

"Bailey and Drew, isn't it?" says Beck, lounging against the cooler behind the bar like he's got all the time in the world. "She was hot."

"Excuse me?" I feel my shoulders creeping up to my ears, my face warming.

"I met her that night at the gala, remember? Then she came by here that day a few weeks ago," says Beck, ignoring my anger. "She asked about you before she went upstairs. Smoking hot, though I can't say I ever had a thing for blondes."

"Mind your own goddamn business," I say, setting the mug down before I can throw it at him.

"She's the kind you'd make an exception for," says Beck, oblivious to the fact that I'm about to kill him.

"That's enough."

He looks at me then. "Funny. Considering you've been in here crying on my bar every night since then, I figured she was a free agent."

Somebody else calls for a drink and Beck walks away, leaving me to stew in my own rage. I might still have to kill him, but he's made his point. Bailey's not mine. She and Drew are free to see other people. Or each other. Or any combination thereof. The thought makes me want to hurl.

"Drew, on the other hand," says Beck, coming back like he was never interrupted at all. "That guy is exactly my type."

"You've made your point," I say, gritting my teeth.

"That ass," Beck says with genuine enthusiasm.

"I'm going to kill you."

Beck meets my eyes, his gaze level.

"Then maybe you get what I'm saying," says Beck.

"I got it," I say through my teeth.

"So why are you sitting here sulking in my bar and driving away my business?"

"Name on the building says Rusty's."

"Semantics." The corner of his mouth turns up a little. I feel the last of my aggravation seep out of my shoulders and put my head on the bar.

"I'm an idiot," I say, not bothering to sit up.

"I know," he says. "But turns out that particular condition isn't always fatal. The question is, what are you going to do about it?"

I think long and hard before I answer. I'm still thinking about it twenty minutes later, when Beck's long since stopped waiting for me to speak and is helping take care of a thirsty group of sports fans on the other side of the dining room.

Bailey told me she wouldn't beg, that she was done taking scraps from men. I didn't catch on at the time, but I'm pretty sure she wasn't talking about me, or even Drew. She's had several serious relationships in the past, and while I don't know much about why they ended, I do know that Bailey said she always felt unseen, like her boyfriends didn't respect her enough to see her for who she really was. If that's the case, me calling it off when things got hard probably just reinforced every bad feeling she ever had, putting me firmly in the camp with her exes.

That thought doesn't sit well. At all.

Bailey deserves better. For the first time in nineteen days, instead of being angry or sad, I'm proud of her for walking away. She deserves better than being flaked out on by some drunken asshole, even if that asshole is me.

Even Drew had the balls to stand up to his family and make them acknowledge her. He respects our relationship enough to put himself on the line in more ways than one.

Our relationship. The idea feels strange and new; every time I turn it over in my mind, I sit a little bit taller. The coffee cup in front of me somehow never goes empty, though I've lost track of how many times I've picked it up for a drink.

Drew deserves somebody who'll stand up for him the way he stood up for us. They both do. So what if his family doesn't approve? And so what if it costs me that contract with Sizzle? It hasn't cost me my audience—at least, not all of it. I'm still making enough money to pay the bills, though lately things have gotten a little thin.

But so what? I built a career out of thin air before, just these last couple of years. I can do it again. So the TV gig door is closed. So what? It's done.

Is it worth closing the door to the best relationship I've ever had? To the two best people I've ever met?

Not to mention the sex.

For the first time in nineteen days, my body stirs with interest, causing me to shift in my chair. Maybe not the best time for that, but it's kind of a relief to know I'm not dead inside. Not dead at all.

"You look better when you're caffeinated," says Beck the next time he comes around the bar to top me off.

"Better than you, that's for sure," I quip. Beck does a double take, then smiles.

"You wish," he says. I snort.

The man's got a point. He's seriously hot. If I weren't taken—

But I am. And damned if that thought doesn't bring a smile to my face for the first time in weeks.

"There we go," says Beck, watching me with approval. "So what's the plan, Coop?"

"Good question," I say. I tap my fingers on the bar. "Yeah, I gotta run. What do I owe you for the coffee?"

"On the house," he says, waving me off. "Go."

I grin and head back up to my apartment to plot.

THIS IS A MISTAKE. Surely, this a mistake. This is possibly the dumbest thing I've ever attempted in my lifetime.

I'm nervous. I never get nervous. Never. Yet here I sit, tapping my foot, sweating like a pig. I can practically smell the nerves.

They're just people, says the grown-up part of my brain. Just adults, same as you. Human beings.

They're not just people, though. They're Drew's parents. And Bailey's mom. I couldn't find out anything about her dad, so I'm banking on this being enough.

I couldn't believe they'd agreed to meet with me, any of them. Especially after the earful I got from Bailey's mom about being a bad influence on her daughter and how they're Rosses and Rosses are better than that. Among other things.

I don't remember Bailey talking all that much about her childhood, but I was under the impression she and her mom had it kind of rough. Maybe I was wrong.

Anyway, none of that matters. What matters is that they agreed to come here, to hear me out.

Now I just have to figure out what the hell I'm going to say. The speech I wrote down seems so... so trite. You don't write speeches for an audience of only three people, do you? I should have looked this up.

Chill out, dude. You're going to freak them out before they even get to the table.

I'm startled out of my nerve-induced jitters when the bell over the cafe door jingles. I'd picked Bill & Jillie's Market on Market Street because they catered the party for Drew's parents a few weeks ago. I thought it might seem like home turf to them, and I'll take any points I can get in this battle.

The woman standing at the door glances around and I rise to my feet, waving her over. She's a slightly older version of Bailey. If I thought my girl was beautiful now, it's nothing to what she'll be in thirty years based on what Mrs. Ross looks like.

"You must be Mrs. Ross," I say, extending a hand. She raises a brow at me but shakes my hand delicately.

"You're Cooper Lawson," she says.

"I am. Will you have a seat?" I've occupied the largest table in the cafe in the hopes it'll buy us some privacy. Fortunately, the place is mostly empty.

"Can I get you something to drink? We're only waiting on Mr. and Mrs. Hicks," I say.

"Right," says Bailey's mother. "I'd forgotten they were coming." The way she pats her hair makes me think that's a lie, but I've got too much on my mind to care. I've only just retrieved her espresso from Bill at the counter when Drew's parents arrive.

"Mr. Hicks, nice to see you again," I say. Considering how things went at the party, I'm not surprised when he declines to shake my hand, though I make it a point to offer. "This must be Mrs. Hicks."

"Hello," she says, giving me a small smile. Drew favors his father in looks, but the sweetness in her smile tells me everything I need to know about where he gets his generosity.

"It's nice to meet you," I say. "Will you join us?"

"Oh, Sandra, so nice to see you again," chirps Mrs. Ross as we take our seats. "Hello, Roy. How have you two been?"

"Hello, Nina," says Mr. Hicks coolly. He looks as though he'd just as soon be licking the dumpster out back as sitting here, so I clear my throat to get their attention. Everyone turns to look at me. I'm no stranger to being the center of attention. I've been known, on occasion, to seek it out, even.

Sitting in front of my lovers' parents feels like facing down a firing squad.

"Thank you all for coming," I say, swallowing down my nerves and straightening my posture. "I won't keep you long, but I wanted the chance to clear the air…"

"**B**eezy, you know I love you, but it's been three weeks," says Evie, tiptoeing around the pile of clothes on my living room floor. "You've got to get out of here, get some air. Something."

"I know."

"Showering also would be good," says Evie, giving my pajamas a long, judgy look.

"Hey, these are clean," I say, picking at Cooper's shirt. At least, it was clean when I put it on. But I think that might have been several days ago.

Evie considers me for a moment, then yanks the fuzzy blanket I've been hiding under for the last little while.

"Hey!" I say. "It's fucking freezing in here."

"You'd be perfectly fine if you were wearing pants," says Evie, not batting an eye at my bare legs, not even a glimmer of sympathy in her expression. "Shower. Now."

"Serves you right," I grumble. "What if I'd been naked under that blanket?"

"It's a price I'm willing to pay to put an end to that smell."

I'm pretty sure she's bluffing about the smell. My apartment's a wreck and yeah, I probably look like I've been hit with every ugly stick in the state, but it's not that bad. Admittedly, my judgment's not the greatest these days.

The thought has me hauling ass through my shower routine, scrubbing myself down with more energy than I've had in weeks.

Three weeks, to be exact.

Since I'm upright, I might as well at least give cleaning the apartment a shot, though my heart's not remotely in it. When I emerge from the bathroom, freshly scrubbed and fully clothed against the chill in my apartment and demonstrably not smelly, I find Evie's made herself at home on my couch, tapping at her phone with her feet propped up on the coffee table.

"Better?" she asks, glancing my way. I nod. "Good. When's the last time you ate something?" I don't even get my mouth open when she adds, "Besides ice cream."

It takes me a minute to remember. "I had a sandwich yesterday." I'm pretty sure that was yesterday. I know I had ice cream this morning, though. Thank God for grocery delivery.

"That's what I figured," she says. "Takeout will be here any minute."

"You're a good friend." I say it like it's a joke, but she knows I mean it. Considering I've only known her a couple of months, Evie's been a rock, the one person checking on me after Cooper and Drew and I broke up. Even my own mother hasn't called, though I'm hardly surprised by that after our last conversation.

"Damn straight," says Evie. She gives me a long look but whatever she's about to say is interrupted by a buzz. "There's the food."

"Pizza?" I ask.

"Salad for you, Mrs. Ben & Jerry."

"Polygamy jokes. You're fucking hilarious," I say, rolling my eyes. Only Evie. While she's picking up the food from downstairs, I unearth my phone from the mountain of pillows on the couch, taking a moment to clear the clutter off the coffee table so we actually have somewhere to put the food when she gets back.

I've gotten in the appalling habit of checking my phone every forty-five seconds or so, which is particularly unhelpful given the lack of communication from my lovers. Ex-lovers. Whatever.

I don't know why this breakup is so bad. You'd think getting dumped by three fiancés would have been worse than the end of such a short, wild fling.

Except it wasn't a fling, was it?

It was wild and it was crazy and it only lasted six weeks and a handful of days. But somehow those rat bastards wormed their way in and took over every last inch of my heart. There's no room in there for anybody else—not even the men I thought I loved enough to marry. And the thought of ever letting anybody else get that close again, after Drew and Cooper... it makes me physically ill.

You did the right thing. You know you did.

Cold comfort. I have my self-respect, though, and that's enough. At least, that's what I keep telling myself.

The vibration of my phone startles me so hard, I drop the phone on the floor, not a little alarmed to see my mother is calling. Something must be seriously wrong.

"Mom?" I answer. "Are you okay? What happened?"

"Oh, calm down, Bailey," she says, sounding annoyed. It's a relief to hear. If Mom's annoyed, probably nobody died. "Is that really how you answer your phone? Honestly. I raised you better than that."

It's a testament to how hard my heart is pounding that I don't call her out on that extra heaping pile of bullshit. Before I open my mouth to answer, she continues.

"I'm calling to find out whether you've seen that video your... friend posted."

"What friend?" I ask, looking around for my laptop. It's around here somewhere. "What video?"

"That Lawson boy," she says. "Honestly, Bailey, if I'd known he was going to air his dirty laundry on the Internet, I'd never have agreed to that meeting."

I stop looking for the laptop and pull the phone away to stare at it.

"Mom, I'm going to need you to start over," I say slowly, bringing the phone back up to my ear. "You met Cooper?"

She sighs. "Pay attention, please. Yes, I met Cooper Lawson. He called me a few days ago and asked if we could meet to discuss some things."

Cooper called my mother. My mother.

"What things?"

"Ugh, all manner of things," she says, her voice heavy with disgust. "Including a great deal about your personal life that I did not need to know, thank you very much." My face goes hot. Evie picks that precise moment to come through the door, loaded down with enough takeout bags to feed the pair of us for at least a week. I shake my head at her questioning look, holding up a finger.

"He made it clear that the three of you are seriously involved in a committed relationship," says Mom. "Mr. and Mrs. Hicks were not pleased, let me tell you."

"Drew's parents were there?"

"Bring your voice down, young lady," says Mom. "There's no need to shriek at me. Yes, Alan's parents were there. I expect your former fiancé probably has some things to say about your little arrangement with his brother and his boyfriend."

I don't doubt she's right, but I can't spare mental energy for Alan right now.

"You said Cooper posted a video?"

"Yes," says Mom. "I still get alerts about your cooking competition. I was so proud to see you competing, dear, before all this distasteful... Anyway. I still get alerts, and since the show was tagged in this morning's video, I watched it."

For once my silence seems to register and my mother doesn't try to fill it.

"Well?" I ask, my heart in my throat.

"I can't believe you haven't seen it yet," she says, sighing again. "It's all very romantic, I'm sure, though that sort of gesture never appealed to me personally. He goes on and on about you and Andrew and how much he loves you. There's a great deal about an apology for denying your relationship when that nasty tabloid piece came out a few weeks ago."

Cooper made a video. About us? An apology.

"Mom," I say, trying to get a word in. "Mom. Thanks for letting me know about the video. I have to go now."

"Why—"

"Bye, Mom." I feel a twinge of guilt for hanging up on her but this is more important. "Have you seen my laptop?" I ask Evie, already running back to my bedroom to check for it there.

"Kitchen counter," she calls. Thank God.

Evie's setting out Styrofoam containers on the coffee table when I retrieve the computer and sit on the couch to get it booted up, pulling up a browser and cursing every long second it doesn't load.

"Come on, come on, come on," I mutter.

"I think maybe you've officially lost it," says Evie. She sits down next to me, fork in one hand, kung pao chicken in the other. "What's going on?"

"That was my mother on the phone," I tell her, clicking through Cooper's website until I find a video with today's date on it. "Apparently Cooper posted a video about us."

"Huh," says Evie. Something in her voice has me looking up.

"What?"

"Um, that's actually why I'm here," she says, sounding slightly apologetic.

"You knew?" I know I'm shrieking again, but for fuck's sake.

"I was trying to be a good friend and feed you first," she says defensively. "I didn't know it was an apology, just that he posted a video about you. I haven't seen it yet. What if it were something bad?"

"We are going to talk about this," I say, turning back to the screen and checking the volume. Cooper's voice cuts through my living room.

"—probably saw the kerfuffle a couple of weeks ago online, right?" It looks like a reposted livestream. Cooper's looking at the camera, reading the comments as they come in and responding right away. "Yeah, you could say that was unexpected."

God, he looks good.

"He looks like hell," murmurs Evie. Once I get past the shock of seeing his face again for the first time in weeks, I realize she has a point. He's got dark circles under his eyes and his hair is drifting into his eyelashes, like he's been running his hands through it all day.

"I'll keep it short. The fact is, I need to make a couple of apologies," Cooper continues. In the video he's out walking somewhere, walking down a street that looks familiar but that I can't quite place. "First, I need to apologize to you all. I should never have lied to you like that." The comments start appearing on screen faster, but I don't bother reading them, my eyes glued instead to Cooper's face. He smiles.

"I know, y'all. I shouldn't have lied, but that's why I'm here. To tell you the truth." He looks at the camera, all traces of humor gone. "I'm sorry, guys. The truth is, I'm in love with them. With both of them."

Evie sucks in a breath beside me. I can't breathe at all.

"That's the other apology I need to make," says Cooper. He's staring off camera at something. The scenery around him looks really familiar now. "Bailey, Drew... I'm so sorry. I should never have responded to that article without talking to you both first. I sure as hell shouldn't have shut you out like I did." Cooper focuses back on the camera, determination all over his face. "I don't even know if you'll see this but in case you do, I want you to know I'm going to make it up to you. I'll spend the rest of my life making it up to you, if you'll let me."

Cooper takes a couple more steps, and I realize he's walking into that cafe on Market Street, the one with the croissants Drew likes so much. It feels like years since the last time we met for coffee there.

Cooper starts talking to his audience about subscribing and I recognize the pitch he uses to sign off with every video, so I tune him out, focusing on his gorgeous face.

I walked away from him three weeks ago because I deserved to be fought for, to be recognized. If he's ready to take a step like that, coming out publicly even though I know it has to cost him...

Maybe there's still a chance.

"I have to go," I say, closing the laptop. Evie's already packing up the boxes of food with a grin on her face.

"Thought you might say that," she says. "Lemme just pack this one... yep, that'll do it." She leaves the rest bagged up on the table and stands up to hug me hard.

The downstairs buzzer goes off again. Evie pulls back, frowning.

"Do you think it's him?" she says.

"More likely you forgot to tip the delivery guy," I say dryly. Evie scoops up the rest of the food, carrying it into my kitchen as I buzz up the delivery guy.

"I did not forget—" she calls out, but whatever else she has to say gets lost when I spot Drew Hicks through the peephole, walking up to my door.

"Holy shit," I breathe. Evie comes up behind me.

"Not the delivery boy, I'm guessing," she says, shouldering me out of the way so she can look for herself. She stands up, her grin opening up to a smile.

"Right on cue," she says, pulling me into another hug. By the time she gets the door open, her smile is gone and a vicious glare has taken its place.

"Oh. Hello," says Drew.

"You better not fuck this up again, Hicks," says Evie. Tall as she is, she stares Drew down eye to eye and leans into his personal space. She gives him a glare, effective enough to have Drew stepping back to let her pass. "Call me later, Beezy."

A moment later, the hallway is empty, and we're alone. Drew makes no move to come inside, so I step back and wave him in.

"Got a new guard dog?" he asks.

"If that's a bitch joke—"

"It's not, I swear," he says, holding up his hands in surrender. We stare at each other in silence for a long moment after I close the door behind him. He looks miserable.

"I owe you an apology," he says, finally. "I should never have made it sound like you and Cooper didn't stand to lose anything by us being together. I know better, especially now."

I nod tightly. I'm not ready to give him any ground yet, despite the fact that I'm so relieved he's here that I could burst into tears at any moment. Play it cool.

"And you were wrong," he goes on, looking down at the floor. "I think you're worth it. You're worth everything to me, Bailey." Drew takes a step closer, his voice thick. "You are everything to me."

He takes my hands in his, tangling our fingers together. "I was tired. After my family... it doesn't matter anymore. I know what we have isn't going to be easy. If we do this... if you'll have me, I know it'll take work. I can't promise I won't get tired again." Drew lifts my chin with his finger, forcing me to meet his gaze through watering eyes. "But I promise, Bailey, if you take me back I'll never give up. Not ever again."

"Oh, shut up already." I use his grip on my hands to yank him down for a kiss. It's brief, and when I pull back I don't know if the tears on my cheeks are his or my own. Drew scoops me up, carrying me over to the couch to cuddle me on his lap.

"I missed you," he says, his hands cruising over my back. "God, I missed you so much."

"Missed you too," I say, still struggling with tears. "But hey," I say, knocking him back with a hit to his shoulder. "We're not done yet. What about Cooper?"

Drew groans. "What about him?" The quirk of his lips tells me he's joking, but I haven't quite forgiven him that far.

"Have you seen the video?" I ask. He nods, his expression turning serious.

"I figured if he could man up and apologize publicly like that, the least I could do was apologize in person," he says sheepishly.

"Have you talked to him?"

Drew shakes his head. "You?"

"No," I say, climbing off his lap. He pouts until I hold out a hand to help him stand up.

"Where are we going?" he asks.

"To go get our boy," I tell him, grabbing my coat.

32

DREW

I wake up to soft snoring coming from the pillow to my left. Cooper's still sleeping hard, as is Bailey, curled up on his other side. I slip out of bed as quietly as I can, trying to let them rest a while longer. Considering how late we stayed up, I'm not surprised they're worn out.

The memory of just how we wore each other out brings a smile to my face, so wide it makes my muscles hurt.

I duck into Cooper's kitchen to start some coffee, taking the opportunity to send a quick email to Tyler letting him know I won't be in the office today. Bailey and Cooper's schedules might be more flexible these days, but Sizzle still has me punching a clock. What-ever. They can deal without me for a day.

I'm digging around in Cooper's refrigerator to see if there's enough ingredients to put together breakfast for three when I feel a warm hand slide across my ass cheeks before getting a firm grip on one side.

"You brought it on yourself, honestly," says Cooper, his voice rough with sleep and overuse. The roughness makes me flush, memories swamping me again. "If you didn't want to get groped, you really shouldn't be dressed like this."

"Rape jokes aren't funny," I say, grabbing the eggs and setting them on the counter. His hand stays with me the whole way.

"They're really not," says Bailey, coming into the kitchen with a yawn. "But I have to admit, Coop's got a point." She looks me up and down, not bothering to conceal the lust in her eyes as her gaze moves to Cooper's hand fondling my ass. "Also, why are we out of bed? It's cold out here."

"Sustenance, woman," I say. I grab Cooper's hand and use it to spin him around, bending him back over my arm. "And good morning to you too." I kiss him softly, grinning when I hear Bailey sigh.

"Let me up," says Cooper, doing his best to look disgruntled.

"I dunno, I kind of like you off balance like this," I say, backing him up against the counter. It gives him just enough leeway to push at my shoulders, but I keep moving, hoisting him up on the countertop next to the stool Bailey's sitting on.

"Fucking cold," he says, his body jerking as his back touches the marble.

"Should have thought of that before you left the bedroom naked," says Bailey.

"That's rich, coming from you," says Cooper. The stink-eye he gives her falls short, considering he's lying on his back naked as a jaybird on the counter between us.

"Hey, I'm wearing a shirt," she says, before pulling it over her head and dropping it on the floor. "Well, I was."

I can't help but laugh, though it comes out a little choked at the sudden appearance of Bailey's perfect breasts, her nipples hardening in the cool morning air.

Cooper seems to be having a similar problem, turning his head to look at the bounty right next to him. He licks his lips as his erection thickens and rises up against my belly.

"Come here," he tells her, nudging her breast with his nose. Bailey turns toward him and moans as Cooper puts his talented tongue to work on her body.

"What about breakfast?" she asks, gasping.

"Later," I say, bending to take Cooper's cock down as deep as I can. He groans, pulling away from Bailey to watch me take him down again, both their eyes on me. I put some flair in it since I've got their attention, twisting my hand around the base of his cock and keeping my eyes on them while they watch.

"Fuck, that's hot," says Bailey, one hand coming up to squeeze her breast.

"Get up here, Ross," growls Cooper. Bailey climbs up on the counter, kneeling next to him, clearly torn on what she wants to do next. Cooper takes the decision out of her hands and pulls her astride, his muscles flexing as he arranges her to sit on his face, facing me.

"Oh, God." Bailey's eyes roll back in her head as his tongue makes contact with her flesh. Her gaze snaps back to mine as Cooper thrusts his hips up, fucking into my mouth. "God, Drew, look at you. You take him so deep."

Cooper moans at that, his hips snapping up like he's losing control. I like taking him this way, but this morning I have something else in mind. Cooper goes still as I slide my hands under his knees, canting his hips in the air and exposing his hole. Bailey's breath hitches, and it turns my arousal up another notch to know she's got a front row seat for this. That she's into it. That she wants it every bit as much as Cooper and I do.

Moving slow, so I don't startle him, I kiss the inside of his thighs, working my way inward. When I trace his balls with the tip of my nose, Cooper whines, the sound muffled by Bailey's body. Bent down like this, I can see his tongue dipping into her as she rocks on his mouth. They're fucking gorgeous like this.

"Do it," Cooper says, lifting Bailey's hips off his wet mouth. Her pussy is gleaming. "Fucking do it already."

"So impatient," I say, but because I love him I do as he says, swiping the pucker of his ass with my tongue. After that, all bets are off. I work him over with my tongue as Cooper rides my face like Bailey's doing to him. By the time I manage to work my tongue into his body, Bailey's got a hand between her legs, crying out her orgasm while Cooper fucks her with his fingers and tongue. I wet a finger, pressing it deep into his body, moving my mouth back to his dick just in time to catch his release when he comes. When I curl my finger to hit that spot inside him, Cooper starts to shake, almost like he's coming a second time. I catch every drop, holding him there until he comes down. Bailey's already climbing off him, sliding toward my edge of the counter as I press a kiss to his hip.

"Get over here," she says, pulling at my shoulders. A heartbeat later, I'm sliding into her, unable to stop. It's all I can do to hang on until she comes again, squeezing and clenching around my cock before I lose it, crying out as I come inside her.

My hand falls to the counter, my fingers twining with Cooper's as we all catch our breaths.

"Shower?" Cooper asks lazily, still panting, still laid out on the counter like he hasn't got a care in the world.

"Probably a good idea," I say, grinning at him. Bailey lifts her head from my shoulder.

"It smells like sex in here," she says, wrinkling her nose and making me laugh. Cooper snorts.

"I'm shocked," he says, his ab muscles flexing as he pulls up to sit on the counter next to her. He slides his fingers in my hair and tugs me toward him, kissing me deeply before turning to Bailey and doing the same to her.

"Glad you two came to your senses," he teases, softly. It still feels a little too soon to joke about it, but Bailey smiles. The warmth in her eyes when she looks at him makes me want to cry, and I'm not really a crying kind of guy.

I'm going to look back on this part of my life and forever wonder how I got so damned lucky. Every touch, every kiss, every word between the two of them seems to feed this thing between the three of us. There's so much inside me for them, sometimes I feel like I'm coming out of my skin. I don't think I can take it if things get any more intense between us.

But since I'm not going anywhere without them ever again, we'll just have to wait and see.

"What's that look for?" Bailey asks, turning her sparkling eyes my way.

"Just counting my blessings," I say. I tighten my arm around her waist and slide the other around Cooper's, my throat getting thick. Bailey hugs me back. Cooper kisses my shoulder and hides his face against my neck for a long moment.

We spend the day at Cooper's, laughing and talking and loving on each other. Occasionally, somebody cries—sometimes it's even me. The more time I spend with them, the more certain I am that we've made the right decision. This thing between us... it's worth it. No matter what.

THE WEEK that follows feels much like I figure a traveling circus must. We spend two nights at Cooper's, then a night at Bailey's, then three nights at my apartment. Whose apartment we sleep at depends on who needs to be where and when, but also who has food in their fridge, because none of us want to take time away from each other to go to the damn grocery store.

"I'm telling you guys," says Bailey. "Grocery delivery."

"Or we could just get takeout," says Cooper. It's the third time we've had this conversation this week.

"Enough." I say it loud enough to get their attention, crossing my arms and deploying what Cooper likes to call my teacher voice. "Get dressed. We're going shopping."

Bailey mutters under her breath but heads back to the bedroom to get dressed. Cooper glares at me, but the bulge tenting the front of his shorts gives him away.

"Who died and made you boss?" he gripes.

"Face it, Coop," I say, leaning over to give him a quick kiss. "Somebody's got to be in charge around here." I spin him around by the shoulders and give him a swift smack on the ass to get him moving.

"We're going to talk about this," he says. Given the way he's adjusting what's now a full-blown erection, I've got a pretty good idea what he means when he says "talk."

My phone chimes with an incoming call.

"Hey, Ty," I say, swiping to answer it. "What's up?"

"Got a second?" asks my boss.

"More than one, if you need it."

"I have news about the investigation," he says. My heart starts to pound.

"And?" Surely if they were going to fire me over this, they'd have done it while I was in the office earlier, right? Probably. Surely.

"I think you're familiar with an employee named Mila Hague," he says.

"We've met." Mila had finally stopped asking me out once the cooking competition pilot aired a few weeks ago. "What's she got to do with anything?"

"The IT department was able to confirm that tabloid article was submitted by one of the computers at Sizzle HQ," says Drew. "Specifically, the laptop issued to Ms. Hague."

"You're joking."

"Not in the slightest," he says. "Once HR got her to admit to sending the photo and starting the rumor about you and Cooper and Bailey, she confessed to tampering with the equipment during the live event as well."

"What the hell?"

"She claims she was just trying to get your attention," says Ty. "And, ah… once the security footage came out, she wanted to get back at you. She didn't elaborate about that though." Of course, Ty had seen the footage of Cooper and me making out backstage that day. He'd gone out of his way never to mention it until now. Swallowing my embarrassment, I clear my throat.

"We went out once, Mila and I," I explain. "I don't make a habit of going out with colleagues, I swear."

"None of my business, Drew," says Ty. "I just wanted to let you know, case closed. The network isn't pressing charges, but as of today Mila Hague is no longer employed with Sizzle."

I tell him thanks and hang up the phone, scrubbing a hand over my face. Given her reaction to Bailey at the gala all those weeks ago, I knew Mila might have been a little unbalanced, but I never would have guessed—

The doorbell keeps me from pursuing that train of thought any further. When I open the door, I'm stunned.

"Mom."

"Hello, Andrew," she says quietly. "Can I come in for a moment?"

"Um, sure." I double check over my shoulder just in case Coop or Bailey changed their minds about getting dressed, but so far we're clear. "Come on in."

Mom shakes her head when I offer to take her coat.

"I won't keep you long, dear," she says. She studies my face intently. Uncomfortable and probably being pretty obvious about it, I clear my throat.

"Cooper and Bailey will be out in a minute," I say. She needs to know they're here, at least. I square my shoulders, ready for a fight.

"Of course," she says. "That's why I'm here. But before I say what I came here to say, I need to ask you something." Mom reaches across the sofa and takes my hand. "Are you happy?"

"Sorry?"

"It's a simple question," says my mother, smiling a little. "Are you happy?"

"I'm... Of course, I am," I say, confused by the question.

"I'm referring specifically to your lovers," she says, her smile growing a little. My face heats.

"Mom."

"We're adults, Andrew. If you can fall in love with two people at once, you'll survive hearing me use the word 'lover.'"

She's got a point, but my face isn't getting any less pink.

"Of course, quite an assumption for me to make," she says, pulling her hand back.

"What do you mean?"

"Are you in love with them? With both of them?" All hint of a smile disappears, leaving her face more serious than I've seen in a long time. I answer her as openly and honestly as I can.

"I am," I say. "I didn't know it was possible to love anybody this much. Let alone two people." I'm twenty-nine years old. I will not cry in front of my mother, goddamn it. Then her eyes well up and she makes a liar out of me.

"I know, baby," she says, moving next to me and pulling me into a hug. She holds me tightly for a long moment, long enough to allow me to pull my soggy ass back together. When she pulls back with a delicate sniffle, she smiles.

"It's not going to be easy, you know," she says, smoothing her coat over her lap.

"We know."

"And as for the rest of your family..." She purses her lips. "I think your father just needs some time. He'll come around. The rest of them, I'm not so sure."

I nod. That's about what I expected.

"I think they'll come around too, except perhaps your grandfather," she says. "It'll take some getting used to."

"We're not going anywhere," says Bailey quietly. I turn to look at her, standing in the door, holding hands with Cooper. I didn't hear the bedroom door or their steps coming up the hall, so I have no idea how long they've been standing there. Hopefully, not long enough to have seen me crying all over my mother.

"Hello, Bailey dear," says my mother with a smile.

"I mean it, Mrs. Hicks," she says. "He's not doing this alone."

"Not anymore," says Cooper.

"Mr. Lawson, it's nice to see you again." Mom stands up and circles the couch, embracing Bailey and leaning in to kiss Cooper on the cheek. He blushes adorably.

"Call me Cooper, ma'am."

"Then you call me Sandra," she says. She lays a hand on each of their cheeks. "And I hope one day maybe you'll both be comfortable calling me 'Mom.'"

Bailey bursts into tears at that, her quiet composure gone as she wraps my mom into a bearhug. Cooper looks a little lost, but pleased.

Despite my lovers' best efforts, Mom can't be persuaded to stay any longer. She hugs us each in turn once more and promises to call soon.

"I won't be stopping by unannounced anymore," she tells me as I walk her to the door. Pretty sure I turn a visible shade of green, because she laughs as she waves goodbye.

"Right," I say, turning around and resting my back against the door. "So that was unexpected."

"And weird," says Cooper.

"Not that weird," says Bailey, elbowing him. She grabs their coats from the hall tree, tossing Cooper's at him and pulling her own on. "Drew's mom is amazeballs."

"You could have downplayed it," says Cooper, looking at me.

"What do you mean?" I ask.

"You could have told her it wasn't serious," he says, shrugging into his coat. "Given her something easy to tell the family so you don't have to be excommunicated anymore. We don't—"

"Yes," I say firmly. "We do. We are." I take both their hands in mine. "Do you need me to spell it out for you?" I thought we'd covered this in the last week, in between the lovemaking and the talking and all the stupid goddamned crying. Does he think I cry for just anybody?

"It wouldn't hurt," says Bailey.

I can't let myself forget what led us here, both the good and bad. Especially the bad. They only doubted us because I failed to fight for them.

Never again.

"You're my family," I say. "You're the ones I fight for now. If somebody has a problem—even my own blood relations—you're the ones whose side I'm on." Bailey beams; Coop looks a little thunderstruck.

"Don't you get it?" I say, kissing him softly. "You're mine."

Bailey nearly tackles us over in her hurry to hug us close, and I know this is it for me. This is all I want.

They're mine.

"Hey," says Bailey, pulling back to look up at me. "Who was on the phone earlier?"

"Bailey girl," I say, hugging them tight. "You'll never guess what Ty just told me..."

EPILOGUE

Cooper
A few months later...

"Y ou'll find instruction sheets on your workstation," says Drew. "Take a moment to review the list of equipment you'll need. There should be enough blenders for everybody, but if we turn up short, just let me know and I'll get you situated. All right, everybody ready? Go ahead and get started."

"Got your equipment right here," I mutter, just barely loud enough for Drew to hear. The rest of the class is already buzzing with activity. Sizzle had to rearrange the workstation setup since Drew's cooking classes have gotten so popular. There's nearly twice as many people in here as there were when I took his class last summer.

"Knock it off, Lawson," he murmurs, not looking at me. He's in instructor mode, so he's only got eyes for his students right now.

I can fix that.

"I mean it," he says sternly, catching my eye before I can slide off the stool next to him. "We had an agreement."

Right. No shenanigans in class. Because we're grownups now and shenanigans happen at home.

Maturity blows.

Then again, Bailey's at home, and shenanigans with all three of us are always worth the wait.

I snicker. And go figure, that's what gets Drew's attention. His eyes narrow, like he's trying to see inside my head. Good luck with that, Coop.

I've been acting as Drew's assistant ever since he resumed teaching this class a couple of weeks ago. When he first asked me to do it, I thought it was just an excuse to get me away from my computer—I've been working on a new angle and as a result I don't get out of the house much. But turns out Drew and I work really well together. Maybe I shouldn't have been so surprised, considering how well we work together under less professional circumstances.

Sizzle hasn't officially hired me, but neither have they barred me from the premises. Since I don't do any of the actual teaching, nobody's at risk of getting hurt. And Drew seems to enjoy the company, though I do my level best to give him as much shit as I did the first time I sat through his class.

"You're humming again," he says. He doesn't look up from the paperwork on his desk.

"Can't help it," I say. I've had "Hot for Teacher" stuck in my head since we started doing this together. Drew got all flustered the first time he heard me humming it. Cute as hell. Made me want to fuck him over his desk.

Still haven't struck that one off the bucket list yet, but I have high hopes for next week.

Not tonight, though. Drew's already warned me he and Bailey have big plans for dinner tonight, and they sadly don't involve anybody getting fucked over a desk.

Which is just as well. I'm supposed to be paying attention right now anyway. Drew and Bailey tell me the best way to learn something is to teach somebody else, so my new video series is all instructive: first-timers learning to cook. I don't think they expected me to take their advice so literally, but that's exactly what I'm doing with these videos—step by step how-to's for people who, like me this time last year, can't boil water.

I really hate to admit it, but they're right. The lessons I had such a hard time retaining even after Drew's class are starting to stick. I even take a turn cooking at home one night a week. Half the time we have to pitch it and get takeout instead, but it's getting better. I'm getting better.

Truth is, they make me better. It's easy to get over feeling frustrated when you've got the kind of cheering section I've got. Drew provokes me until I stop being mad at myself, and Bailey soothes any leftover frustration until I'm ready to try again. Anybody in the world would succeed under those circumstances.

"You've got that look on your face again."

I look up from my own desk and grin at Mrs. Weaver. She's hardly a novice, but she still swears by Drew's classes.

"You still here?" I ask. "Drew really needs to step it up if you haven't learned how to sauté onions after paying for all these classes."

"Oh, funny," she says, smirking at me. "Nice to see your eyebrows have recovered."

I scowl. I'd forgotten about that one.

"Oh yeah?" I say, getting into it. "Well, you—"

"Mrs. Weaver, how are you doing today?" interrupts Drew. I have no doubt he's been listening this whole time. Which fucking sucks, because if I'd forgotten about the singed-eyebrow incident, I bet he had too. Thanks a lot, Mrs. Weaver.

"Happy as a clam," she says with a wide smile. "My boy's getting married."

"No kidding? Congratulations," says Drew.

"Thanks," she says. Her smile takes on a hint of mischief. "His fiancés are wonderful. We're really very lucky." She takes herself back to her workstation, stopping to chat with other students along the way.

"Did she say 'fiancés'? Like, plural?" I ask.

"I think she did," says Drew.

The rest of class passes quickly. Apparently Drew's in a hurry to get home, given that he actually beats me back to the car for once when we're finished cleaning up. Winter seems to have finally passed, if the humidity is any indication. Spring is in the air, which for us means rain and lots of it. I don't mind, for once. Everything feels new and fresh.

There I go again.

"What's that frown for?" Drew asks, glancing at me as he points the car in the direction of his apartment where we've been spending most of our time lately. I miss being able to run down and chat with Rusty and Beck anytime I want, but not enough to stay at my own place. I keep wondering whether Drew's getting tired of having us around so much but can't seem to find the nerve to ask him outright.

"You've turned me into a damned sap, that's what," I say. "First Mrs. Weaver rags on me, now this. Ugh."

I don't elaborate any further, but Drew's smug expression tells me he knows what I'm talking about. Fucking feelings. Ugh.

Bailey's already home when we get to Drew's. She's found a tiny restaurant that rents their kitchen to her a couple of times a week for her catering business, so her hours are all over the place. It's been a rocky couple of months for her and me both, but things are looking up. And between the three of us, things couldn't get any better, which helps us get through the rest.

Drew managed to get through the competition incident with his career more or less intact. Turned out that vicious bitch Mila was the one responsible for both the equipment tampering and the tabloid article outing our relationship. Sizzle only caught her because she used Wi-Fi at work to send that photo of us—she fessed up to the rest once they questioned her. Apparently she'd been so furious that Drew was screwing around with "so many other whores" that she was determined to get him fired. It was a close call, but in the end, she failed. Drew says things are still weird with some people at work, but he thinks it's getting better.

Personally, I'd have flipped them all off and walked out a long time ago, but I'm not exactly the people-person my boyfriend is.

"There you are!" says Bailey, leaping on me as soon as I get in the door. She wraps her legs around my waist as I hitch her up, walking us both inside.

"Oof," I manage. "Good thing you're tiny."

"Funny," she says, laying a kiss on me that almost takes me to the floor for real. "Missed you."

"Missed you too, Ross."

"Hello to you, too," says Drew, dryly. Bailey grins at him and winks, unwrapping herself to go to him, giving him the same kiss. I keep waiting for the jealousy to kick in—either jealous of her or jealous of him. It's been months now.

Nope. Still nothing. All it does is make me think we need to get a proper desk here at Drew's so I can fuck somebody over it.

"Knock it off," says Drew, looking at me.

"I didn't say anything!"

"I know that look," he says. "Save it."

"Fine," I grumble. "What's this big plan about tonight, anyway? Do you know?" I ask Bailey.

She shakes her head. "He wouldn't tell me anything, either."

Drew tells us to go sit at the table without him. I can hear him rummaging around as we take our seats.

"I'm starting to get a little worried," says Bailey quietly.

Me too, but I don't want to make her feel worse, so I take her hand. "I'm sure he's just winding us up. What on earth could it possibly be?"

"He could be asking us to go back to our apartments," she says, ticking off each item on her fingers. "Telling us both he wants to see other people. Telling me he only wants to be with you, and not with me after all."

"You can't be serious," I say, actually shocked by the last one.

Bailey flushes. "It's crossed my mind."

"Andrew!"

"For crying out loud, I'm right here," says Drew, wincing as he walks up right as I'm in the middle of shouting for him.

"Tell Bailey you're not about to dump her so we can be a couple."

Drew's face goes blank with shock. Bailey groans and covers her face with her hands. Drew sets some papers down on the table and goes to his knees next to her chair. He pulls her hands away from her face, holding them tightly in his own.

"Never," he says, forcing her to look at him. "Never. Do you hear me?"

"I know it's stupid," she says, squeezing her eyes shut.

"It's not stupid," I say.

"And I'll tell you as many times as you need to hear it," he says, nodding to include us both. "Both of you. I need you both." He squeezes her hands again, lifting them to press a kiss to each one. "Okay?"

"Okay," Bailey whispers. She reaches for me blindly; I catch her hand and wind our fingers together, squeezing.

"Right," says Drew, standing up to take his seat. "So. I've asked you here today—quit snickering at me, Coop, I'm serious—I've asked you here today because I think there's something we need to discuss."

"Obviously," I say, glancing at Bailey. I'm trying to lighten the mood, but I'm afraid she's still not appeased. There's a really excellent way to get around that; Bailey's shit at being upset when she gets naked, but Drew's adamant about talking about whatever this is.

"You know I love you both," he says, waiting until he's sure he has our attention. "And you know I respect you and I value your opinions."

"Okay, now I'm starting to get scared," I say. Drew presses on.

"So if you say no, we can still back out of this." Drew taps on the papers on the table. He doesn't say anything else.

A long moment passes.

"Back out of what?" Bailey finally prompts.

"Oh," Drew jumps a little. "Yeah. Um. Here." He pushes the papers at us.

Bailey reads faster than I do. She looks up at him almost immediately.

"Is this what I think it is?"

Drew rubs a hand over the back of his neck. "If you think it's an offer for the house over on Melbourne Street then yes, it's what you think it is."

"You made an offer on a house?"

"It's got five bedrooms," says Drew defensively. "The owners are really motivated. It's a great time to buy."

The man looks positively terrified, so much so I can't help but laugh. And once I start, I can't seem to stop. Bailey catches my eye and starts laughing too.

"What?" says Drew, looking between us. "Why are you laughing?"

"I'm laughing," I say, wiping my tears of mirth out of my eyes, "because you're an idiot."

"What? Why?"

"Bailey thought you were asking us to move out," I say. Bailey nods, still chuckling.

"What? No!" Drew takes her hands again. "I wanted to ask you to move in with me, not move out."

"Maybe just lead with that next time," I suggest.

"It would save some time," agrees Bailey.

"If we're talking about next time, does that mean yes?" Drew asks. He doesn't bother to conceal his hope.

I look at Bailey, drumming my fingers on the table like I'm mulling it over.

"What do you think, Ross?" I ask. "Time to make it official?"

"I don't know," she says, playing along and drawing it out. "Paying for two extra apartments has its perks."

"Five bedrooms," says Drew, jabbing at the paperwork. "Five. Plenty of space to get away if you need privacy."

I have to give him credit for thinking it through that far ahead. Just because we don't need privacy from each other right now doesn't mean we won't need it someday.

"Or maybe just a couple of home offices," he says, looking between us. "Considering I've gone and fallen for a couple of jobless drifters."

"Funny," says Bailey, kicking him under the table. Drew grins.

"Wait till you see the kitchen," he says. "So is that a yes?" His grin is infectious.

"Why not?" says Bailey. "Coop?"

I shrug, ignoring the sudden burst of butterflies in my stomach. I look at him, and at her, and remember how bleak my life was without them in it. Every cell in my body is ready to tell him yes, but I hold it back, determined to savor this moment.

Drew appears to take my hesitation personally.

"I bet we can talk him into it," he says to Bailey. Her eyebrows go up.

"What do you have in mind?" she asks. My heart starts to pound as Drew stands up.

"Come on," he says, heading for the bedroom. "I'll show you."

And they do. Over and over again, until late into the night, they make me tell them "yes" until it's the only word I know, until it loses all its meaning and all that's left is them and me. Just us.

That's all that matters anyway.

ALSO BY WHITLEY GREEN

Sizzle

She works for him. He lives with me. I want them both...

Alex

We've been best friends and roommates for a long time but Elliot still doesn't know I'm into men and women both. When he hires the luscious Joelle to save his restaurant, I can understand his need to keep things professional between them. But there's no reason I have to...

Elliot

I need a miracle; Joelle needs a job. When she turns out to be sweet, smart, and sexy as hell I can't blame Alex for wanting her, too. But Joelle wasn't there the night he left his bedroom door open. I could have sworn I was straight, but now they're *both* in my head.

Joelle

I've got too much on the line to lose my head (or my heart) over my boss, or his hot-as-sin roommate. Both at the same time? Out of the question... until they convince me otherwise.

Smoke

Three lovers. A second chance. One little white lie.

Anna

I cut loose for one night and they fell asleep before we sealed the deal. It's for the best—I'll never see Ben again but James and I have to work together... until the restaurant closes and we go our separate ways.

Months later, what are the odds that they'll turn up right when I'm meeting a blind date?

Ben

Anna rocked my world that night. And James... my best friend doesn't know it changed the way I look at him. That's my cross to bear.

Then Anna turns back up, hot as hell and every bit as drawn to us as we are to her. When James makes up a story to keep her around, I play along.

Because I can't lose him. And I *won't* lose her again.

James

I've wanted Anna for years. Now she's back and I've got the second chance I've been waiting for.

Now how do I tell Ben that I want them both?

One little white lie won't hurt anybody.

ABOUT THE AUTHOR

Whitley Green writes hot ménage romance because she can't help herself. She likes coffee, scotch, and Sherlock Holmes in any incarnation.

Printed in Great Britain
by Amazon

19819404R00161